NOMINATED FOR "BEST PERFORMANCE BY A CLEVER KILLER"...

RONNIE FORDYCE—A TV critic with a poison pen. Has he decided to give someone a more lethal dose?

MICKEY SAMISH—His favorite song is the theme from *The Godfather.* Have his latest offers been refused?

SHELDON WALTERS—A gag writer whose wisecracks cut to the quick. Has he decided that some people should die laughing?

DEBBIE WEINTRAUB—A production assistant who's a plain Jane in Glamor City. Is she setting the stage for death?

SAPPHO DURKIN—A PR advisor who's been dropping names in deadly places. Has she found murder more effective than bad press?

And in supporting roles: Johnny Carson, Mike Douglas, Jack Paar, Merv Griffin, Dick Cavett, Dinah Shore, and a host of others—including, of course, Steve Allen.

"A brilliant gimmick."—*The Minneapolis Tribune*

"Irresistible."—"TV Topics," *Buffalo Evening News*

"Steve Allen has made his mark in a new genre."
— *The Indianapolis News*

Books by
STEVE ALLEN

BOP FABLES
FOURTEEN FOR TONIGHT
THE FUNNY MEN
WRY ON THE ROCKS
THE GIRLS ON THE TENTH FLOOR
THE QUESTION MAN
MARK IT AND STRIKE IT
NOT ALL OF YOUR LAUGHTER, NOT ALL OF YOUR TEARS
LETTER TO A CONSERVATIVE
THE GROUND IS OUR TABLE
BIGGER THAN A BREADBOX
A FLASH OF SWALLOWS
THE WAKE
PRINCESS SNIP-SNIP AND THE PUPPYKITTENS
CURSES
WHAT TO SAY WHEN IT RAINS
SCHMOCK-SCHMOCK!
MEETING OF MINDS: VOLUME 1
CHOPPED-UP CHINESE
RIPOFF: A LOOK AT CORRUPTION IN AMERICA
MEETING OF MINDS: VOLUME 2
"EXPLAINING CHINA"
FUNNY PEOPLE
THE TALK SHOW MURDERS

THE
TALK SHOW
MURDERS

Steve Allen

A DELL BOOK

Published by
Dell Publishing Co., Inc.
1 Dag Hammarskjold Plaza
New York, New York 10017

Dell ® TM 681510, Dell Publishing Co., Inc.

ISBN: 0-440-18480-0

Reprinted by arrangement with Delacorte Press
Printed in the United States of America
First Dell printing—January 1983

Acknowledgments

I should like to acknowledge the assistance of Jeffry "Flash" Freundlich of my office staff; Walter Sheldon, an expert in mystery writing; Betty Kelly of Delacorte Press; and Sheri Lail, Kim Saunders, and Monte Montgomery, who transcribed endless dictated drafts of this manuscript. And while I'm at it, my thanks, too, to Merv Griffin, Mike Douglas, Johnny Carson, and all the other talk show hosts and hostesses who grace these pages.

What you are about to read is purely a work of my imagination. No matter what I say in the following pages, don't believe it. This is a novel of suspense, and I have chosen to work with the situations I know best to make it more credible and, I hope, fun—but as I said, don't believe a word of it.

STEVE ALLEN

A Kind of Preface

I sit in the hot, carcinogenic southern California sunshine, beside my swimming pool on a low hillside in the Royal Oaks section of Los Angeles, from which I can easily overlook the mortgage. A small pocket-size tape recorder in hand, I begin a report of events connected with the talk show murders. Perhaps Merv Griffin, Johnny Carson or one of the other fellows in the trade might someday decide to write about the crimes committed on their programs, in full public view. But I'm getting into print with the story first, simply because I also write books for a living and had the good fortune to run into a publisher who knew a good story when he heard one.

In reconstructing what happened, I must employ a degree of literary license, and I hope it doesn't expire before I finish the book. You see, I'm going to have to report on a number of events at which I was not actually present and get into the heads of the people connected with this sensational murder case. Literary people call this being omniscient. I call it the only way to fly.

Actually, I *was* on hand when some of these things happened. I know most of the principals well enough to reconstruct what they said and did, even on occasions when I was elsewhere. Come to think of it, I've been elsewhere most of my life. I used to worry about this, but my agent tells me it's better than being nowhere.

In any event I've talked to everybody involved with the case. The first and most important of these people is Roger Dale. Dale's a private eye who, because of the murders, became a public eye. Which, in a sense, was what he wanted, even though I tried to tell him that being recognizable to large numbers of people isn't all it's cracked up to be. You really have to watch your hangups when that happens.

I first met Roger Dale some years ago on a plane. He happened to get the seat next to mine and, as he said later, recognized me but assumed that I wanted privacy and pretended to ignore me, the way dogs sometimes do with each other in alleys. As it happened, I'd just wrapped up a few projects I'd been working on, was taking a breather, and was willing to make small talk with a stranger. From one look at Roger I guessed that his talk would be of the smallest kind, which was fine with me.

He was dressed in an Edwardian suit, which I somehow remember as having ruffles at the sleeves although it probably didn't. His hair was obviously styled and the colors of his accessories added up to an effect of languid—if offbeat—good taste, no doubt carefully worked out beforehand, like most comedian's ad libs. I decided that anyone who paid so much attention to his own packaging must lack depth, and that was all right at the moment too, since I wasn't in the mood for subject matter any more complicated than the weather or the pennant race. But I assumed that the stranger in the seat next to me wanted *his* privacy, so I didn't say anything either and we both sat there in awkward silence until the stewardess brought salad and I spilled a drop of oil and vinegar on Roger's well-creased trousers.

"Damn! I'm sorry," I said. "Let me pay for the cleaning. Or new pants—"

"Okay," he said.

I hadn't expected that, so I blinked.

He grinned. "Just wanted to see if you really would."

I laughed. "I'm not so sure. But it's the thing to say, isn't it?"

"I guess it is. Anyway, forget it. Could have been my salad oil on your pants. One of the risks of air travel."

"Well, I *am* sorry. Really. My name's Allen." I extended my hand.

"I know," he said. "I'm Roger Dale."

We shook hands, elbows in the way in the confined space of the airline seats. "Look," I said, "I do feel bad about the pants. Let me send you something. I don't know what, but I'll think of it. Got a card?"

He had one, expensively embossed. It said Dale Security Agency and named him as president. According to the legend the agency offered everything from private investigations to guard service. The motto was "Total Security."

"Interesting," I said, looking at it. "You know, I've always been something of a crime buff. Mildly, anyway."

"I know," said Dale. "I've read your book, *Ripoff*. I must say, even though I'm in the business I hadn't realized the problem of white collar crime was that bad. You know, that's an interesting point. Obviously I know more about crime than you do but often an outside observer can see things that the man on the ground doesn't notice, because his nose is too close to the grindstone."

"I know what you mean," I said. "Same way a tourist may notice things about a city that a lifelong resident would never see."

"Right," said Dale. "But the odd thing about crime is that everybody is interested in it, to a degree. Most people secretly fantasize about committing crimes themselves. I even have a theory that if everybody who ever *thought* of committing murder—even as a passing fancy—actually committed one, it would go far to help the problem of overpopulation." Since I was obviously going to be talking to Dale for the next few hours I was relieved to see that he had a sense of humor.

I didn't get my small talk. Instead we kicked around the psychology of the criminal mind. Dale had a lot of ideas on the subject. I revised my opinion of him. The man was a walking encyclopedia of crime, criminals, abnormal psychology, history, philosophy, the arts. I couldn't reconcile it with the fancy dress and kept thinking he ought to be in rumpled tweeds with elbow patches, but anyway I enjoyed it and for a change listened more than I talked.

"As for me," he said presently, "I'm a TV buff."

"Everybody's that, too," I said.

"It's the exposure that fascinates me," he said. "The fantastic power of it. Never before in history has anyone been able to reach so many people in such a short time and with such impact. I don't care who you are or what you do—get on the tube and you're just about guaranteed success. In fact," he continued, "I've often wondered how any of the famous speeches of history managed to make their obvious impact in the absence of radio and television. I mean, today a man can say something on TV and be heard by thirty or forty million people. Think how few actually heard the Gettysburg Address, the Sermon on the Mount, or Pericles' funeral oration. And even then it must have been difficult or impossible for everyone in those small crowds to hear exactly what was going on. Everything I've ever read, for example, about Lincoln or Jesus Christ suggests that they were soft-spoken. So when Christ was speaking that day there must have been a few people in the back of the crowd who were saying 'What did he just say? Blessed are the freaks?' "

It occurred to me at that moment that Dale would make a very good guest for a talk show. Little did I know that he soon would be.

Later the seat belt lights went on and the pilot said something on the speaker about landing soon. "Well, it's been nice talking to you, Roger," I said. "Maybe we'll meet again."

"I doubt it," he said. "You're so busy."

"I imagine you are, too."

"Busy getting nowhere," he said, shrugging.

That should have been the tip-off that Roger Dale was not as prosperous and fulfilled as he seemed, but frankly, I wasn't all that interested in the affairs of a passing stranger, whatever they might be, and would wrap up our chance encounter and expiate my clumsiness with the salad oil by sending him a case of Scotch. That, I'd learned, was what he drank, though private eyes are supposed to prefer bourbon—or was that just a detail dreamed up by Raymond Chandler or Dashiell Hammett?

So that's how I happened to know Roger Dale, and what led to my subsequent meetings with him when things started happening. I sensed from the beginning that in spite of the Edwardian bit and carefully styled hair—the reasons for this became apparent later—the guy was very bright, much brighter than most. It all had a bearing on the talk show murders. And it's partly why I make so bold as to take the omniscient viewpoint in the events that follow. So I make bold. Sounds like I'm manufacturing a new detergent.

The arrival of young Elmo Finstetter was, in some respects, like that of an Arab prince. His ragtop, silver-gray Lamberghini came to a halt in the parking lot near the old Hollywood tan-stucco building, stage 4 of station KTLA, which stood tall in the sun, as an ancient desert palace might have stood in the days of Sinbad and Ali Baba.

There was a bright sky over all of southern California, a favorable wind this day having blown the smog elsewhere. At the gate there had been a surging crowd to welcome Elmo. He had slowed down and stopped to acknowledge them, at least the groupies, predominantly young and female, who, by some mysterious intelligence-gathering technique, had learned of Elmo's scheduled appearance on the Toni Tennille talk show.

They had converged upon his gleaming automobile in a great, squealing implosion. Forcing himself to smile, Elmo had paused only to scribble autographs, receive a wet kiss or two he could not avoid, and admire a well-shaped pair of hips, budding breasts in T-shirts, or a flat stomach set off by tight bluejeans.

Accompanied by Danny Moss, his agent, Elmo

drove on to the lot slowly, with only one button on his open-chested shirt and a necklace missing. He had taken care to wear only a cheap, gold-filled chain; he kept a supply of these specifically to lose whenever he exposed himself to those who loved him.

Inside the building the air conditioning was cool and comfortable. Elmo turned to look for Danny Moss, reflecting that he always had to look for him, even when the man was right beside him, for Danny had a way of fading out of any scene. And there he was, small, self-effacing, dressed in a dark summer business suit with narrow tie.

"What the hell've you got me into this time?" Elmo's speaking voice was high-pitched and breathy; an occasional consonant sent out a fine spray of saliva.

"Exposure," said Danny. "The kind you can't buy."

"Bullshit," said Elmo. "Who needs it?"

"You need it. That last album of yours hasn't broken gold yet. Just go through the motions, will you, Elmo? Trust me, okay?"

"For a lousy four hundred and fifty bucks."

"Right." Danny nodded. "Minimum scale. Of which I get a whopping forty-five. So don't complain."

"It's a waste of time. And I don't even get to do a number. Just sit there, right? It's dumb."

"It's like I told you," said Danny with bland patience. "Toni does her own singing. Anyway, they can hear *you* sing anytime. What they want is to get to know you personally when Toni talks to you. Be nice this time, okay, Elmo? Don't blow it."

"Balls," said Elmo, shaking his head so that the tangled Medusa strands of his long, yellow hair rippled and shimmered.

A stocky young woman emerged from one of the backstage doors and clicked toward them in sensible, low-heeled pumps. She wore heavy hornrimmed spectacles and her dark hair was drawn tightly back across her skull. She clutched a clipboard to one swelling breast. "Hi," she said, "I'm Debbie Weintraub, one of the talent coordinators. I'll take you to the greenroom, where you can be comfortable—unless you'd like to use one of the dressing rooms."

"None of the above," Elmo said sourly. "Where's the men's room?"

"There's one in your dressing room," said Debbie, indicating the direction with a nod.

"Be right back," said Elmo. One quick glance had told him that, by his standards, Debbie Weintraub was not beddable. He had at once lost interest in her.

"Oh, did you want any makeup?" Debbie called after him.

"No, thanks," said Elmo. "I'm gorgeous enough."

When Elmo was out of sight, Debbie said to Danny Moss, "He was kidding, of course."

Danny shrugged. "Don't ask. With Elmo, I never know."

Debbie and Danny traded comments about the weather and such matters until Elmo returned. Then Debbie led the two men to an area that was a cross between a living room and a prosperous doctor's waiting room. It was done in cheery buff, and the accents were colonial, with bullseye mirrors and imitation Duncan Phyfe side tables. No one else was there.

"There's no goddamn green in the greenroom," said Elmo.

"That's right," said Danny. "But that's what they call 'em, no matter what color they are."

Danny shrugged. Debbie smiled. It was the smile of someone who knows trade secrets and isn't about to give them away. "Just make yourself at home here,

Mr. Finstetter. Some of the other guests ought to be along pretty soon. I'll pick you up when we're ready. The audience will be coming in in a little while. After the warmup we'll be ready to go."

"Yeah, sure," said Elmo absentmindedly. He sat on the sofa, then unzipped the airline bag he'd brought with him. From it he retrieved a fresh shirt—one with a plunging chestline designed for him alone by Mr. Gerald, who did all his clothes—and then a pint bottle of vodka, which he placed upon the coffee table. He looked up at Debbie. "Got a glass?"

"Glass," said Debbie, frowning. "Let me see. Glass. There are some plastic cups around somewhere, I think."

"Plastic?" Elmo's tone was contemptuous.

"I'll find a glass," said Debbie quickly. She swiveled toward Danny. "Want to come with me, Mr. Moss? Our producer wants to check something with you—I almost forgot."

Danny looked at Elmo. "Will you be okay without a baby sitter?"

"Get the hell out of here," said Elmo.

When Debbie and Danny had left the room, the tangle-haired rock star took a gold cigarette case from his bag, opened it, not in the least surreptitiously, and contemplated the neatly rolled joints in it. Then he shook his head and snapped the case shut. He'd wait for Miss What's Her Name and the glass. One thing was certain: he wasn't going out there, without even a guitar to keep his hands busy, unless he had a small buzz on. Danny had said take it easy; give them, you know, the all-American-boy thing, and he could do that better if he didn't feel too tight inside, which was the way he always felt without something to relax him. He opened the vodka bottle and took a short belt.

Lousy. Funny what a difference a glass made. Like those wine nuts always made a thing out of the shape of the glass, and maybe they had something.

The door opened again. Elmo thought it would be Miss Weintraub returning. Instead, a portly, bearded man stepped into the room.

Elmo looked up blankly.

"Ah! Excuse-a me!" The bearded man, who spoke with some kind of accent, was smiling. "I think this is where we wait, is it not?"

"I guess so." There was a pause while Elmo tried to decide whether he should say something else, and if so, what it should be. He finally settled for "You on the show, too?"

"Yes. I do not think we have met. I am Luciano Pavarotti."

"Yeah," said Elmo. The lack of animation in his voice made it clear that he did not recognize the name.

Holding his smile, Pavarotti said, "I am a singer."

"So'm I," said Elmo.

Pavarotti's smile broadened as he came forward with a burly stride. "You have not heard of me, have you, Mr. Finstetter? Well, that is refreshing."

"Yeah?" Elmo was wondering what this guy seemed to find so amusing. He looked around vaguely. "Where the hell's that broad with the glass?"

"I do not think I know to what you are referring," said Pavarotti, with the bookish correctness of one to whom English is not a natural language. He crossed to peer at a Van Gogh reproduction on a wall.

"What kind of stuff you sing?" asked Elmo.

"Opera," said Pavarotti, chuckling. "I am a tenor."

"No kiddin'?" said Elmo. "So'm I. Real high. Way the hell up there when I use my head voice."

"Ah!" said Pavarotti. "Falsetto."

"Yeah. That's it. You ever use it?"

"I do not have to." Still smiling, Pavarotti continued to examine the Van Gogh.

Elmo sensed that what the older man had said was some kind of a zing, but he couldn't decide exactly why. Frig it. He was probably jealous of Elmo's success, like everybody else.

Frig everybody else, too.

Still searching for an acceptable glass for Elmo, Debbie Weintraub entered an office that contained a sofa, a coffee table, and, against one wall, a highboy that served as an occasional bar. Strictly speaking, Debbie, now that she had become a talent coordinator, should not be rummaging about to find a glass—there were gofers around for that sort of thing—but she'd thought it would be easier and quicker to find a glass than to find a gofer to go for one. More efficient.

Above all, Debbie was efficient. Had been ever since she'd gone to night business school in New York, somehow lucking into a behind-the-scenes TV job the time she came out to L.A. to visit her sister Sylvia, who was married to a computer engineer. She'd started out as a production assistant on a local station, had gone from there to the Dinah Shore show, and after that had gone off the air, had been picked up by Toni Tennille's group.

It had all come rather swiftly, and there were times when she could hardly believe she was genuinely part of the glamorous world of showbiz rather than a nice Jewish girl with a lot of old-fashioned ideas about sex, morality, marriage, and all the rest, which her mother, back home, thought she still was, and which, as a matter of fact, she was indeed at heart, though she tried mightily to match the sophistication she imagined she saw all around her. Mama still wondered why she hadn't found a husband out there on the west coast. What Mama didn't know was that she almost had, or at least thought she had, until the producer she'd so willingly given herself to for a couple of months dumped her cold and left her wary of liaison with anyone else. She learned later that it was his pattern to carry on with a young woman for sixty days or so, murmuring words of love and marriage he didn't mean in the slightest, and assuming that his partner knew very well he didn't mean them. At times she didn't know which memory was the more painful: her disappointment in love or her chagrin over having been so naive about it. She now detested the sophistication and permissiveness she'd once thought she admired. But she was part of that milieu now so she'd have to learn to live with it. And not think about that jolt to her psyche from that bastard of a producer. The job, which kept her busy, helped with that.

As she entered the office now, she saw a short, badgerlike man in his early fifties sitting on the sofa. His face had the sags and wrinkles of someone inherently plump who has recently lost weight. There was also upon it a lugubrious expression: a weariness of the eyes and a downturn of the mouth that was almost, but not quite, sour. Smiling, Debbie told herself that if she had not known Sheldon Walters she would never in a million years have pegged him as a gagwriter—and one of the best, at that.

The ashtray of the coffee table was full of cigarette butts. Walters was lighting a new cigarette. Scattered before him were numerous sheets of paper with typing and scribbled notes upon them.

"Greetings, me proud beauty," Walters said.

"I'm no beauty so I can't be proud about it," Debbie said, picking up his bantering tone—all women on talk shows carry on playful word games with all comedy writers in a kind of folk rite that has to be observed. "So why do you call me that?" said Debbie.

"I submit, your honor," said Walters, "that the question is irrelevant, immaterial, and possibly fattening."

"Shel," said Debbie, "you make a lot of sense. If you're writing anything for today's show it's probably too late to get it on the cue cards, unless it's for one of the late interviews—maybe Elmo What's His Name."

"No," said Walters, "I'm knocking out questions for tomorrow."

"Why are you working on this show at all? Toni doesn't do comedy per se."

"Because," Walters explained, "Carol Burnett has gone off, *The Big Show* was canceled, and Dinah Shore, for whom I might have done questions, has gone off too and lastly, but hardly leastly, I'm too proud to stand in the unemployment line. And now that you've got all that, and I wouldn't be surprised if you haven't, what can I do for you?"

"I'm looking for a glass," said Debbie. "A real *glass* glass."

"The best kind," said Walters, muttering the line to himself rather than for its effect on Debbie. "But let me divert you from your quest for an unholy grail with a query of my own. Is Regis Philbin still set for next Monday?"

"Yes."

"His name always sounds to me like doubletalk. The krelman is attached to one end of the spatulum and at the other end is the Regis Philbin, where it fits into the croyden. I thought Elmo Finstetter was supposed to be on Monday, too."

Debbie was still laughing at the doubletalk. It pleased her to know that she'd now been around long enough not to get caught by it. "Elmo was supposed to be on Monday," she said, "but somebody else fell out today—I forget who—so they moved Elmo up."

"I believe you might get a Finstetter to fit into the croyden, too," said Walters.

Debbie laughed again. One of the reasons she kept her job, in fact, was that she laughed so readily. She followed the dictum of the boss who had once said, "Miss Jones, feed the goldfish—I want to see happy faces all round me." She'd laughed at that one, too, when she'd heard it. Laughing was another way to keep from getting too furious. "Shel," she said, "how long have you been in TV, anyway?"

"Since before you were a gleam in your father's whatever. I worked with Dinah Shore back in the fifties, when there were actual sketches on her show."

"But you don't get to write jokes these days, do you?"

"Not often," Walters said, sighing. "I console myself by thinking that I'm stealing money. Not that writing jokes is all that difficult, but writing dumb questions is a lot easier."

"But don't you want to, you know, do your thing?"

"I do my thing all the time," Walters said. "I call up Pat McCormack, Bill Larkin, sometimes Pat Paulsen, who used to be a member in good standing of our honorable profession, or maybe Bob Hope, who buys stuff from me for benefits and special gigs, and cut them to ribbons. If I can get a laugh out of Harry Crane thirty seconds after he picks up the phone I'm a hit for the day."

He paused to think things over.

"Actually," he continued, "I should thank God Toni is not doing sketches on this show. I shudder to think of writing repartee for her to bat about with the likes of Elmo Finstetter. As a matter of fact, I always shudder to think. I may just stop thinking altogether and concentrate on shuddering."

"Elmo kind of makes me shudder, too," said Debbie. "What he stands for, anyway. You know—women as pure playthings. All that. But you have to admit he's kind of cute. In a jerky sort of way."

"That's what this country needs more of. Cute jerks. That's what I should have Toni asking him about." He put on an imitation of Toni Tennille's broad, buttermilk smile—as broad as her sexy shoulders—and adjusting his voice to a level of utter earnestness, said, "Tell me, Elmo, which of your qualities do you think is more important, your cuteness or your jerkiness?"

Debbie laughed. "I don't think," she said, "that Elmo would be a very good straight man. Or should I say straight person?"

"That sounds too much like a heterosexual," said Walters, "and they're getting to be an oppressed minority these days."

"Well, you'll work it out, I'm sure," said Debbie. "I'm not sure what it all is—just that you'll work it out." She headed for the highboy. "There's got to be a glass around here somewhere. For a kid from the sticks Elmo's turned into quite a connoisseur. He thinks plastic spoils the taste of vodka."

"I know," said Walters, nodding. "He always has that glass of his around, even when he's doing a gig somewhere. His public thinks it's water. Fats Waller used to do the same thing, only with gin."

"Fats who?"

"Great genius of another time. You're too young to know. The whole goddamned world's too young now. That's one of the things wrong with it."

"I'm too young to notice," Debbie said, which made her feel she'd won the exchange. Advantage, Miss Weintraub. Not bad, with somebody like Shel Walters across the net.

She had found a glass now, in the highboy. Holding it up for Walters to see, she smiled and slipped out of the room, leaving the jokemeister to scowl at his array of typed questions.

The audience was taking seats in the large, tiered, auditoriumlike studio, staring at the set and the cameras and the cables lying like dead boa constrictors on the floor, and the busy, quiet men with headsets riding the camera dollies and microphone booms. In the rear, above the seats, shadowy figures lurked behind double glass in the control room. The viewers came from all corners of the country and all walks of life to attend the great American ritual of the talk show, rather like pilgrims on a once-in-a-lifetime visit to a shrine.

Toni Tennille, who was about to officiate, was a relative newcomer to the time-honored institution of the talk show. Being a host involved nothing more than being an alert and friendly person, rubbing elbows and trading chitchat with people everybody knows, and somehow giving the viewer the feeling that he's right up there with the celebrities himself. Little of significance was ever said, great revelations were seldom made, important news was rarely announced. But that, in a way, was the point of the whole thing—just the chance to be on intimate, smalltalk terms with the mighty or the merely known, or with what few celebrities-to-be were thrown in. It swept the viewer into the midst of the glamorous world of showbiz. Like the skillfully packaged junk food of the soap operas, the sometimes hysterical, forced humor of the sitcoms, and the brain-rotting appeals to avarice of the game shows, it was a convenient escape from the everyday world.

In the greenroom, Elmo Finstetter fidgeted, sipped his vodka, tried gamely to make conversation with Pavarotti, who seemed determined to be amused by him, and later with Burt Reynolds, who dropped in briefly, and who struck Elmo as pretty easy to talk to, considering he was a famous actor and all. After that there was a doctor who looked more like an actor than a medical man and who was supposed to have discovered a controversial treatment for arthritis. He had never heard of Elmo, as Elmo had never heard of him.

Pavarotti and Burt Reynolds got into some glop, which Elmo didn't fully dig, about the differences between screen acting and acting on the operatic stage; the medical man listened with fascination to this, while Elmo fidgeted, bored. Then both the opera star and the actor began to ask the doctor about his treatment, following his answers attentively.

This, Elmo thought, was a goddamn talk show already, here in this dumb waiting room. He'd never seen many talk shows—except sometimes on the road when there was nothing much to do in the afternoon —but in those he'd caught the action was just like it was now: guys sitting around and talking to each other. Which was no damned action at all. The way Toni Tennille did it, he understood, was to bring her guests on one at a time, all by themselves, and not keep them onstage after she was through talking with them, *Tonight Show* style.

To illustrate some point or other, Pavarotti was singing a bar or two from an opera very lightly. "He does not say Mimi is dying, but he sings to her . . . *Che gelida manina* . . . 'Your tiny hands are cold.' "

"Yeah," said Elmo. "That's what the cow said to the guy that was milkin' her."

The other three looked at him almost blankly, and Elmo shrugged and took another belt of vodka.

Burt Reynolds drifted off somewhere; the doctor was summoned to the stage by a young man who stuck his smiling head in the door, and Pavarotti politely excused himself and returned to his dressing room.

At last it was time for Elmo to go on. He filled his glass with what was left of the vodka and picked it up to carry it with him. His staff escort was a tall young man with ringleted dark hair; he looked like a college student. "I can take care of that for you, Mr. Finstetter," he said, reaching for the glass.

"I want it with me," said Elmo.

"I'll see that it gets put out there for you, sir. During the commercial."

"Okay," said Elmo. "But don't lose it."

"No, sir," said the gofer, with the solemn earnestness of ambitious youth.

When Elmo finally stepped on the set, and the applause greeted him, he became a different sort of creature by passing through this flaw in the continuum and into another dimension. His smile, with its interesting suggestion of the feral, returned. Greeted by Toni, he loped to his place like a tame cougar. And then she began throwing questions at him in a surprisingly loud voice.

"These songs you sing, Elmo—they're really **all**

based on the things young people think about all the time, aren't they?"

"Yeah, I guess they are."

"What about your own problems as a young person? What do you think of the differences between the young group and, let's say, those over thirty?"

Elmo frowned. What the hell was he supposed to say? He didn't like this broad. She came on strong. He'd thought at first that swimming-champ build of hers, and how tall she was and everything, was kind of sexy, but now he wasn't sure. On the other talk shows he'd seen, the host kind of murmured to the guests. This Toni Tennille seemed to be letting him have both barrels.

"Once I left home, I didn't have no more problems," said Elmo.

The ripple of sound and scattered applause showed that his remark had pleased at least the younger segment of the audience. Obtuse to people as individuals, Elmo was sensitive to audience reaction and could detect the subtlest shifts of mood out there in the rows of what he considered cabbageheads.

He'd learned to gauge the tempers of others in the rural jungle in which he'd been raised—a small county seat in Oregon's orchard-and-Bible belt, where, in spite of the folksy, God-fearing atmosphere, the dangers were sometimes every bit as real as those of the inner-city ghettos, especially for a high school dropout, who got his first guitar the only way he knew how: by visiting a music store in another town one night, breaking in, and stealing it.

Later Elmo's old man had ranted and raved, and once even taken a swing at him for being in the music business and playing in sleazy taverns, and his mother, looking put-upon, had taken him to her minister for counseling.

(Elmo was now, in response to Toni's questions, giving her a somewhat altered version of this story, making it sound as though his folks, with all their lack of understanding, were the bad guys in the black hats.)

In time an agent from Portland caught Elmo's group and came up with a few modest bookings on the road for the summer. Away from home at last, Elmo smoked pot, drank likker, sniffed coke, and blasphemed to his heart's content.

It came to him after a while that young girls were fascinated by him. The combination of his Presley-style rock music and his feral look seemed a challenge to most of them; there was deliciousness in courting danger. In delighted surprise, Elmo took advantage of the situation. The agent noticed this magic appeal, and before long had other bookings with other groups for Elmo, plus the recording date where one of the songs was "Eat Your Heart Out, Baby," the single that caught fire all across the country and really made him a name.

Not long afterward Elmo dumped his old group and the Portland agent (who was still trying to sue him) and moved over into Danny Moss's stable of thoroughbreds.

At times he wondered secretly if he could keep it up, though he promptly pushed away the thought whenever it came. There were only two activities that kept him from absolute boredom. One was performing with his raspy voice, raspy guitar, and acrobatic hips; the other was sex. Now that he could afford it, he shot for a different chick every night, which made three hundred and sixty-five a year, though the actual total, due to misunderstandings and goofups, was considerably less than this.

He'd wondered once or twice during their conversation whether the superhealthy broad interviewing him might not be worth a play. Her bright red lipstick struck him as pretty. She was married to some keyboard type named The Captain, the way he understood it, but as far as Elmo was concerned, husbands didn't always stand in the way. You took these things the way they came. But the hell with it, Elmo concluded. He liked his chicks a bit slinky and not so goddamned wholesome.

He reached for the glass of clear liquid now in place on the low table beside the edge of his chair, lifted it, and sipped. It tasted odd. Aromatic, somehow; more like gin than vodka. Where had he known a taste like that before? He remembered now. His mother, when he'd been a kid, had had a number of superstitious medications she'd forced upon him for everything from sniffles to nosebleed; among them had been something she'd called sweet spirits of niter. That was what it tasted like. Sweet spirits of stupid, goddamned niter. Must be himself, not the vodka.

Elmo's last moments upon earth passed swiftly, calmly. At least he was not in deep thought, and deep thought was probably not the state in which he would have wished to die. The cabbageheads and the lights out there were a pleasant, multicolored blur to him. Toni was still asking questions, but he was answering without really listening—no mean trick, but one he could do. He was in a happy state, akin to nirvana; he had a gentle high on but was by no means stoned.

The sharp pain burst into his consciousness as though a knife had been plunged into him. His eyebrows rose swiftly and his jaw dropped in surprise. He gagged, coughed, clutched at his middle, and doubled over.

Toni Tennille looked at him in horror.

Elmo fell forward from his chair, twitched several times on the bright yellow carpet, and died.

II

Roger Dale paused before entering suite C-7 in the Fairview Business Park to admire the sign, carved into a teak panel, that said Dale Security Agency. He'd had the sign for three months now but still paused to admire it. It meant that he'd arrived, even though, by his secret standards, he was still on the way. Indeed, Roger Dale probably would have considered himself still on the way no matter how far along he got.

Before he pushed open the plate glass door, he adjusted the knot of his broad tie, performing the gesture consciously and as an onerous duty. Narrower ties were back in—or so the rude little Austrian who was his haberdasher assured him—but Roger had already decided he would stick with his Edwardian image. In the cultural entity set in greater Los Angeles but known generically as Hollywood, you were more apt to succeed if you had an image, which might be anything you chose, from a hayseed look to the thoroughly urbane, as long as it was a clear impression of some kind and made people remember you.

It bugged him that the young hip crowd, which consciously prided itself on being independent in its tastes, was in fact fanatically rigid in its submission to peer group pressure. Whatever was *in*—gold neck chains, sandals, beards, loose jeans, tight jeans, jogging shoes, cowboy boots, old-fashioned legit-looking cowboy hats, new-fashioned cowboy hats with the sides turned sharply up, mass-produced for the urban country-and-western crowd; and with the women, Bo Derek corn-row hairdos, jungle frizzy hairdos, Afros, dumb-looking Shinola-brown cheek and eye makeup, baggy wrinkled painters' pants, jackets with the sleeves pulled up to the elbows—whatever was perceived as *with it*, the lemmings flocked to. Such fads Dale had always resisted. If clothes were that important in southern California pop culture, well then, by God, he'd be his own man and make his own decisions about attire.

Roger pushed back a lock of wavy hair that had escaped the bondage of his morning pump handle hairspray and went into his office.

Charleen Yates was already in place at her typewriter and reception desk.

"Morning, Rodge."

"Good morning, Charleen."

As part of his ritual, he paused for a beat or two to admire Charleen. Both of her, as someone had once said when introducing Dolly Parton. He took in Charleen's blond ringlets, somewhat round face, pouty little underlip, and those *Guinness Book of World Records* boobs. Like 85 percent of the attractive young women in Hollywood, Charleen had vague dreams of someday being on TV or in the movies, but Roger knew that the camera would make her plumper than she actually was, so that unless she had the wit to be a comedienne, which she didn't, she would, alas, almost certainly never make it.

It disturbed Roger somewhat to know all this. He knew a little and sometimes a great deal about practically everything and he had to fight it or at the very least try to conceal it from time to time, if only to avoid a fat lip. Nobody, as we say, likes a smartass. But what do you do if you're born that way? You adjust, you pretend. It can get to be a strain.

An affair with Charleen would have been interesting, but among the several lessons Roger had learned from his brief military service in Vietnam was the wisdom of keeping his pleasures as far as possible from the flagpole. Besides, there were plenty of others out there, equally or more interesting, so there was no difficulty in exercising a bit of restraint at the office.

"Something on your mind, Rodge?" asked Charleen. He realized that he'd been staring at her a moment too long. And the slight flutter of her lashes suggested that she suspected something was on his mind, and had an idea what it was. And didn't mind.

"No more than usual," Roger said with a slight sigh, the closest he could come to a truthful answer without getting into complications.

He broke off and went into the back room of the suite, which served as a working sanctuary for himself and his assistant, Jinny Cantu. Ms. Cantu's title was vice president of the agency, which wasn't incorporated, but Roger felt the billing would make her happy, and that would help ensure her continued presence, even when paychecks were a little late, which they sometimes were.

Jinny, on the phone, blinked at Roger through lenses that looked as though they'd been made from the bottoms of wine bottles, covered the mouthpiece with her palm, and said, "Long distance. Be right with you."

Roger smiled, said "Press on," and sat at his own desk.

Turning the page of his calendar pad, he glanced at the few scribbled reminders on it. Nothing urgent. He listened as Jinny continued her phone conversation.

"You've got a B and E on him? How about the disposition? No charges? Remanded to county officer as juvenile. Yes, I've got it. Thanks. Anybody else call for this info? Los Angeles police. Yeah, I figured they would. Thank you very much. Appreciate your courtesy."

Jinny hung up.

"What was that all about?" asked Roger.

"The Elmo Finstetter thing. His hometown in Oregon. You asked me to look into it."

"Oh, that. So he's got a yellow sheet, huh?"

"Nothing much," said Jinny, glancing at her notepad. "One juvenile breaking and entering. Seems he stole a guitar from a shop. The owner not only didn't press charges, he let him have the damn thing."

Roger nodded. "Must have been worth it. I'll bet the guy's still telling how he pulled a Bishop of Digne on the now-famous Elmo Finstetter."

"Bishop of who?"

"Digne. In *Les Misérables*. The one Jean Valjean stole the candlesticks from."

"Oh, *that* bishop of Digne," Jinny said.

Grinning at Jinny, Roger contemplated her. It pleased him that she was one of the few women he was drawn to without the slightest sexual arousal. Not that she was physically unattractive: her figure wasn't bad at all, and her medium-brown skin looked as though it would feel very nice indeed under one's curious palm. Without her glasses—which she needed to see two steps in front of her—she would have been comely enough to attract notice even in this town, where every fourth or fifth girl who walked down the street was worth a sharply swiveled neck. But in Roger's estimation Jinny's efficiency and even temperament were far more important than her physical charms. He had liked her on the spot the first day she'd walked in, answering his ad for an assistant. He was proud that he had hired her for herself and not because, as a black female with a Spanish surname, and handicapped to boot, she fulfilled virtually all of his equal-opportunity requirements.

The handicap was Jinny's borderline blindness. As an LAPD policewoman, she'd walked into a shootout in a barrio one night, and a bullet creasing her head had done something to the optic nerve, giving her a medical discharge she would rather not have had. She talked about it dispassionately, however, and without complaining, so Roger assumed, and certainly hoped, she was at least moderately contented here at the agency.

"How come?" Jinny asked.

"How come what?"

"This sudden interest in Elmo Finstetter."

"It's kind of on spec," said Roger, getting up and crossing to the drip machine to pour himself some coffee. "Did I tell you I got a call from Johnny Carson's office?"

"*The Tonight Show*? We're coming up in the world."

"We can use it. I wish the books looked as great as the office does."

"We're in the black," said Jinny. "Except if we buy a bottle of black ink to enter it, we'll be in the red again."

"Ha, ha," said Roger, without mirth.

Jinny shrugged. "I didn't think it was all that bad. Maybe it's just too early in the morning."

Roger sat and sipped his coffee. "Out there," he said, waving his hand vaguely to indicate greater L.A., "they don't know how a business like this runs. They think we slink around in seedy hotels running into peroxide blondes, making like Sam Spade. Anyway, we'd really go broke if I concentrated on P.I. Look what's showing our biggest profit now. Installing burglar alarms. Pushing the damn things makes me feel like a salesman."

"Is that bad?"

"It's an honorable profession," said Roger. "They're all honorable professions. Just not my bag, that's all."

"You're off the track again. You said something about Johnny Carson."

"Yeah. Some guy on the phone—one of his staff people. They want to book me for the show Thursday. He apologized for the short notice, but they want me to comment on this Finstetter thing while it's still news. So I called up Steve Allen over in Van Nuys and asked him if he thought I should do it and he asked me if I was crazy to ask a question like that, and I said okay I'd do it, and he said nice talking to me again and why didn't we have lunch sometime. I wonder if he meant it."

"But this is great, Rodge! Looks like all your PR efforts are starting to pay off!"

Roger nodded. "Could be. I put a lot of time into those cases—even some expense. And it wasn't easy, getting credit in the media for cracking them. Someday, when I can afford it, I'm going to have a good public relations counsel to do all that. Everybody should have a woman, a head doctor, and a public relations man."

"Everybody who can afford it." Jinny rearranged some scribbled notes on her desk. "Want me to start a P.P. on whoever wasted poor Elmo?"

"Might as well," said Roger.

She rose and went to a bright yellow supply cabinet to retrieve a fresh manila folder. "The FBI does it, too, you know," she said.

"Does what?"

"Keeps P.P.'s. At least they teach it at Quantico in the Behavioral Science unit. They had a whole article on psychological profiles in the last *Law Enforcement Bulletin*."

"Glad they finally got around to it. It's not a new idea, you know. They had it in the days of Bertillon—called it a *portrait parle*. Actually, it's what any good cop does by instinct when the perpetrator is unknown. Asks what kind of person would do this particular deed. Reconstructs said person, then looks for somebody to match the model. Simple. Only, in keeping with our enlightened times, the professors have given it big names and made it complicated."

"You were born in the wrong century, Rodge."

"Oh, I don't know," he said. "Ever see the photos of the chicks they had in those days? All overweight. I'd say something funny about them, but that would be making jokes at their expanse."

"Ha, ha," said Jinny, in the same tone Roger had employed before.

"Okay, one bomb for you, one for me. Go ahead with a workup on Elmo, okay? Be fantastic if I could close it in time for the show. Too much to hope for, I suppose."

Jinny laughed. "You're dreaming again." Bringing a folder and a mimeographed P.P. form back to her desk, she sat and began to sing softly to herself in a kind of disco beat.

Roger grimaced. He hoped Jinny would not look up and note his reaction. He has as much courage as the next man, he supposed, but the one thing he'd never been able to bring himself to do was tell Jinny about her singing. Perhaps that was *her* dream—to be someday what Sam Spade would have called a canary. But Jinny, alas, was tone deaf. In a remarkable way, too. Most tone deafers, which you could check out on *The Gong Show* if you wanted to go to all that trouble, sang flat. Jinny sang sharp. Or maybe it was sideways. Anyway, to hear it was to wince. Roger sighed. If none of Jinny's flaws were any worse than this, he was ahead of the game.

The working day, for the denizens of greater Los Angeles, lazed away under a faintly hazy sun. The proprietors of countless small businesses fretted, as Roger did, over the state of their books; employees of big and small outfits did their best to rip off the company in little ways, like taking home envelopes or stamps, and in some shadowy places avarice loomed even larger as freelance crooks in every field from auto theft to narcotics pushing conspired to make their scores.

A few people either dreamed of or actually planned murder. Mostly, their motives were rational, or let us say, comprehensible. Revenge, elimination of business rivalry, even honor thought to be at stake. But some, by ordinary standards, were freakish.

The one who planned the next talk show murder fell into that category.

* * *

The chimes went dingdong. Meg Arlington strode to the front door of her apartment, opened it, and there was Roger Dale.

"Hi."

"Hi."

They kissed.

She noted that his suit this evening was a shimmering gunmetal gray—some kind of silk, probably Thai or Italian. His tie was maroon with a paisley design. It would have made a better story if Meg could have said that she had fallen in love (or *toward* love, anyway) with Roger Dale the first moment she saw him; the fact was that she had initially reacted to him negatively, searching the midden of her mind for a single word to describe whatever it was about him that struck her, and coming up, finally, with *popinjay*. It took several encounters before she began to be attracted to Roger. There was much inside, she discovered, that didn't show on the surface. It was drawing Meg to Roger with increasing intensity.

"Nice pad," said Roger, looking around.

"Make yourself at home. I'm still cooking." She nodded toward the kitchenette, which was separated from the small living room by a bar counter.

"You're not only cooking, you're sizzling," said Roger, admiring her trim figure.

"I try," said Meg, laughing.

Roger sniffed. "Smells good."

"*Carbonnade de boeuf flamande*," she said.

"Wasn't he the eldest son of Louis the Twelfth?"

"Beef stew, dummy."

"I love it already," Roger said, smiling.

Meg had a small apron over her pottery-blue shirtwaist dress. Compact of build, pert in her movements, she wore her sandy hair in a disciplined ruffling. A constellation of almost invisible freckles crossed her nose. "You can have a drink if you want it. Scotch, isn't it?"

"Scotch. Thanks."

"But maybe you don't want it right now."

"Why not?"

"It might spoil the taste of the wine. I've got a Cabernet from a small winery in Sonoma County. Rather choice, I think."

"My cup runneth over," said Roger. "But I'm willing to risk numbing my taste buds with Scotch. What the hell."

"Makings there on the bar," said Meg.

He busied himself putting ice, Scotch, and water into a glass, as Meg, across the counter, made a final check of the stew simmering in a Dutch oven on the electric stove. "Brilliant idea, spending the evening here," said Roger. "Charming, old-fashioned. Might have known. That's your stock in trade—good ideas."

"I get a few from time to time," said Meg, laughing, and slipping on a pair of padded gloves so that she could remove the pot from the stove. "Turning them into cold cash is something else again."

"Hang in there," said Roger. "The world is yours. It just doesn't know it yet."

"And maybe never will. Sometimes I wonder if I've done everything right. And if not, where did I go wrong? I started out to be a successful public relations person. All I am, so far, is still a person. I suppose that's something."

Roger carried his drink to the sofa, lowered himself into the cushions, and set the glass on the coffee table. He glanced at the card table Meg had covered with a tablecloth, in the center of which sat a red candle in an old, straw-jacketed Chianti bottle. "It's possible," he said, lifting his drink to taste it, "that you acquired too much wit and good taste for your professional good. Some people mistrust it. Political candidates, for example, don't dare have it. Or conceal it if they do."

"What about Ronnie Reagan?" Meg said.

"Please," Roger said. "Not while I'm eating. But seriously, Reagan's kind of humor is okay in politics because it's totally square humor and that can't get you into trouble. But humor with true wit—the real article—*can*. It makes you too hip for the room, as we say."

"Well, anyway," Meg said, "witty or not, here I am, dreaming dreams of success, and I can't even promote myself, let alone the clients I can't get. So much for the old degree in mass communications."

"Don't knock it," said Roger. "It got you a job."

"Yes," said Meg with a sigh. "On the tour bus. The mansions in Beverly Hills. Where Rudolph Valentino used to live. I suppose that *is* mass communications."

Smiling, Roger watched Meg bring the plates to the table and complete the setting. He liked her deft way of moving—it reminded him of a ballerina. He'd found her pleasing the first day she'd wandered into his office, not, as he'd thought initially, to seek a job, but to enlist him as a client for the public relations agency she wanted to get started in her spare time.

She had not attempted to snow-job him in the slightest. That was one of the things he'd liked about her immediately. She'd told him right off that she was a guide on a tour bus, but that she was trying to get her own PR career off the ground and was visiting small businesses at random to get their accounts. She'd heard about him, figured he might be a likely prospect, and wandered in. Maybe *that* was where she'd gone wrong—telling the truth so openly, as much as he admired it. Maybe, hoping to make her way in the world of hype, she was already doomed by her own compulsive integrity.

He had told her that he, too, was struggling, and that for the moment, at least, couldn't afford PR, though someday he meant to have it, and had explained how he'd already made a few gestures on his own to spread the word about the services he offered. And then, somehow, without either actually suggesting it in so many words, they'd made a date, with the tacit understanding that if it worked out there would be more. It had worked out, and by now there had been several.

This was their fifth date. "Dinner at my place," Meg had said. "To show you I can cook. And I really can."

"As a buildup to what?" Roger had asked, playfully feigning suspicion.

"To whatever," Meg had said, meeting his eye.

And here she was, across from him, the lights turned down, the red candle on the table flickering between them. The beef stew with the French name was delicious. The wine, as she had said, was choice. He rolled it on his tongue and nodded. "Yes. Full-bodied, chocolaty, like a Médoc. A touch on the bland side, maybe. I like a suggestion of astringency, if possible. This reminds me of a Margaux '78. The '77s had more bite."

There was the faintest touch of irritation in Meg's honest laugh as she said, "Roger, is there *anything* you don't know about?"

"I keep looking," he said blithely. "As for the wine, well, I had this buddy in Vietnam."

"You had time to talk about wine in Vietnam?"

"Yeah, between ducking, running, shooting and—in some cases—dying." His face grew somber for a moment, then he pulled himself back to the present. "Anyway, my friend's old man owned a winery near Livermore. He got me interested and I went on from there. One of the things I got out of that stinking war. They're all stinking. But I guess you can find dimes in a cesspool if you're immersed in it long enough."

"Nice table talk," said Meg sarcastically.

"Sorry. Inappropriate image," said Roger. "But I was thinking of how what's bad sometimes breeds what's good. Like how the war led to my career. They made me a military policeman. I came back and finished school on the G.I. Bill. Soash, with a minor in criminology. And here I am. Selling burglar alarms."

Meg studied Roger for a moment. It had struck her before that there was something elusive about his physical appearance, and now she thought she knew what it was. At first glance he gave the impression of being handsome, but he really wasn't. He wore his face rather as he wore his carefully selected clothes. Take away the confident, insouciant air and you had a countenance that vaguely resembled that of a sleepy camel. She was delighted to find this. Concealing her discovery, she continued the conversation. "I had an idea," she said, "that the private eye business wasn't nearly as glamorous as everyone thinks. But there must be more to it than peddling burglar alarms. After all, you *did* solve those cases I read about."

"Well, I didn't exactly solve them, though I had a hand in it. The big break was getting the first one mentioned in Ronnie Fordyce's column. One of those happy accidents. Ronnie somehow met the captain of detectives I'd called—at a cocktail party or someplace—and the captain, telling the story to Ronnie, was good enough to give me credit for what I'd contributed. It looked to Ronnie like a good story, and I guess it was, so he put it in his column."

"The park strangler thing?"

"Right. I have this clipping service—crime news from out-of-town papers. Research, grist for the mill, et cetera. You see, after I came back from Nam I told myself I'd be the best goddamn criminal investigator ever. I poked into anything and everything that might help. Books, lectures, law enforcement publications. Psychology, forensic medicine. I was born with a pretty retentive mind, like some guys are born with a good pitching arm or a fast left hook. Add to all this a couple of years with the sheriff's department in Tucson —best opening I could find at the time. Anyway, you get the idea. The clippings are a part of it. Am I off the track again? What was the last station we passed?"

"Park strangler."

"Oh, yeah. He committed thirteen murders in L.A., then stopped for a while. To me it seemed like he'd left town. Then they had one in Minneapolis that was exactly the same m.o.—knife pricks in private places. I'd already worked up a P.P. on the guy, just for prac- tice, and I called Minneapolis and gave it to them, with one added entry. He would be recently arrived from California. Then I called the captain of detec- tives here who had originally caught the squeal and told him he might hear from Minneapolis soon. You know the rest. The strangler's serving life now, though he should be on a squirrel farm."

"You do good work," said Meg. "More wine?"

"Only for drinking."

"How about the missing heiress?" she asked. "Didn't you locate her when nobody else could?"

"Lucky break. Her P.P. showed that she had this

thing for sauna baths—psychological overtones we needn't go into. At my suggestion, they looked and that's where they found her body, buried behind this real estate operator's sauna. Ronnie Fordyce picked up on that one, too, and it also made regular news stories. By this time I figured it was good publicity and ought to bring in some business. It did, but not much. Evidently you've got to keep a P.R. campaign going, which you'd know more about than I do. Anyway, the bread and butter is still rent-a-cops and those damned burglar alarms. An occasional divorce case. Not too many laughs."

"What about the Harrington case?"

"Mostly hunch. The way the secretary said she found him at his desk, dead of a heart attack, just sounded a sour note to me. I made a quiet check, found out she was big in his will, and suddenly guessed what she must have done. She knew he had a bum ticker and gave him the most vigorous roll in the hay she'd ever treated him to. Not a bad way to go, if you have to. I don't imagine they'll ever convict her on it, though."

Meg looked across the dancing candle flame and saw Roger's eyes gleaming. "You do love your work, don't you?"

Roger looked surprised for a moment, then said, "I guess I do. It's creative. It's the therapeutic basket I weave. But I know some other creative activities," he said, looking at her steadily.

"I'll bet you do," she said.

"Meg," he said, "I don't want you to think this is some sort of a line or standard ploy with me, because it isn't, but—"

"Yes?"

"I would very much like to make love to you."

"That's a nice way to put it," she said. "So much

better than I'd like to sleep with you, make it with you, have sex with you."

"After we get through with the semantics," he said, smiling slightly, "I wonder if we might get around to an answer to my question."

"We might," she said, toying with a breadstick. "The thing is, with you, you'd probably spend more time analyzing than enjoying."

"The two are not mutually exclusive. But if you prefer it I promise to withhold analysis."

"Really?"

"You'll be astonished at my self-control. I probably will myself."

Meg laughed, rose, and picked up the plates to bring them back to the kitchenette. "Time for coffee. And Grand Marnier."

"Perfect evening," said Roger.

"Which isn't over yet," she said with a smile that had, like the astringency of good wine, just the right touch of salaciousness in it.

III

There were papers in J. Duffy Griswold's *in* basket and, even more annoying, in his *hold* basket, too. Always those goddamned papers. Statistics from the district offices, congressional inquiries, complaints, requests for investigations, interpretations of new Supreme Court rulings (usually in favor of criminals), and amendments to or modifications of the old regulations.

Et cetera.

Griswold had had a crazy dream the other night. The commies had come up with a new secret weapon, a gas that destroyed paper. It would be subtly sprayed throughout the FBI building and everything would come to a grinding halt. In his dream he tried to warn about it, but nobody would listen.

That was par for the course.

J. Duffy Griswold always came to work an hour early and left an hour late—two or three hours sometimes—but he never even came close to catching up with all those papers that kept coming. And coming.

It was now seven minutes after eight in the morning. He had arrived nine minutes ago. Mrs. O'Reilly, his secretary, was still making coffee in the room outside the spacious office. The only possible good thing about this morning, which was otherwise like any other morning, was that Mrs. O'Reilly, thin, gray-haired, gentle, settled-down, was not caught up in women's lib or any other form of contemporary madness and did not object to making coffee, even though the chore was not specifically referred to in her job description.

He hunched over his desk like a bear over a bone and sighed, his massive shoulders moving up and down. As he had all his life, he disciplined himself inwardly to accept his burdens. After all, he'd known it would be this way when he'd accepted his post, a year ago, as one of several assistant directors to the director, himself, of the Federal Bureau of Investigation.

His corner office overlooked Pennsylvania Avenue. That was one of the beanies of his exalted position, like the old-fashioned wooden desk instead of one of the cold gray steel kind issued by the General Services Administration to those of mere middle rank. He could hear the growling of automobile engines outside as hordes of other bureaucrats made their ways to early arrivals in countless offices in and around Washington, D.C.

It was a far cry, thought J. Duffy Griswold, from the little southern town where he'd started out as a cop twenty-five years ago. A lot of water had passed under the bridge since then, eroding away a great many rough edges. With his J. Press suit, his striped rep tie, his buttondown shirt, and his cordovan wingtip shoes, he looked like one of those persons from the eastern establishment who came down to Washington so earnestly to serve and in such noticeable numbers. He was almost beginning to talk like that particular breed of Yankee, too. He needed another fishing trip back home—an annual event he planned but didn't always get around to—if only to retrieve some of his lost accent.

Mrs. O'Reilly stuck her head in the door. She could have used the intercom but knew its sudden electronic bark annoyed him, especially in the morning. Showing the half smile that was her standard, unruffled expression, she said, "Mr. Peterson is here."

Griswold looked up, scowling. "Vern Peterson? What's he want?"

"He had to see you, remember? You said twelve minutes after eight was the only time. He came in early."

"Oh. Yeah. I forgot. Well, a little VOT won't hurt old Vern. Show him in."

Without quite knowing why, he vaguely resented Peterson, the director of public affairs. Maybe it was because Vern, in the nature of his job, wasn't in a constant state of harassment the way the rest of them were. He didn't have to demonstrate his diligence, for instance, with a lot of voluntary overtime. The VOT custom, a vestige of J. Edgar Hoover's iron reign, still obtained throughout the bureau, and sometimes Griswold wished it would die out. Vern, appointed to public affairs because he'd once worked on a newspaper, had it made.

Peterson came in. He was plump—too plump for an FBI man, really. He wore a bow tie and huge black hornrimmed glasses. His face was mobile and he smiled too readily. Old J. Edgar would have got rid of him faster'n a 'gator can chomp on a tarbaby, thought Griswold, but these were other times, and the whole damned world was not as structured and predictable as it used to be.

"Morning, Duff," said Peterson. "Glad I finally caught up with you."

"Yeah. Well, you know how it is. Busier'n a hounddog in a manure pile. What have you got?"

"It's this rock-and-roll singer who was poisoned on that television show."

"What's this?"

Peterson, much to Griswold's irritation, hooked his well-upholstered buttock on the corner of the desk. "You didn't hear? Kid named Elmo Finstetter. He was appearing on the Toni Tennille show and somebody slipped him a Mickey in his glass of vodka, which, of course, everybody thought was water."

"Who is Elmo Finstetter? Is, was—?"

"Very big with the kids. Like I say, he died right there in front of the cameras. They're showing the tape in most parts of the country today, I guess just to take advantage of all the publicity."

"I thought they taped these talk show things quite a long time in advance."

"They do," said Peterson, "except for *The Tonight Show*. But maybe they were afraid that if they held this particular show up for three weeks or so somebody might stop 'em from running it. Anyway, it's on this afternoon in most cities, and tomorrow evening in Washington. You'll probably want to get a look at it."

"Sounds like lousy taste to me. Even rock-and-roll singers are human beings. Sort of."

"Right," Peterson said. "But they got out some press releases that maybe if enough people watch the show somebody might come up with a helpful clue—a theory about the motive or something. Personally, I think it's crap, but I'm just telling you what they're doing. I'm surprised you didn't hear about it. It's been on all the front pages; John Chancellor mentioned it."

"I've been working so goddamned late here," Griswold said, "that I've missed the early evening news the last coupla days, and by eleven o'clock I've usually passed out. But I still don't know why you're telling me this. We certainly don't have jurisdiction. We could, maybe, TV being interstate and federally regulated and all that shit, but we don't."

"It's nothing like that," said Peterson quickly, shaking his head. "LAPD's investigating and getting nowhere, though they'll probably break it in time. Seems like Elmo, who was not exactly beloved, except by his stupid fans, had so many enemies they've got to sort through them. But Johnny Carson—you *have* heard of Carson, haven't you? Well, Carson would like to have an FBI official on the show to talk about the case."

"What the hell is this, anyway?" Griswold's habitual scowl deepened. "The whole damned country's going to pot from emasculated law enforcement and he wants *me* to talk about some rock star that got poisoned?"

"I agree it doesn't make sense," said Vern. "But you've got to understand these things. The case is in the news, you see, and they just want somebody from the bureau to talk about it in general terms. They asked for the director himself."

"Then why doesn't he do it?"

"Too busy. He said it would have to be you."

"Oh." Griswold's expression collapsed. It stayed that way for a moment, then his scowl returned. "I guess that's what assistant directors are for. To take the stupid jobs."

"I guess they are, if they want to become directors someday," said Peterson blandly, unable to resist tossing a little dart. "You'll have to fly out to L.A. to tape the show. Figure a whole afternoon, getting there from the airport and everything. I'll have a complete run-down on the case you can study on the plane."

"God damn!" said Griswold. "A whole day wasted. Maybe more."

"Not wasted," said Peterson. "Good PR for the bureau. I couldn't place us on the Carson show if I tried, and here they are asking for us. Remember, the director's behind this."

"I heard you the first time. I still think it's a boon-doggle. And I still don't know why in hell they came to *us*."

"It's what I'm trying to explain. You see, I kind of caught the overtones when I was talking to this staff guy of Carson's on the phone. They want a conversation that strikes sparks, so it'll be interesting. Basically, that means some kind of conflict—a suggestion of it, anyway. What they're doing, you see, is squaring you off with somebody who has a different, sort of un-official, approach."

"Who?"

"A guy named Dale. You probably haven't heard of him, either."

"Can't say as I have."

"He's a P.I. who cracked a couple of cases out there and got a big play out of it. The park strangler, for one. He has his own methods, and they're supposed to be pretty sharp. Probably has a hard on for the bureau —most of these characters do. It's up to you to make us look good against him. Efficient. Sensible. Dignified. Dedicated. What we really are. Just play it cool and you'll do fine."

Griswold shook his head sadly. "Sounds to me like a dirty old pail of crawdads."

"Probably, but it's one of the things we have to live with. Look at the bright side, Duff. You'll enjoy the holiday and get to meet some celebrities. Know who else is going to be on the show? The author of *In Cold Blood*. Truman Capote."

"God, isn't he the one who posed holding lilies in his mouth?"

"That's the one," said Peterson.

"Jee-*zuss*!" said Griswold. He continued to shake his head. Mrs. O'Reilly came in with the coffee, and he gratefully poured his first cup of the day.

Roger Dale paced back and forth in his office, pausing now and then to contemplate the huge placard he had set upon an easel against one wall of the room. It was neatly ruled with lines and columns, and these were labeled with a Leroy lettering set so that it was, in effect, a blowup of the psychological profile form he'd had mimeographed for office use. Whenever Roger wished to concentrate on a case he had a blowup made and kept it where he could see it constantly so that his subconscious—which he firmly believed to be much smarter than *he* was—could be constantly fed with data and whir away upon it while his conscious mind met everyday demands.

Jinny, at her desk, was going over recent data she had collected, entering it upon a yellow, legal-size pad, then adding notes and corrections to be included in the final typing.

"Any ideas yet?" she asked. It was rhetorical; he'd have let her know quickly enough if he'd had any.

"Uh-uh." He shook his head. "Not enough data yet."

"I did the best I could," said Jinny.

"You did fine," said Roger quickly. "A hell of a lot for a short time. I don't even want to see the long-distance phone bill when it comes in."

"Business expense." Jinny shrugged.

"Right," said Roger. "A few more tax deductions like that and I'll be in line for food stamps. Well, let's see just what we *have* got here." He halted his pacing and squinted at the placard.

At the top of the chart it said *Perpetrator, Finstetter Homicide*. The lines that continued below were labeled with such designators as *Race, Sex, Age, Marital Status, Criminal Record, Residence, Reputation*. In a separate section were *Motive, Opportunity, Relation to Victim, Alibi Time and Place*, and other entries for the elements of the crime in question.

"All we do now," said Roger, "is apply Ockham's razor."

"A new twin-blade?"

"William of Ockham. Fourteenth-century philosopher. To find the truth you slice away what is irrelevant. As Ockham put it, '*Entia no sunt multiplicanda praeter necessitatum.*'"

"Language dropper."

"The trick is to know just what *is* irrelevant," said Roger, ignoring Jinny's comment. "Which ain't easy. Like, let's say, the size and build of the pigeon we're looking for. Anybody of any size could have done it, theoretically. But since the weapon was poison, we might make a tentative assumption that the killer is not a large or vigorous person, because if somebody has physical strength he tends to murder with it."

Jinny had been treated to Roger's soliloquies—and to this information—before, but she went along with the game and nodded. "All right. Could be anybody. Male or female. Big or small."

"More relevant at this stage," continued Roger, "is 'Attitude Toward Victim.' Obviously, the killer had it in for Elmo. It was a planned crime, not spur of the moment. Elmo didn't have a will; nobody stood to gain in a business way from his demise—you've already dug up enough to establish that. So I think we can safely say that whoever did it hated Elmo's guts."

"That ought to narrow it down." If there was sarcasm in Jinny's remark, it was elusive.

"Yeah," said Roger dryly. "Elmo made enemies the way a tornado makes broken houses. That agent from Portland who's suing him. The record companies he broke commitments with. The endorsement contracts he reneged on. Danny Moss, whom he treated like dirt. All the women he enjoyed and tossed aside. Their husbands and lovers—maybe their parents."

"Well, that's a lot of suspects, but it's a start," said Jinny, with mock cheerfulness. "Look, you don't really have to crack this thing in time for the Johnny Carson show, do you?"

Roger grinned. "Why not try?"

"Because you've got other things to do. You're supposed to go see that aircraft factory this morning to bid on their guards."

Roger frowned. "Rent-a-cops. Burglar alarms. Tracking down deadbeats. What ever happened to police work?"

"It's alive and well. Late at night on TV. You have to stay up late to get your violence these days."

"I'll go see 'em at the aircraft factory," said Roger, turning abruptly from the easel and picking up his glen plaid jacket where he'd hung it on the back of the chair. "And Jinny—If I start acting like a spoiled brat again, do me a favor, will you?"

"Sure. What?"

"Kick my gluteus maximus for me."

"All right. If that's what I think it is."

He grinned again, finger-waggled a good-bye, and left the room.

Danny Moss, looking and feeling hot in his dark business suit, came down from his room, crossed the hotel lobby, and emerged into the white glare of the desert sunshine. When his eyes became accustomed to the unholy light he saw that even at this hour there were at least half a dozen very good-looking young women in the area of the swimming pool, all in suits that covered little more than the basics.

He looked around the pool. Some of the girls glanced at him with interest they pretended wasn't there. He understood. Only too well. They had their eyes open for showbiz powers-behind-the-scene, millionaires on gambling holidays, even racket guys. His for the asking, if he wanted it.

Well, of course, in a way, he wanted it. He was human, after all. And as a top Hollywood actor's agent he'd had it thrown at him enough times. But Danny had a theory about that sort of thing and, because of it, disciplined himself fiercely. His disapproval of licentiousness in general wasn't out of any religious ethic, though there was maybe some of that left over from his childhood—funny how the fear of Jehovah stayed with you even when you knew better—but out of a commonsense appraisal of human behavior he'd worked out for himself. It had begun in his mind when he'd become acquainted with Masters and Johnson's findings in their work on sexual behavior in the human male. Not that he'd read the book—he didn't have time for actual books. One of his clients had had a script idea based on the property, and it was still a helluva title for a screenplay, come to think of it. One of the findings—the one that stuck with Danny—was that those who disported themselves sexually early often tended to achieve less material success in life. Which figured. There was only time for so much, after all. But it wasn't easy, keeping one's putz in one's pants—not with temptation all around you. He'd come to resent that temptation, even, in an odd, emotional way, to hate it. But he took care not to show it. Somebody's agent, like somebody's psychiatrist, should never seem to disapprove. That, too, was a strain, keeping it up—

Feeling his anger become shaky, as though it might turn into momentary madness, Danny steeled himself and stopped a passing waiter. The man was swarthy, had a drooping Fu Manchu moustache, and looked like a Mexican bandit. "Excuse me," said Danny. "Have you seen Sonny Pearson around this morning?"

"The tennis champ?" asked the waiter in a flat, Midwest American voice, which disturbed Danny's sense of typecasting for a moment.

"Yeah."

"I think I did see him, sir." The waiter angled his head in another direction. "He was headed for the courts, I believe."

"Thanks," said Danny. Compulsively generous, he reached into his pocket, peeled off a fiver, and gave it to the waiter.

"Thank *you*, sir!"

Danny stalked across the poolside area and, beyond a redwood windscreen, found the tennis courts surrounded by a chain link fence. He saw Sonny Pearson immediately. Lithe and tan, boyishly good-looking, wearing shorts and one of the bright red T-shirts that had become his trademark, Sonny was moving about easily on his side of the net, hitting gentle ones back to a young woman who wore a halter and had long blond hair falling well below her shoulders.

Danny frowned for a moment at the young woman. The *very* young woman. Only fourteen or fifteen, he'd guess, in spite of her chestiness. He moved silently beside the net and into Sonny's view.

"Hi, Dan!" said Sonny, grinning. He reached out and returned the volley the young girl had sent his way.

"Got a minute?" asked Danny.

"Sure." Sonny caught the next ball with his left hand and called to the girl, "Don't go 'way. I'll be right with you."

The girl giggled and said, "I'm not going anyplace." She went to a bench by the fence and began to pat her pretty face with a towel.

Sonny, racket under his arm, came to where Danny stood. "What's up, oh, swami?"

"Did you forget we have an appointment?"

"Oh, migosh. Lost track of time. This Mickey Samish person."

"With him, make it personage. And don't forget it."

"Sure, Danny. God, I'm really sorry I forgot. Judy over there wanted a lesson."

Danny compressed his slender, hollow-cheeked face into another frown. "Look, Sonny, I think I better drop a few cards on the table."

"About what?"

Danny glanced at the girl, then at Sonny again. "Sonny," he said, "I've handled a lot of talent and I've seen a lot of careers either take off or crap out. Will you believe me when I say I know what I'm talking about, and that I have only your interests in mind?"

"Well, sure. You're the best, Danny. That's why I got you."

"It's not that I give a frig about my clients' private lives," said Danny—who did give a frig but just didn't want it known—"it's just that in this business you can hardly ever keep them private."

"What are you talking about?" For Sonny Pearson, Danny Moss, who acted like a combined guru and favorite uncle, was a new experience. Out of tennis now because of a trick knee, and broke from bad investments, Sonny had decided upon a career as a singer and, with this decision, had entered another world.

"Lolita over there," said Danny.

"What about her?"

"Jailbait. This seems to be a thing of yours."

"Now, wait a minute, Danny. What's it to you what kind of girl I like? Am I supposed to go around with old bags or something?"

"You got in trouble before, Sonny. Statutory rape if you hadn't had that fancy lawyer handling the case for you. You must realize that. But this—uh—preference of yours is dangerous for other reasons. You can't afford the slightest scandal, especially right now when things are startin' to break for you real good."

Sonny scowled. "What I do on my own time is my own business."

"No." Danny shook his head. "Not to all the fans. Especially with the kind of thing you're going to do. We're makin' another Donny Osmond out of you. The nice boy next door. You've got to start actually *bein'* that, see? If you were some punk-rock jerk it wouldn't matter."

"Where do you get off, poking into my private life?"

"Business," said Danny. "Nothing personal—business. And, take my word for it, I know this business. I ain't Billy Graham, like I said, but Mickey Samish, who we'll be seeing shortly, is."

"Are you kidding?" Sonny Pearson's finely cut eyebrows rose.

"When it comes to nonstandard sex the guy's a square John. Get the usual picture of a mobster out of your mind when you think of Mickey—at least in that department. And frankly, that's one thing about him I kinda admire."

Sonny's scowl deepened. "I'm still not sure I like the idea of going to Samish."

Danny shrugged. "You want a good start on this new career of yours, this is the best way. It wasn't easy for me to set up. Take it or leave it."

"All right, dammit," said Sonny. "I'll go along. I just hope it works out right, that's all."

"Get dressed fast," said Danny, "and meet me in the lobby in"—he glanced at the gold Patek-Philippe on his slender wrist—"let's make it twenty-five minutes. On the button. Mickey doesn't like to wait. And, Sonny—"

"Yeah?"

"Ditch Lolita."

"Jeez, Danny, I just met her!"

"Cold turkey," said Danny. "Never see her again as long as you live. Or anyone like her."

"I'm not sure all this is going to be worth it."

"Your choice," Danny said.

Sonny's scowl reached its nadir. "Okay, dammit. I'll play it your way. For now." He took the racket from under his arm and made practice swings in the air as he stalked toward the young girl, presumably—and Danny fervently hoped—to dismiss her.

IV

Relaxed in a corner of the sofa, Johnny Carson scanned the type-script in his hand, smiled at three of the jokes, crossed out two others, then handed it back to Sheldon Walters. "Not bad."

"I thought it was superb," said Walters, who had just been hired by *The Tonight Show* to replace a writer who had quit. He was pleased to be writing jokes again instead of straight talk show interview questions for Toni Tennille.

Johnny smiled. "No, it's a funny bit, Shel." He wasn't sure yet whether Walters was a touchy sort. Being a boss wasn't easy, in the creative or other world; you were never sure how people were going to take even innocent remarks. Johnny's mien and manner of speaking were straightforward, sincere. Like many comedians, Carson, unless he was with personal friends or other comics, was not particularly funny off-camera—didn't try to be. If anything he was businesslike, shy.

Walters, straddling a chair he had turned back-wards, examined Johnny with mild envy. The guy was at least as old as Shel himself—and, except for the white hair, still looked boyish. Must be genes or something. "I think the stuff on Sonny Pearson is a little forced," he said.

"Oh?"

"Dragged in by the scruff of the neck," said Walters. He butted his cigarette in the ashtray and reached into his shirt pocket for his pack of low-tar hundreds and a new one. "It's a matter of, you know, unity. Here we have a crime theme buildup and all of a sudden up pops an ex-tennis champ."

Johnny shrugged. "Well, Sonny's already booked, so we'll have to work him in. It's not easy, getting exactly who you need all the time. At least that's what Shirley Wood keeps telling me. Personally, I hope the guy goes over with his song. And it doesn't hurt when people remember they got their start here, either."

"Oh, he'll go over, all right," said Walters. "I caught him at a benefit a few weeks ago. He did okay. Now that he's got himself a trick knee—and that match with McEnroe was enough to give anybody a trick knee— he's going to have to do something else or end up working as a pro at some country club."

"There might be a kind of crime theme with Sonny Pearson at that."

"How so, exalted one?" asked Walters, and was gratified to hear Ed McMahon's familiar hearty chuckle from the next room.

"I heard the mob was backing him," Carson said.

Walters shrugged. "Maybe. They've backed singers before."

"Right," Carson said. "In our business, how the hell can you keep totally away from those guys anyway? They're still in Vegas, whether the law recognizes the fact or not, and they can still call a certain amount of shots there. They're even in television."

"Is that right?" Walters said.

"So I hear, anyway," Carson said. "Who the hell knows?"

He glanced at his notes and questions which had been prepared by talent coordinator Shirley Wood for the next guest. "Griswold. J. Duffy Griswold, of the FBI. I'll bet the 'J' stands for John, which he doesn't want to be known as. Now, I don't want to zap him in any way. It's easy enough to put the FBI on after some of the stuff they've pulled in recent history, but it would be gratuitous. Unless, of course, he asks for it."

"So play it straight with him," said Fred de Cordova, the show's producer, who had just come in. "You can have some fun with this Roger Dale, though. That foppish outfit of his has got to be a put-on, anyway. I hear he makes Beau Brummell look like a bum."

"Is this guy Dale as good as they say?"

"Sherlock Holmes," Walters said. "I wouldn't be surprised if he smokes shag in a calabash and sniffs coke for inspiration. I tried to sniff coke once, but the bubbles got in my nose—"

"Ba-rump-bump," Carson said, giving him a verbal rim shot.

The applause was gratifying after Sonny Pearson had finished his song. He was no stranger to the sound on the courts; he'd heard it before after a particularly good volley or drop shot, but this, he thought, was even headier. It was as if all those people out there, beyond the cameras, and in their tiered seats, were almost in love with him. Sonny decided he was going to like this new career of his very much indeed.

He took his seat. Truman Capote was on one side of him, perched like an elf on his chair. His round, little-boy's face was beaming. He was applauding, too.

Where, Sonny wondered, had he ever found that Windsor tie he was wearing with his velvet-lapeled jacket?

"I think that was fine, Sonny," said Capote. "Just fine. I love that song, anyway. So sentimental. I almost cried."

"Thanks, Mr. Capote," said Sonny.

"Mister? You make me sound as though I'm *married*, for God's sake!"

The audience laughed.

J. Duffy Griswold of the FBI looked blank and stolid, wondering what was so funny.

(In the control room, the director said, "Okay, number two, a little tighter on Johnny—that's it—that's nice—okay, take two.")

Johnny Carson showed his impish smile. "Sonny Pearson definitely doesn't murder a song, but if he did—or committed any other kind of murder—chances are Roger Dale would find him out."

It was, as Sheldon Walters had said, a weak way to make the connection, but what the hell, he had to get into it somehow.

"I said earlier," Johnny continued, "that we were going to meet a supersleuth, a modern-day Sherlock Holmes, and that's what our next guest is. It was Roger Dale who gave police the clues that led to the arrest of the park strangler. It was Roger Dale who guessed where heiress Jennifer Cartwright's body might be found. He uncovered the alleged hanky-panky in the Harrington heart attack case and led police to the suspect who, as we all know now, later confessed. How does he do it? Maybe we'll find out tonight. Ladies and gentlemen, Roger Dale!"

Roger came on the set to cordial applause, the band playing the now-ancient *Dragnet* theme. He smiled and nodded, liking it as much as Sonny Pearson had. Johnny greeted him casually and in a moment he was in the hot seat, as some of the staff members called the Ed McMahon chair beside Carson's desk. For the occasion—and at the suggestion of de Cordova, Roger had donned a flashy Donegal tweed norfolk jacket and a ruby stickpin in his flowing tie to give himself a somewhat Holmesian look. He crossed his legs and sat comfortably.

"Mr. Dale," said Johnny, "I'm wondering, like everybody else, just how you go about finding murderers, especially in cases where the police can't. Do you do it with some kind of ESP?"

"Mostly," said Roger, "I use what is really a very old method—the *portrait parle*—the modern version of which is the psychological profile. For short, the P.P."

Johnny did his Jack Benny look into the camera as four or five young people in the audience tittered at the phrase "P.P."

"Just how do you go about taking one of these P.P.'s of yours?" said Carson quickly, overriding the laugh. That got another laugh.

"Well," said Roger, pointedly ignoring the distraction and, as an amateur performer, coming in on top of the laugh a little too soon, "it all goes back to motive. As we know, murder can have any number of motives, all the way from monetary gain to sudden, uncontrollable anger. Now, motive springs from character, and if you can reconstruct the perpetrator's character from the crime itself you can—sometimes, anyway—zero in on the killer, or at least eliminate a good many possibilities. In fact, sometimes it works out that the crime was an almost inevitable result of a clash of characters—those of the victim and the murderer."

"And you believe *all* murders can be solved this way?"

"No, no, not at all," said Roger quickly. "Only those that fit the classic pattern of an unknown perpetrator who has some actual connection with the victim. Ninety percent of murders are sordid, obvious affairs and produce quick confessions. Mostly, it's not your enemies who murder you—it's your friends, neighbors, or a member of your family. The toughest kind to solve are those where the killer has no direct connection with the victim. Like those done by professional hit men. Hundreds of those still on the books."

"I should think," interjected Capote, "that the *crime passionel* would be the most difficult to solve. Here the motivation is always so hidden—so enshrouded in a miasma of dark and vaporous psychological forces. Consider the two killers I wrote about in *In Cold Blood*. Very ordinary young men. Even likable young men. Who could have foreseen what terrible, swirling rages were inside them?"

"That's true enough," said Roger. "But in a crime like that you can nearly always connect the killer with the victim. And the crime of passion shows itself for what it is. It may have kinky overtones. Brutality. Sadistic aspects. That sort of thing."

"Do you see it this way, Mr. Griswold?" asked Johnny, turning to the assistant FBI director.

Griswold showed his square scowl. "Most murders get solved on informant's tips," he said, "or by plugging away at the files. All this brilliant deduction stuff may work in mystery novels, but not much in real life."

"But Roger, here, seems to have employed it successfully," Johnny said, warming up to the prospect of an argument among his guests.

Griswold shrugged. "He lucked out a couple of times.

That can happen, even to professionals. But it doesn't prove anything. Every big murder comes along, we get a bunch of amateurs trying to solve it. You should see the mail. Good thing it's only mail. There's nothing puts a burr in your saddle more than some amateur meddler getting in your way while you're trying to conduct an investigation." He leaned forward to glance at Roger. "No offense, Mr. Dale."

"That's all right," said Roger, smiling. "In principle, I agree with you. But every once in a while there *is* a crime that doesn't lend itself to solution by routine police methods."

Johnny hopped on it. "Like the poisoning of Elmo Finstetter? Was that such a crime?"

"Exactly," said Roger. "Let's see what we've got in the Finstetter case. Obvious premeditation, for one thing. Time to procure poison; time to plan how to administer it. A definite knowledge of the victim's habits—such as the vodka he always drank, pretending it was water. The autopsy showed napelline, an aconite derivative recently developed as an animal tranquilizer. Aconite is the deadliest of ordinary poisons—one four-thousandth of a milligram is fatal. We can assume that anyone able to procure it—perhaps from a veterinarian—would be well educated and have a more or less prepossessing manner. This helps us form a character picture of the killer right away. In short, a P.P. —a psychological profile."

"It sounds as though you might already have some theories about whoever killed Elmo Finstetter," said Carson, looking serious.

Roger smiled. "I wish I could say I had. There just hasn't been time to gather enough data. We haven't narrowed it down much so far: dozens of people who knew Elmo and have apparent motivation still fit what we've got."

"May I make a suggestion?" said Truman Capote. The camera pointed his way showed its red light. Off-camera, Johnny signaled for him to go ahead. "If I were you, Roger," said Capote, "I'd add a deep, psychological disturbance to that list of traits. This crime, done in full view of an audience of millions, has overtones of the bizarre. Your killer probably has a twisted sense of the dramatic. He may be someone who *needs* an audience. It's the same psychological syndrome you find in those poor old men who compulsively open their raincoats. The ones the police call flashers."

"I agree again," said Roger. "In fact, I've been thinking along the same lines, though not the part about the raincoats."

"This murderer, I'd say," continued Capote, "is really quite sick inside. Someone, I'd guess, who has never loved or been loved, by man or woman. Or else he's had his love rejected, poor fellow."

"Do you agree, Mr. Griswold?" asked Johnny, his instinct telling him Griswold wouldn't.

The assistant FBI director shifted heavily and uncomfortably in his chair. "First of all," he said, "we don't know yet that we're entitled to use the word *fellow*. The crime might have been committed by a woman."

Two teen-age girls in the audience booed playfully.

Carson did his slow head turn to them, riding the laugh. "Listen," he said, "if women's lib means anything it means women have just as much right to commit murder as men do."

"Recent statistics show exactly that," said Griswold,

playing it straight. "The bureau's always right on top of all these trends—a valuable service that doesn't always get proper credit with the general public. But," he continued, turning back to Roger and Capote, "it sounds to me like you two actually cotton to this killer. How are we going to cut down on crime if we keep joking about it or mollycoddling those who commit it?"

Scattered applause.

Griswold drank of it for a moment, then continued. "Things are tough enough as it is, what with Escobedo and Miranda and the courts letting a lot of characters loose when they do get caught."

Roger smiled condescendingly. "Would you rather go back to the days of the rubber hose, Mr. Griswold?"

"Of course not," Griswold answered coldly. "And you know I wouldn't, Mr. Dale. But—to get back to the point—the great majority of crimes are solved by solid, professional police work, such as we do in the bureau, and not by fancy razzle-dazzle."

"You mean plain old police procedure," Carson said.

"Yes, and administered with a firm hand. And that means a hand not tied down excessively by liberal interpretations of the law."

(Fred de Cordova, the producer, fidgeted in his canvas chair next to camera one, stage right, and muttered to himself, "Christ, it's getting like a panel discussion on PBS. Come on, gang, brighten it up a bit.")

As though he had heard him, Johnny leapt into the breach.

"There are ways of knocking people off I'll bet Roger couldn't detect," he said. "Like, bore 'em to death. Or give 'em one of those looks that can kill." He mugged a fierce face. "Kill 'em with kindness? Smother 'em with kisses? That wouldn't be a bad way to go—"

What he was saying was not remarkably funny, but somehow, in the way he said it, it became so. The audience was enjoying his brief performance. Their eyes were riveted on Carson. The guests, grinning, were looking at Johnny, too. Even J. Duffy Griswold was wearing a smile that looked as though it might start cracks in his cheeks if it got any wider.

And with everyone—even the ushers in back—watching Johnny, no one noticed what happened to Sonny Pearson. Sonny was also watching Johnny and grinning. Then he felt a sudden, sharp prick of minor pain in his torso, on the right side, just below his ribs, and was thoroughly surprised at it.

He glanced down at his side. His eyebrows exploded upward; his mouth opened and his jaw hung. He could not believe what he saw. Some kind of small dart with what looked like a cork on the end of it was sticking in his side.

He reached down to pull it out and began to feel the first numbness. . . .

A palpable sense of relief filled the air when somebody finally came into the room with hamburgers and coffee. It was one of the gofers the homicide detective in charge had permitted to leave—accompanied by a uniformed policeman. The regular LAPD cops, summoned along with the ambulance, had arrived barely ten minutes after the call, and the detective, accompanied by several assistants, including a fingerprint man and a photographer, had shown up in another fifteen.

The detective's name was Sergeant Willoughby. He was tall and balding and looked more like an insurance agent or dentist than a detective. The first thing he said was "Nobody leave. But nobody."

"Sergeant," said Griswold, flashing a small folder with his ID in it, "I'm Griswold, FBI."

"Hi," said Willoughby. "Sir, even if you're the queen of the May, I'd like all hands to stick around just now."

"Sergeant, that just doesn't make any sense in my case. Anybody who could have done this here thing has already left. Nobody even knew Pearson was dead till the audience was half filed out."

"Yes, sir," said Willoughby imperturbably. "Please sit down."

And here they all still were, sitting and waiting. Johnny Carson and Truman Capote were in a dressing room off the adjacent hallway. The technicians, production assistant, and even Doc Severinsen and the musicians on deck were milling about, onstage. Sergeant Willoughby, as Roger understood it, was in one more room, talking to witnesses one by one. With Roger in his dressing room now—almost two hours after Sonny Pearson's slumped, open-eyed body had been noticed in his chair—were J. Duffy Griswold and Danny Moss, the agent. Moss was pulling his usual trick of seeming to fade into the wallpaper. Griswold was in a chair across the room, wrapped in a mighty scowl.

"I'm gonna have that sergeant's ass if it's the last thing I do," he said.

"He's just being firm," said Roger. "The way you said cops ought to be."

Griswold turned a radioactive glare upon Roger.

"I thought FBI men were always patient," said Roger, then smiled. "Relax. This'll blow over any minute now."

"Damn right it will. My own people ought to be

barging in here pretty soon, and then we'll see who the hell counts around here."

"Okay, the sergeant's overdoing it," Roger said, "but strictly speaking, he's within his rights to hold us here until he talks to everybody."

"We'll see who has rights—and jurisdiction on this one."

Roger raised his eyebrows. "What do you mean, jurisdiction?"

"I'll tell you what I mean, Mister Amateur Detective. Somebody shot a poisoned dart at us, right?"

"Right. Blowgun, for a guess."

"I don't care how he did it. The dart came at us— that's the point. How do we know it was meant for the tennis player?"

"We don't. But we can assume—"

"Assume, my ass. That dart could have been meant for me, and attempted ADW on a federal official is a federal crime, and that, by God, gives the bureau jurisdiction! How do you like them apples?"

"Not much," said Roger.

Griswold let a grin show under his scowl. "Didn't think you would. Well, I've just got half a mind to take jurisdiction. And if the bureau gets on it you'll see this one wrapped up the way it should be— professionally."

"I'll be working on it, too."

"Not if we take jurisdiction. Fair warning, Mr. Dale, with all those fancy theories of yours. Stay out of my hair. Don't obstruct justice. That's another federal crime."

"Are you threatening me?" Roger almost seemed to be amused.

"No, we don't do that in this day and age. What we

do is take poor, underprivileged lawbreakers by the hand, look sweetly into their eyes, and say 'You don't have to say a word, and we'll even get a nice lawyer to lie for you, absolutely free. So, if you want to confess —but only if you really want to—please do.'" He quirked his lips as though he had just spat in disgust. "No," he added, "I guess we don't even go that far. The judge might call it coercion."

"Careful, Griswold," said Roger. "You're about ready to blow your stack."

"It's already blowing," the FBI man grumbled. "Has been for some time."

V

The trumpet climbed upon the framework of the tune and circled around it, like wistaria growing on a trellis in a fast-forward-motion film. The clarinet and tenor sax counterpointed, weaving themselves into the pattern. Underneath it all, the acoustic bass went *gump! gump!*, the upright piano tinkled, and the drums slammed in a medium-tempo four-four beat. The tune was "Sweet Lorraine."

I stood with Augie Kretschmeyer at the end of the bar. I said, "Nice."

Augie, speaking softly, and putting the word in like a soft cymbal crash, said, "Yeah!"

Augie was the proprietor of the bistro we were in, the Jam Session. Before losing his lip when it was stitched following an auto accident, Augie had been a trombonist with such luminaries as Tommy Dorsey and Tex Benecke. Small, slender, silver-haired, mellowed now, he stood in his usual spot and beamed upon his customers.

Most of the customers were regulars—recidivists, as

he sometimes said with a smile. Some were older folk, afflicted with a nostalgia for the swing music of the thirties and forties; some were younger but had also discovered its joys.

Augie said to me, "You wanna sit in, Steve?"

"No, no," I said, smiling. "Like to, but I haven't time. I just dropped in to talk to you about that jazz special idea. In the neighborhood, had a chance. Besides, that kid on the piano's *really* good."

"Well, glad to see you," said Augie—and whenever he spoke I could somehow see guys in zoot suits lounging around the old Brill building at Forty-ninth and Broadway. "Must be celebrity night."

"How come?"

He nodded toward a smoke-filled corner. "Over in that booth. Ronnie Fordyce."

"Oh? Ronnie is here?" I looked that way.

"Yeah. He's got that private eye character with him. What's his name? Dale."

"I know Dale, too. I'll go over and say hello."

"Why not? You get a free drink." Augie blithely and dreamily returned his attention to the combo on the stand.

When I said hello, Ronnie insisted I sit and have a drink. The girl with Roger Dale was Meg Arlington, and Roger introduced me. I liked her fresh, sincere smile immediately. There was the usual how-have-things-been talk for a moment, and then Meg resumed the conversation she'd apparently been having with Fordyce before I arrived. "I wasn't kidding," she said. "I do love those beads you're wearing."

"Thank you for noticing," said Ronnie. Except for the doelike look in his eye, he could have been a handsome male juvenile in the movies—the mother's boy forced into the cattle drive; the kid you just know is going to get killed before the end. He touched the necklace. "Navajo turquoise. My TR-6 broke down in Flagstaff one time. There was this Indian lad. Gorgeous! But don't let me get sidetracked on *that*."

"I like your sidetracks, too," said Meg, laughing. "Like in your column. They're the funniest part. In a nasty sort of way."

"Why, thank you, dear lady," said Ronnie.

"Of course," she continued, "you hardly ever like *any* TV show, and you sting like a wasp, but most of them deserve it. And you *do* write—to use one of your own words—exquisitely."

Ronnie grinned and sipped his Wallbanger. "Your taste is as impeccable as my own."

"But I'd hate to be a producer and not have you like one of my shows," she said.

Ronnie nodded. "They tremble in their Guccis. I love it. I'm not sure I can actually make or break shows, but my power intoxicates me. I don't really need these Wallbangers at all. You have now got me on another of my favorite subjects. Myself."

"Well, why not?" Meg tossed some sandy hair back with a flick of her head. "It's hardly a dull topic."

"*Love* this lady!" Ronnie said to Roger. "Where did you ever find her?"

"On a tour bus."

"No kidding," said Meg.

Ronnie nodded. "Good a place as any for a great romance to start. Didn't Romeo first glimpse Juliet in some sleazy marketplace? Or was it a tacky ball? No matter. Let us get on with the agenda." He opened a steno pad and poised a gold Mark Cross ballpoint over it. "Roger," he said, "I want something *exclusive*. Something you didn't give all the other newspeople. Something you held out. There *must* be something."

"What's this all about?" I asked, feeling a little like the bird who flew into the badminton game.

"That *marvelous* murder on Johnny Carson's show," said Ronnie.

"Oh," I said, trying to think, as Ronnie apparently was, of a murder as marvelous, and not succeeding.

Roger said, "I don't think I held out anything, Ronnie."

"You must have. Perhaps something you don't want the murderer to know."

Roger laughed. "Well, if I had something like that I wouldn't give it to you, would I?"

"You would. Because you owe me. Remember who it was that first brought Roger Dale into the merciless glare of the public eye."

"Fat lot of good it's done."

"Don't hand me that. You love it. Be abnormal if you didn't. And if it's payoff you're looking for, be patient. The heady musk of success will come in time."

Roger smiled. "That's what I'm not so sure about now. There I was, me and my big mouth, telling how to solve murders, and—*whammo!*—one is pulled off right under my nose. How's that for being hoisted with your own petard?"

"What *is* a petard, anyway?" asked Meg.

"As a matter of fact," said Roger, "it's an ancient—"

"No. Please," Meg interrupted. "Not another esoteric lecture. Sorry I asked."

"Right," said Ronnie. "All of us will have rich and rewarding lives without ever knowing what a petard is. Anyway, Rodge, you must have some theories about this second murder."

"I'd be interested in hearing those, too," I put in, although the three by now were more or less ignoring me. What the hell; with friends, I don't mind.

"Well," said Roger, shrugging, "the second murder didn't add much to the assumptions generated by the first one. Assuming, of course, that it was the same murderer. Which seems likely; the m.o.'s are similar, though not identical. Poison in both cases. The blowgun the second time throws me off, though."

"It *was* a blowgun, then?" asked Ronnie.

"Had to be," said Roger. "The dart was in an ordinary cork, and the only possible means of propulsion would have been a blowgun. A simple tube. Could have looked like a cane, an umbrella, or anything else. I must have asked a hundred people in the audience if they saw anyone carrying anything like that. Nobody did. The police, incidentally, also got nowhere and have now more or less dropped that lead. But they *are* looking into the poison. Curare this time. You don't just pick it up at your nearest Seven-Eleven."

"Where do you pick it up?" I asked. Ronnie frowned faintly, as though he didn't want anyone but himself to ask the questions.

"Almost any hospital pharmacy, believe it or not. You need a prescription, but there are ways to get or fake those. It's a muscle relaxer. They give it for spastic paralysis and sometimes in shock therapy. Or as an inhalant combined with cyclopropane for anesthesia in abdominal surgery."

"Oh, goody!" said Meg. "Everything I always wanted to know about curare."

Roger went on as though he hadn't heard her. "The dart itself was a hypodermic needle which you can damned near get at a toy store these days."

"Delicious!" said Ronnie.

Roger frowned. "I mention all of this not to show off but because it tells me more about the killer. He's clever. IQ way up there somewhere."

"It takes one to know one," said Meg.

Roger looked at her. "A killer?"

"No, a smartass."

We all laughed, and Roger had to laugh, too, though I don't think he wanted to. It was my guess he realized he needed Meg, in a way, to take him down a peg or two once in a while. He continued. "The murderer knows how to research—maybe has hospital or medical connections. Devising that blowgun probably makes him manually dextrous. So at least we have a little more in the way of traits to look for."

Ronnie jotted something down. "Well, all that's interesting," he said, "but not in the bombshell category. People read my column for bombshells, not firecrackers."

"Sorry," said Roger. "It's all I've got today. I need more time to work on this, Ronnie."

"You *are* going to work on it, then?"

"Of course. The first murder was not all that unusual. I wouldn't have bothered with it if they hadn't asked me to go on *The Tonight Show*. But this second time —well, it's a challenge. I have this queer feeling the murderer knows it's a challenge. Maybe he did it because I was there. Consciously or unconsciously. His twisted personality, with its compulsion to be dramatic, even ironic, just might demand that. See what I mean?"

"I do see exactly what you mean, dear boy. And that's it." Ronnie scribbled busily.

"That's what?"

"My exclusive angle. Killer throws gauntlet at supersleuth—taunts him with murder under his very nose. Supersleuth accepts challenge. It's scrumptious; I love it!"

"I think I will have another Scotch and water," Roger said.

"And I another Wallbanger," said Ronnie. He turned to me. "Steve?"

"Gotta go," I said. "I'm picking up Jayne at CBS."

"You should stay and hear the music," said Ronnie. "I wonder if that troupe of wandering minstrels up there knows 'On the Sunny Side of the Street'?"

"Ever think about the words to that?" asked Roger. "They have to do with passing. Blacks on the light side pretending they're white. Which some did in the old days. The honkies, hearing the song, never knew it. Poignant."

"I wish they'd play something romantic," said Meg.

"Like what?" asked Roger.

"I don't know. 'Three Little Fishies in an Itty Bitty Poo'?"

"Those were the days," said Roger, laughing. . . .

Detective Stefan Radmilovich of the Las Vegas police leaned back in his chair, clasped his hands behind his head, and drew a bead upon Roger, using the tip of his nose as a forward sight. His was one of the memorable noses of all time, like those of Cyrano de Bergerac, Jimmy Durante, Danny Thomas, and Jamie Farr. It protruded in a great scimitar curve and came to a point like the inverted bow of a Nova Scotia schooner. Radmilovich had said once, "Danny and Jamie like to think the Lebanese have got noses, but we Yugoslavs can show them a thing or two." He was wearing—as Roger had been sure he would be—one of his wildly flowered sport shirts. It hung outside his trousers and there was a little bulge on one side where his holstered detective special .38 rested.

"So how the hell have you been, Rodge?" asked Radmilovich.

"Busy. Healthy. Solid and sound outside; inside,

vaguely discontented. Same as always." For his sortie into the wilds of Las Vegas, Roger had donned a khaki bushjacket with epaulets.

Radmilovich laughed. "Adjusted to peacetime and civilization, no doubt. Which, in some ways, is as hairy as Nam used to be."

"It can be, I guess," said Roger, smiling. "You know, I can't say I miss the leeches and ducking mortar rounds in the elephant grass, but there's one thing I do miss about Nam."

"What could anybody miss about that patch of hell on earth?"

"The birds."

"The what?"

"Don't you remember? Whenever we got R and R in Saigon we'd sit at these sidewalk cafés and watch the birds go by."

"Oh, *those* birds," said Radmilovich. "Yeah, I remember. One of our favorite sports, birdwatching."

"There they were in those wooden clogs with French heels, and their *ao-dais* slit on the side all the way up to their great trochanters—some of the greatest trochanters you ever saw. Their glossy black hair hanging down. You know, Stef, from a middle distance, anyway, there was no such thing as un ugly Vietnamese girl."

"I remember," said Radmilovich, nodding, his eyes fogging over with it for a moment. He came back to the present. "So what brings you to our swinging metropolis?"

"Trying to get a line on a few things," said Roger. "I guess you know about those talk show murders."

"I heard. Did somebody really knock off that tennis bum right under your nose?"

Roger nodded. "That's how it happened. And I'm looking into it. Mainly to repair damaged prestige, which sounds like foolish pride, but which can actually have a bearing on future earnings. Anyway, I heard that Sonny Pearson had some kind of mob backing from Las Vegas, which may or may not be significant. I thought you might know something about it."

Radmilovich shrugged. "Just what they say on the street."

"What do they say on the street?"

Radmilovich squinched his eyes for a moment. "That Mickey Samish came up with a bundle, or at least promised it, to get Sonny's career launched. The connection was Danny Moss, Sonny's agent, who, somehow, is on speaking terms with Mickey. Now, just why Mickey goes into something like this, I don't know. It could be a good investment, especially if Sonny turns into a superstar—which he won't, now. Maybe Mickey just digs the kind of songs Sonny liked to sing. About sweet young love, home and mother, and all that. You know Mickey."

"No, I don't."

"He doesn't bat an eye when somebody tortures a stool pigeon or hangs him on a meathook, but he's shocked when somebody cheats on his wife. He's got this thing about the family. A new button joins his mob, he makes the poor son of a bitch get married and wants him to settle down. He loves weddings even better than funerals. Jesus, I think he cries at them."

Roger took a moment to think. "It sounds ridiculous, Stef, but do you think Samish might put out a contract on, say, somebody like Sonny Pearson, or the other one, Elmo Finstetter, just on account of their moral turpitude?"

"Christ knows what Mickey Samish would do," said Radmilovich. "You don't predict guys like him. Maybe that's how they last. Like shifty boxers."

"What's Mickey into, mainly?"

"Depends on how you look at it. If you're talking about the last twenty-five years he's been into everything—narcotics, extortion, hijacking—and, of course, gambling—you name it. No prostitution, though. Even at his worst he wouldn't touch that. But once he became a big man in Vegas he got more—" Radmilovich paused.

"Honest?"

"No way. These guys never get honest. Just more careful. He'll still put money out into the old stuff, but between him and the action now there's always one or two other guys so we can never touch him, even though sometimes we later find out that he had a piece.

"And on the legit side he does so well that I don't know why he even bothers about the old crap. He's big with real estate, owns a couple of restaurants, has a piece of a liquor distributorship. And of course, a big chunk of the Mecca Hotel, where he stays when he's in town."

"So the boys are still in town?"

"Are you kidding? We'll never get them out. Oh, individual guys know they can't hang around the town like in the old days, but Meyer Lansky and the others have never had too much trouble getting around the new rules. They just set up fronts, arrange for loans from the Teamsters' Central States Pension Fund. It's a snap. And what they don't make on top of the table —which is plenty—they simply steal, by skimming. So they get it both ways."

"Is it going to be that way forever?"

"Sure. Only one thing could stop it."

"What's that?"

"A president in the White House who is hip to organized crime and sends out the word that the circus is over. I voted for Reagan because I thought maybe—with all the law-and-order talk he's been laying out for so many years—maybe he was gonna do it."

"And?"

"I shoulda known better," said Radmilovich. "He got in bed with the Teamsters during the campaign. It's a little tough, after you pose for pictures shaking hands with those bastards, and go to dinner parties with them—it's a little tough to turn around and start trying to put them in jail."

"Tell me something," Dale said. "I'm not all that familiar with the organized crime situation. How can people like Samish have so many defenders when time and again the FBI, the IRS, the congressional crime committees have publicly labeled them as gamblers, racketeers, people with organized crime backgrounds?"

"Money," said Radmilovich. "Money is all it takes. If you've got enough you can pretty well buy yourself any kind of reputation you want."

"Aren't you exaggerating?"

"I don't think so."

"Do you mean these guys simply bribe newspapermen, officials, sheriffs—?"

"No, it's not that simple. Oh, that happens once in a while, but I wish that were all there was to it. No, about all you have to do to keep out of trouble is give a lot of money to charity. Then they'll say that you're recognized and respected in your community for your work in numerous charitable and civic endeavors. And generous donations to politicians who are running for election don't do any harm either."

"Are people really that stupid?"

"Looks like it."

"I still have the feeling it can't be that simple."

"It isn't. There are a lot of people—in this town, in Hollywood, hell, all over—a lot of people who frankly don't give a good God damn whether these guys have organized crime connections or not. In other words, it's perfectly okay with them if they do. Oh, they may feel a little guilty if some square like you or me walks in and says 'Hey, why are you playing golf or posing for pictures with a guy that has killed twelve people, a schmuck who has dealt in heroin, pornography, prostitution?' They may feel a little guilt at moments like that. But nobody likes to feel guilt, so they're on the lookout for any evidence on the other side of the ledger, any sign that the hood is not a total monster, just a monster now and then. So that's where you get all this crap about the five thousand dollars the schmuck gave to this Las Vegas hospital, the ten thousand dollars he gave to the last Jerry Lewis telethon, the ten thousand dollars he gave to the Boy Scouts, the Variety Clubs, the March of Dimes, or whatever. But the truth is most people don't give a crap how crooked the guy is. If he gets *caught*, if he fails publicly, they'll walk away from him; but up to that point they're attracted to his power. Jesus, I'd love to see those Moral Majority cats tackle that problem. But they won't because the politicians they support are out in Palm Springs playing golf with people that in a really law-abiding society they would be trying to put in jail. I'm kind of a reactionary son of a bitch about a lot of things myself. Maybe just 'cause I'm a cop it makes me sick when I see politicians —conservative Republicans as well as Democrats—

hangin' out with those guys. Anyway, if you're looking for Samish you can probably find him at the Mecca."

"I'll bet they didn't anticipate all the rich Arabs when they named the Mecca Hotel. An insult, in a way, to a devout Moslem. In Mecca they have the sacred territory of *haram*, where the killing of any living creature is not allowed, and in the mosque of Namira they—"

"My God, you still give lectures."

"Sorry. Can't help myself sometimes. About Pearson and Samish. You don't know anything specifically about their relationship?"

"Only that Sonny and Danny Moss came here to talk to Mickey. I could ask around some more. How long you gonna be here?"

"Just overnight. I'm in the Kingston Motel. Poverty Row. Only one swimming pool."

"I know the joint." Radmilovich nodded. "You want to do some birdwatching tonight? I could set something up. Or we could just tell each other war stories."

"Thanks, but I'll take a raincheck. No time to mix pleasure with business on this trip."

"No problem. Anyway, good to see you, you old bastard."

"Same here," said Roger. "Keep your eyes on the birds."

Roger spent the rest of the afternoon, which soon became evening, in the Mecca Hotel, wandering, nosing around, not sure precisely what he was looking for. He was vaguely hoping to run into Mickey Samish without bearding him in his den, which, he understood, was in the hotel's penthouse. That might give away what he was after. He had a couple of drinks at the bar, stuck a few rolls of quarters into the slots, then dropped a fifty at the blackjack table and wondered whether he'd be able to claim it as a business expense. He strolled through the pool area several times and took in the solo women. Very nice birds, indeed. He'd have to come back and see them again sometime when he was less busy and more prosperous. If that day would ever come. Seemed that whenever he gathered a little momentum some setback would come along—like Sonny Pearson getting it right beside him. He could almost hear the snickers, and Ronnie Fordyce, with his angle on the story—the murderer taunting Roger—hadn't made it any better.

Late dinner. Alone. Salmon steaks with truffles and a fairly decent Gewürtztramminer to go with it. A little on the sweet side for salmon; maybe he should have stuck to Chablis.

He took in the show, having slipped the maître d' a twenty to give him a good seat. Feature attraction was an up-and-coming comic, Larry Lawson, a little butterball of a man with a rubbery face, who mugged his way through a series of rapidfire gags about the ultralow middleclass environment from which he'd evidently emerged. Roger felt that Lawson was repeating someone else's ideas and didn't really have many of his own.

The long-legged beauties of the chorus line danced with remarkable precision.

He had another couple of drinks and tried the crap table. Came out twelve bucks ahead. Back to the bar. Buttonholed there by some guy from Cleveland or someplace who owned a couple of dry-cleaning establishments and had won a contest giving him three free nights in Las Vegas. The guy had a system to beat blackjack and that was all he wanted to talk about. Roger listened to him spout about the permutation of odds and the maturity of chances, finally asked how the guy was doing, and the guy said, well, at the moment, he was a thou' or two behind—but it took time. They argued a little about who should buy the next drink and Roger finally managed to duck away.

He was now slightly more light-headed than he had meant to be—the drinks went down faster than you thought when you strolled through an evening this way. He taxied back to the Kingston Motel, which looked deserted at this hour, and went toward his room, looking forward to a good sleep.

Maybe his trusty subconscious would come up with something as he slept. Good ol' subconscious—even the drinks never reached it.

He slipped his key with its purple plastic tab (did anyone ever really drop the damned things in mailboxes when they went off with them?) in the lock and opened the door.

The bedlamp was on. In one patch of shadow on one side of the bed sat a large man. In the other patch of shadow, on the other side, sat a small man.

Roger stared and said, "Am I in the wrong room?"

"Do come in, lover," said the large man.

"Yeah. Get your ass in here," the small man said.

The big man had a fleshy face and looked like, maybe, a running back; the little man looked like a racetrack tout. Not that such persons always looked like that, but anyway, they looked like such persons ought to look. Roger felt his mind going in irrelevant spirals and decided it was the drinks. He stayed near the door. "Do I get an explanation?"

"Sure," said the running back. "We're not hard to get along with. Allow me to introduce myself. I'm Varsity. He's Gee-gee."

"I'm Annette Funicello," Roger said, thinking the light touch might help.

"Listen to him!" said Varsity, glancing at Gee-gee. He rose from the chair. "We already tossed your room. Now we toss you."

"The hell you do," said Roger.

"The hell we don't," said Varsity. "Over to the wall. Assume the position."

"Just a minute. I suppose you've got a warrant. And some ID."

"You hear that, Gee-gee? A warrant. ID. This guy's cute."

"Yeah, cute," said Gee-gee, also rising.

"You're not cops?"

"Do we look like cops?"

"Yes."

"Flattery will get you nowhere," said Varsity. "Come on, assume the position."

Roger did not move. Okay, he was telling himself, though not in words all clearly laid out in his mind, how to explain what he felt? He'd be damned if he'd let these creeps, whoever they were, frisk him or do anything else to him. Why did they want to, anyway? They looked too prosperous to be simple muggers. Anyway, toss him they would not. More intelligent, maybe, to let it happen and avoid a hassle, but the Scotch and water, or maybe just his stubborn mood, had taken the edge off the sharp logic he usually tried to think with.

"Hey, Mac," said Varsity, coming toward him, "when I tell you real nice to do something, I expect you to do it."

In his training as a military policeman Roger had gone through a course the Army called Combat, Unarmed, Hand-to-Hand, in the backward way the Army, U.S., usually called things. For his own edification later he had studied *ninjitsu* in the *dojo* of Kazu Hashimoto, right behind the Cherry Blossom grocery in Little Tokyo, near downtown Los Angeles. Both disciplines had one principle in common. When you know it's coming, according to this principle, don't wait for it—strike first.

Being careful not to telegraph his movements by so much as a flickering of his eyes, he lashed out with what old Hashimoto called the dragon hand, one of several in the *ninjitsu* inventory. His curled fingers, forming a sharp angle at his knuckles, struck Varsity in the Adam's apple and sent him staggering backwards, pained and surprised.

"God damn!" he croaked.

A couple of millimeters off, thought Roger. If he'd caught the *kyusho*—the sweet spot—Varsity wouldn't have been able to say anything at all. Roger was rusty; he needed a few workouts at the *dojo* again.

Varsity now came back with a left hook that flashed out of nowhere and was not bad at all. It came too fast for Roger to avoid entirely, though he did manage to suck in his midriff long enough to take some of the force out of it. Some, but not all. Roger heard himself whoosh. He bent forward a little—couldn't help it. Varsity caught him with an excellent right cross to the jaw. The room rocked and blurred in Roger's sight.

A flurry of blows and counterblows from the two men followed, with Roger, to his surprise and disappointment, suffering more damage and doing less than he had hoped for. Definitely rusty. The Scotch didn't help, either. It was Gee-gee who slipped the unexpected kick to his groin. Painful. Even summoning up the *ki* from its seat, somewhere deep in his viscera, failed to counteract the pain entirely. Roger had booted it; he should have kept up his sessions at the *dojo*, damn the expense.

Time passed. Minutes? Seconds? It was not the sort of time you measured. They had his arms twisted painfully behind him now, and they were slamming him up against the wall. Varsity was cursing him foully. Most of his epithets had to do with incest. Sticks and stones will break my bones, thought Roger, but names will never hurt me. Like most old saws, it didn't cut a damn thing for him.

So now they had him. The bastards. He did the intelligent thing at last, limped up on them, and submitted to their search.

Varsity spun him around so that he faced them again, and tossed his wallet back to him. "All right, smartass, are you going to be nice now?"

Roger, panting, nodded.

"That's better," said Varsity. "Now, what you are going to do, lover, is take a little ride with us."

"Ride?" Roger's eyebrows came up.

"You see too many gangster movies," said Varsity. "The ride is to go see somebody who wants to see you. Come on, let's go out to the car. Like a lamb, lover. Like a fucking lamb."

Roger was tempted to say "Ba-a-a!" but thought better of it.

Like a lamb, he went. He did not even succumb to the temptation to break away as they arrived at the Mecca Hotel but strolled through the lobby, into the elevator, and up to the penthouse. By now he had guessed who it was that wanted to see him. Gee-gee pressed the buzzer and Mickey Samish himself answered the door.

"Hey there, good evening, Mr. Dale," said Mickey Samish. "Nice of you to drop around. Come on in and have a drink, hey?"

"My pleasure," said Roger, dry-mouthed.

Samish was small and dapper. His gray hair was slicked back from a center part in a coiffure right out of the days of F. Scott Fitzgerald. He wore a brocaded smoking jacket with satin lapels and a ring with a huge star sapphire in it.

There was a large, expensively furnished living room inside. The decor was moderne. Not modern—moderne, Roger reflected. There's a difference. Moderne is not only more expensive but doesn't let you forget it.

Mickey Samish glided behind a small bar on one wall. "Whaddaya like, Mr. Dale?"

"Nothing, thanks."

"I invited you here for a drink."

"Okay," said Roger. "Scotch and water."

"That's better." Mickey retrieved a bottle and began pouring. "MacKeckneigh's Dew of Killduggan," he said. "That's the most expensive kind."

"It would be," said Roger, and was immediately sorry he'd said it. Samish might just catch its meaning.

But Mickey kept fixing the drinks. Varsity and Gee-gee found seats elsewhere in the room, smiling, watching to see what would happen now that Roger was in the boss's hands. Mickey finally brought both drinks to the coffee table and sat across from Roger. He waited, smiling coldly, as Roger took his first sip. "How is it, hey?" he asked.

"Not bad, if you like it smoky."

"Yeah, that's what I always say," said Mickey. "We're gonna get along just fine, aren't we?"

"I hope so," said Roger. "It'll be easier when I know what's up."

"So it is your position that you don't know, is that it?"

"Haven't the faintest."

"I wonder." Mickey Samish's small, dark eyes were sending out laser beams. "Okay," he said, "let's start out by learning a little about you. You married, Mr. Dale?"

"No."

"You should get married. Everybody should get married. That's why the country's falling apart. No family life. Everybody should get married and have kids and a fine home environment."

Roger shrugged. "I suppose I will someday."

Mickey Samish shook his head. "Don't put it off. All you do when you're single is waste your energy screwing around. You get married you don't have to screw around. I mean, banging an occasional broad is okay—like when you're traveling or something—but you don't waste time looking for it, hey?"

"An interesting philosophy," said Roger. He tasted the Scotch again. It *was* good.

"I hear," said Samish, "you run a private detective agency in L.A. They say you're another Shylock."

"Sherlock."

"Yeah. And I also hear that you were there when Sonny Pearson got knocked off and you'd like to find out who did it, hey?"

"Yes," said Roger. "I would like to."

"So would I," said Samish. "I was about to make something of the kid. You ever hear him sing? Clean, nice. Make Pat Boone sound like some coon shouter.

That's another thing tearing down the morals of our society—all that nigger music."

"I don't use the word," said Roger.

"One of the liberals, hey? Well, you'll get over it. A little right living, a little success, you get over it. Now, Mr. Dale, I can understand why you're looking into the Sonny Pearson number, and why you came to Las Vegas to see if he had any connection with me, which he did. It takes a pretty big roll to get a singer started right; all the publicity he needs, and recordings and clothes, and payoffs for bookings you can't get just by applying a little pressure. You follow me?"

"With morbid fascination," said Roger.

Mickey's eyes flared. "Mr. Dale—no zings. Okay? I mean, for your own good—dig? Now, like I was saying. It takes a bundle. Even then it's a gamble. You might like what the kid does, but you never know about the public. Anyway, I already laid out plenty and was looking forward to the payoff, and now some son of a bitch has come along and ruined everything."

"Better luck next time," said Roger.

"Yeah. Maybe." Samish went off into a brief reverie, then came back to the world again. "Now, what I'd really like to ask, Dale, is who sent you here to Vegas to snoop around?"

"Sent me?"

"You don't hear good?"

"Nobody sent me. It was my own idea."

"You're sure about that?"

"Cross my heart and hope to die."

"Don't hope too hard." Mickey studied him for another moment. "Maybe you're leveling. You must know it wouldn't be very nice for you if you're not, hey?"

"Look," said Roger, "I don't get it. What is it you

want me to say? If it's not true, whatever it is, I can't say it. Have these apes of yours beat hell out of me—I still can't say it."

"Who you callin' apes?" asked Varsity from across the room.

"Shut up," said Mickey softly. He kept his eyes on Roger. "You were on that talk show with Griswold of the FBI."

"So I was. I thought it ridiculous to have him there, but I don't book the show."

"Do you know, hey, that Mr. Griswold's favorite thing is going around making trouble for free enterprise and the American way by calling everybody a gangster? The Mafia, he says all the time. Shit, we don't use that term at all. He named me as a Mafia guy in one of his speeches. God damn it, I'm not even Italian!"

"Mr. Samish," said Roger, "I don't like J. Duffy Griswold any more than you do. For different reasons, but anyway, I don't like him."

"That's good," said Mickey. "I thought maybe he'd sent you to pick up a few things he might use. Not that there *is* anything, but nobody likes a snooper, hey? I would be very disappointed to learn that this is what you are. Okay. Let's say, for the time being, you're just looking into the Sonny Pearson thing. What have you got so far?"

"Zilch," said Roger.

"You're not holding out, are you? Because if I had a line on who iced the kid I might be able to do something about it. A lot better than the cops or courts might do."

"Mickey," said Roger, "let me try to say this in a way you can really understand. I don't have a personal interest in either Elmo Finstetter or Sonny Pearson, and by that I mean I'm not looking for revenge. My motivation is based on self-interest. Find the killer—if it's the same one who killed them both—and I get prestige out of it. Which can be turned into money. Which I can use. Which, the way things have been going, I can especially use."

"Okay, that makes sense," said Mickey, nodding.

"I thought it would."

"Careful—that's close to a zing," said Mickey.

"Wasn't meant that way. Of course, there *is* a touch of something higher than the profit motive. Civic duty, et cetera. Murderers should get whatever's coming to them."

"Balls," said Mickey. "You know what they ought to do? Give everybody a murder ticket with, say, half a dozen punches on it. Then guys would save their punches and the murder rate would go way down."

"Interesting," said Roger.

"That means you don't like it, hey? Well, why should I solve society's problems when nobody listens? But I'll tell you what, Dale. I had a piece of Sonny Pearson, like I told you. And my own reputation's on the line. What do you say we sweeten the pot? You finger the cocksucker for me—me, not the cops—and I personally will slip you a little bonus of, oh, I don't know, ten big ones, okay?"

Roger stared for a moment, then said, "I don't mean to be difficult, but I just can't do that."

"Why not?"

"Louis Armstrong."

"What's he got to do with it?"

"Somebody once asked old Satchmo to define jazz. He said, 'Daddy, if you got to ask, you ain't *never* gonna know.' That's how it is."

"Okay, I get it. So you're one of these real solid

citizens. Well, maybe it surprises you, but I respect that. It's just that whoever did the number gets what's coming to him a lot faster and surer if he gets it from me."

"I wouldn't doubt it," said Roger.

"Well, I won't push you. So I'm softheaded tonight. Must be getting old. But do me one favor, hey?"

"What is it?"

"Someday," said Mickey Samish, sighing, "I'm gonna ask somebody an important favor and the guy is gonna say just 'Right!' instead of 'What?' On that day, water's gonna run uphill. Anyway, if you finger the killer—"

"Yes?"

"Give him a good kick in the balls. For me."

"Thanks for the Scotch," said Roger. "Can I go now?"

"Yeah. Go on," said Samish. "Get the hell out of here."

VI

Phil Donahue
sprawled on the patio chaise longue in loose slacks
and a sport shirt, a cool drink in his hand, his thick,
prematurely gray hair comfortably ruffled. He enjoyed
being generally casual and ungroomed in his few pre-
cious moments of relaxation. The demands of success
—so much time that was not one's own—were nothing
to complain about, for the rewards far outweighed
them. Nevertheless, he looked forward to the rare
moments when he could be alone, with nothing to
attend to.

He didn't entirely get away from the rat race, even
in such moments. The newspapers and magazines he
constantly consulted were scattered about the chaise
longue. Idly, he wondered what would happen if he
correctly called it a chaise longue on the air sometime.
Most people believed it was a chaise lounge, perhaps
thinking someone named Chaise had invented it.
Chaise longue—long chair—what could be simpler?
Would they think him stuck-up if he called it that?
You never knew.

Phil fixed his attention on the TV set. He'd turned

it on specifically to catch Ronnie Fordyce, whose daily three-minute segment was one of the most popular features of the news-and-features potpourri known as *TV Magazine*, which could have had even higher ratings had it not been scheduled opposite repeat runs of an appalling but immensely popular canned-laughter sitcom on another network.

As Donahue watched, the commercial faded and Ronnie came on. Phil took in the boyish features, the ceramic glint in Ronnie's gray eyes, framed by long lashes any girl would have loved to have. When it came to TV fare, Ronnie struck with the swiftness and deadliness of a krait; praise, with him, was as rare as the whole truth in a sales pitch. As for inside dope, well, you had to hand it to the guy. Somehow, he knew about network decisions practically before they were made. Many a bit of industry news was prefaced with the remark that one had heard it from Ronnie.

It was Phil's guess that most viewers did not actually like Ronnie and his haughty, waspish ways. It wasn't because he was gay—that was his own business. But he was bitchy. People watched him with morbid fascination—as a victim might watch that krait, with its beady eyes, preparing to strike.

"Hello, all of you," said Ronnie. The photo of a well-groomed, well-dressed, thirtyish man was on the screen behind him. Some new actor? Phil did not recognize him.

"Supersleuth Roger Dale may find himself with a case of sniffles soon," said Ronnie, getting right to work. The picture over Ronnie's shoulder, Phil decided, must be supersleuth Roger Dale, whoever he was.

Phil's interest was still only mildly aroused. New

faces, to him, were sometimes potential guests for his own show, so he usually gave them more than mere passing attention. They had to fit his formula, though he liked to think of it as something more flexible than formula. His fresh approach, years ago—seizing upon controversial issues and letting the Ohio studio audiences, predominantly housewives, take part in discussing them—had brought him swift success. But he still looked like the ingenuous young man he had once been and, in spirit, still was.

Ronnie Fordyce was continuing. "The sniffles," he said, "will come from the cold shoulder Dale's been getting from the FBI. You'll remember that Dale, a Los Angeles private investigator, solved the park strangler murders, among other crimes, when the police could not. He is currently working on the murders of Elmo Finstetter and Sonny Pearson, both of whom were poisoned in full view of the audience while appearing on TV shows. Pearson, the tennis champ who wanted to be a singing star, was slain virtually under Dale's nose on *The Tonight Show*. As it happened, FBI assistant director J. Duffy Griswold was also present."

Griswold's stolid, clifflike face appeared on the screen.

"I have told you before," said Ronnie, "how the still-unknown murderer is playing a cat-and-mouse game with Dale, deliberately taunting him. Well, Dale has picked up the gauntlet and accepted the challenge. But he's being stymied in his investigation by the FBI—and in particular by assistant director Griswold.

"According to Mr. Griswold's own admission, when I contacted him by phone, he is deliberately withholding information requested by Dale. It seems the bureau has become interested and has elected to analyze the physical evidence, such as the poisoned dart used to kill Pearson.

"There is some legal question as to whether they have jurisdiction over these crimes. But putting that aside, they've refused to share any of their data with private detective Dale. They're even snubbing the news media. Griswold would not even tell me whether or not the FBI *is* actually making an investigation of the Pearson homicide, though obviously it is.

"Now, as a private investigator, Dale is licensed by the state of California, after meeting certain stringent requirements. In the sense that any attorney is an officer of the court, Dale represents the law enforcement establishment. By common courtesy, and possibly by constitutional right, he ought to have the information he asks for. We may have here a freedom-of-information issue as significant as, say, the previous high-handed refusal of the government to make public the contents of the Watergate tapes.

"I will go out on a limb and make a prediction. The FBI, for all their vast resources, will not discover who murdered Elmo Finstetter and Sonny Pearson. In time, Roger Dale will. And because I have revealed this information, the FBI will blush with embarrassment. Which I can hardly wait to see; they've got it coming.

"This is Ronnie Fordyce saying good day and good viewing—if you can find it."

Donahue swung from the chaise longue and switched off the set. He went into the living room, picked up the phone, and punched out a set of numbers, listening to the tones go *vee-vah-vum-dah-voop*.

"Charley? This is Phil. Glad I caught you home. Look, check out this private investigator, Roger Dale, as a guest possibility, will you? He's locking horns with the FBI on a freedom-of-information thing and it might make a good show. What? Oh, Marlo's fine—we're all fine. Enjoying our holiday. Get on that right away if you can, will you, Charley?"

When Roger Dale opened the door to admit Meg Arlington to his apartment for the first time, she stood there for a moment, staring as though thunderstruck.

"I know," said Roger. "It's me. The real me."

He wore tattered, faded, patched bluejeans and a gray sweat shirt, tattered, with a now almost unrecognizable likeness of Beethoven stenciled upon it.

"The last time I ran into something like this was with some doctor. What was his name? Oh, yes. Jekyll. I don't suppose you got hold of that stuff he—"

"Never touch it," said Roger, grinning. "Too many preservatives. Come in, come in."

Entering, she absorbed the masculine decor. Sailboat prints, bullfight posters. Two sheathed samurai swords on a rack. A rack of The Comoys pipes, a jar of mixture heavy with perique and latakia beside it. A huge, richly piled Syrian rug on the floor. A teak wine stand in the corner.

"Yes," said Roger, watching her. "Early polyglot."

"One of my favorite periods," Meg said. "Though late eclectic isn't bad, either."

"And just so we don't get in a rut—wait, let me amend that. A good rut might be fine later. Imagine; I just found a three-letter word for it."

"The shorter they get the more vulgar they seem," said Meg, taking off her jacket.

"I consider myself properly chastised," Roger said. "I did mean the remark as a joke, particularly because I consider you a lady, or does the movement not recognize that particular word anymore?"

"It does, indeed," Meg said half primly, half playfully.

"Good," Roger said. "In any event we're having Chinese food tonight. Already ordered it. You use chopsticks, I presume."

"Only for eating," said Meg.

"And the perfect drink to go with it," continued Roger.

"Which is?"

"Beer."

"Just beer?"

"Not just any old beer. Not one of the abominations made for the supermarket trade. Why is it that America, which has everything it takes to make good beer, including Germans, can hardly turn out a drinkable one? I've got some Ferdinand Borgstedt in the fridge. Small brewery near Dusseldorf. Airline pilot I know picks up a few bottles for me now and then."

"Pilot?" asked Meg. "I would have thought with you it would be a stewardess."

"This," said Roger with a slow grin, "is a *female* airline pilot."

"Oh. So you think only the Germans can make good beer."

"I didn't say that. One of the best bottles of beer I ever had was from China."

"Really?"

"Sure. It comes from Tsingtao. There's a dealer in San Francisco who imports it. It's sort of a hearty, gutsy beer. But you know something funny?"

"What?"

"Tsingtao was a German treaty port in the old days. The Chinese learned the art of fine beer making from the Germans."

"Those Germans did get around."

"Yes," Roger said. "They were in Japan, for example, long before World War Two—still quite a German colony in Yokohama. The Japanese learned a lot from them and put some of it to work in their phoenixlike renaissance after the war. Pianos, for one thing. That's why the Yamahas and Kawais and some of their other instruments are of very good quality. The Chinese never picked up the same trick from the Germans, so to this day they don't know how to make a good piano. Beautiful lacquer exterior, but forget the sound box."

"But your comments on American beer sound downright unpatriotic. Isn't there any good American beer?"

"I didn't say there wasn't," Roger said. "In Wisconsin you can still find some obscure small-label brands, brewed the old-fashioned way—by Germans, needless to say. It's the mass-produced stuff I can't stand."

Meg found a seat. "You're lecturing again. If you ever write a book it'll be called *The Story of Everything*."

"Not a bad title," said Roger.

Meg sighed and settled back. A Glenn Miller album was on the stereo. The lights were low. A bottle of MacKeckneigh's Dew of Killduggan was open on the sideboard, and seeing it, Meg recalled Roger's account of his meeting with Mickey Samish. There was so much to Roger, and all of it came on so strong, she still wasn't sure whether she was actually attracted to him or fascinated by some sort of danger she thought she sensed.

"So this is your lair," she said, still looking. "And I've been admitted. Am I supposed to feel privileged?"

"Yes," said Roger. "Not many women get brought here. For the same reason supermarket beer doesn't."

"I'm not sure I like being treated like a connoisseur's item."

"Why not? It means you'll be handled with care."

"If handled at all," said Meg.

"That's up to you. I don't get my kicks out of rape."

She laughed. "Only out of seduction. That's *verbal* rape."

"Call it what you will. It's part of the game."

"Keep up this male chauvinism," said Meg, "and there won't be any game."

"Male chauvinism?" Roger raised one eyebrow. "Let's face it. There *are* differences between men and women. Vive la same."

"And," said Meg, "one of the differences is that women can resist getting scored upon when they want to."

"Don't tell me you suddenly—"

"Let's change the subject. Where's that food?"

"On its way, I guess. You know, Meg, you and I—what would be the word? We mesh. We jibe. We were made for each other, as they say. Even the way I go a few pegs up and you bring me one or two pegs down. That puts me exactly where I ought to be. See what I mean?"

"I'll be serious, too. I think it's too early to tell."

He thought about it for a moment, then said, "Possibly. Possibly. What we really should be doing, right now, both of us, is concentrating on our goals. No distractions. Somehow, you've got to get that PR agency of yours started. Somehow, I've got to catch me a murderer."

"This Finstetter-Pearson thing's getting to be an obsession with you."

"It's not so much that as the way everything depends on it. Which kind of sneaked up on me, I admit. At first it was just another game. Now, suddenly, my reputation's at stake. If I boot it, everybody will go out and get themselves ten-foot poles not to touch me with. And booting it will be failing to identify the killer before the FBI or LAPD or somebody else does."

"Then the cool and imperturbable Roger Dale *does* have his insecurities."

"You'd be surprised," he said, nodding. "Though you shouldn't be. Only a freak doesn't have secret hangups, and maybe that's what makes him a freak, letting them hang out instead of up. You know, real early, when I was a kid, I discovered that I had a retentive memory and a well-greased mind. I thought others might admire it, but I learned pretty quickly that they resented it—starting with my parents, who were dear and worthwhile folks of average intelligence. Maybe I'm boring you. Call it the price of admission."

"You never bore me, Roger. That would be impossible. I love your well-greased mind. Has it come up with anything new on the murders?"

He shrugged. "A few more entries in the P.P. Or certain entries deleted, I should say. The Mickey Samish angle, for example. Doesn't seem significant. Unless something else unexpected pops up. I wish I had something new for the Donahue show. Did I tell you they called me?"

"Phil Donahue? That one I've got to see. I like him. He respects women. Not like some people I know."

The door chimes rang. Roger went to the door, peered through the peephole, then slid back the chain-bolt and opened it. A round-faced, round-bodied Chinese with cardboard boxes in his hand stood there.

"*Ni hao ma?*" said Roger.

"Don't speak a word of it," said the man. "Born in Milwaukee. That'll be twenty-seven fifty, sir."

"My God," said Roger, "it *must* have come all the way from China."

"They all say that," said the delivery man wearily. "I wish sometime somebody would think of something new to say."

"*Ch'o wang pu tong,*" said Roger.

"What's that?"

"Chinese cussword. You ought to learn it."

Within moments the savory fare was on plates on the coffee table and Meg and Roger were having at it with chopsticks—but not before Roger lectured on the differences between the blunt-ended Chinese chopsticks and the pointy-ended Japanese ones and how this exemplified the teleological theory that form follows function. Meg's incipient yawn cut him short.

"Delicious," she said, still eating.

"So it is. If he hadn't been such a wiseguy I'd have given him a bigger tip. What ever happened to old-fashioned courtesy?"

"It's with the servility and insincerity that's also disappeared. Fact is, Roger, for all the irritations, these, as Dickens once said, are the best of times."

"Maybe so," said Roger, deftly tweezing out an almond sliver from the oyster sauce. "Though the crime rate and all the shortages and slowness of the mails and a dozen other things would argue to the contrary." He looked up abruptly. "The mails. Forgot to check the box today. Be right back."

"Expecting something special?"

"There are girls," said Roger, grinning, "from here to Singapore who write now and then. Special ones, who know my home address."

"And who have been here?"

"Let me have a *few* secrets." Roger rose and ducked outside briefly. He came back with letters in his hand

and sat beside Meg again, shuffling them, glancing at the return addresses.

Meg, whose mind had evidently been going its own way during the interlude, said, "What *was* that Chinese cussword, anyway?"

"Son of a turtle's egg. Worst thing you can say."

"I like son of a bitch better," said Meg. "More bite to it."

"Which makes it another homegrown product superior to the foreign import," said Roger, tossing it off the cuff. He was still looking at the letters. "Hm. What's this one?"

"What's what one?"

He showed her the address on a manila envelope. "Pasteup letters. Like in a ransom note."

"So it is," said Meg, frowning.

Roger, now holding the envelope by its edges, as a magician holds a card he is about to make disappear, put it down carefully on the coffee table and rose again. "Gloves," he said. "May be fingerprints. You never know."

"Aren't you being dramatic?"

"Possibly," said Roger. "Anyway, don't touch it."

He ducked into the bedroom and came back wearing gray suede gloves—the kind bought for you by the groom when you're best man or usher at a wedding, which was exactly how Roger had acquired them. On his way back across the room he picked up a bronze Thailand letter opener from the desk. He sat beside Meg once more and carefully slit the letter open.

Plain sheet of paper, folded, inside. More pasteup letters. Mostly capitals, in several different sizes. Meg, glancing at the letter as he held it, read aloud. "Dear Mr. Dale," she read. "It will happen again. Right under your nose. All the best. You know who."

"Crank note, maybe," said Roger, refolding the letter carefully and returning it to the envelope. "Not necessarily from the murderer."

"How do you figure that?"

"Every time there's a well-publicized murder case—particularly if there are several victims—the police hear from some weirdo who just wants to get into the act. Sometimes these people talk themselves into believing they've actually done it."

"It gives me the creeps," said Meg, staring at the letter. "So you think it's not from the murderer?"

"I didn't say that. Not enough evidence to warrant a firm conclusion. But one interesting question is, how did the guy know where I live. I'm not listed in the phone book."

"How do you know it's a guy?" asked Meg.

"I don't. I may have some answers by tomorrow. I'll get Jinny to check it out. She's a whiz at that."

"A whiz?" Meg smiled. "Roger, even your slang comes from another age."

"I know," said Roger. "Nostalgia." He sighed. "And nostalgia, too, ain't what it used to be."

VII

It was perhaps the most thrilling day yet in the life of Mrs. Mabel Merriwether. She had not only obtained tickets to this Phil Donahue taping—the eleventh important show she'd managed to attend—but was being permitted to enter the greenroom before the show and actually have a word or two with Phil's guest.

She sat in the greenroom now, reading a copy of *Variety* she'd found there, not understanding a good deal of its jargon—"Nets Still Sit on Sitcoms," whatever that meant—but feeling, in this opportunity to come close to it, part of an inner circle. She kept looking at the incomprehensible periodical, wondering when the guest—Roger Dale, the celebrated detective —would arrive.

Mabel was in her late forties and somewhat dumpy of build, though she was proud of her large breasts. A girdle flattened her stomach, and her dress, carefully chosen today, had vertical stripes that slimmed her down a bit to the eye. Her nails were done in jungle red, and the two-carat diamond her late husband, Theodore, had given her on their tenth anniversary, after he'd made a go of his plumbing business and was able at last to afford it, glittered on the third finger of her left hand. God rest his soul. Theodore, on the whole, had been good to her even if he had been mostly too tired at night to do much in bed. But perhaps that had been her fault. She would not think of it now. It was past. The present was pleasant enough and she would enjoy it to the fullest.

A few minutes earlier she had met Phil Donahue himself. Imagine! Actually stood in the hall with him, while he smiled and shook her hand and asked a few personal questions about herself, looking over her shoulder at someone else only twice. My gracious, but he was cute! He'd talked to her before on the show, of course—they sort of made a joke out of her "always" being there, in the audience, like Dorothy Miller in Merv Griffin's audience (and mine, too; S.A.)—but that wasn't the same as actually meeting Phil in person and having him all to herself, so to speak, if only for a few seconds.

In the course of things, during the last show she'd attended, which had been taped in Lincoln, Nebraska, because the guest was some psychiatrist named Dr. Albrecht, who was with some college there and whose specialty was the study of rape—a subject the contemplation of which always gave Mabel a pleasurable chill—she had managed to corner one of Phil's assistants in the corridor before entering the auditorium serving as a studio. The assistant, Charley Higgins, had been a busy-looking man in short sleeves and with a big moustache—not bad-looking, come to think of it, though he didn't respond to her flirtatious chatter —and he'd said he'd see what he could do next time about her being allowed to go backstage before the show and maybe meet Phil himself.

"Don't you find it expensive, Mrs. Merriwether, following the show from city to city all the time?" he'd asked.

"Oh, I can afford it," she'd said. "And it's what I want to do. Now that I have the time for it, it's what I want to do. I started with Bob Barker, but after one time they never seemed to call me up to bid on all those things. He's handsome, too, don't you think?"

"Yes, I suppose he is. But both he and Phil are married men, you know. Very much married."

"They all are," said Mabel, with the sense of a sigh. "But they're still men. And men don't ever really stop looking around. My late husband, Theodore, had a glint in his eye up to the very end."

"Well, good luck, Mrs. Merriwether." Charley Higgins grinned at her. Mabel Merriwether, he knew, had made semipasses at almost everyone on the show, from the audio engineers to the coffee gofers. "She reminds me," Charley had said to Phil one day, "of those women who used to follow the Foreign Legion from fort to fort in the desert."

"What women?"

"The whores-de-combat," Charley had said.

It was good to work for Phil. He didn't mind being your straight man.

And now Mabel Merriwether sat in this chamber they called the greenroom—it was powder blue—and told herself, dopily enough, that if she could arrange a delightfully wicked assignation with one of these attractive men all around, why, then, her day would *really* be complete. It hadn't happened yet, but you never knew, you never knew. . . .

The door opened and another decidedly attractive man entered. To Mabel's eye, anyway. When she looked close she could see that he was not collar-ad handsome—put glasses on him and he might resemble Hale Irwin, the golf champ, or maybe Steve Landesberg in his role as Dietrich on *Barney Miller*—but something in his bearing and his dress gave him, for her, a kind of romantic appeal. He was impeccably groomed. The suit he wore looked British and somehow out of the last century.

"Oh, hello," said Roger Dale. "Didn't know anyone was here."

"I'm Mrs. Merriwether," said Mabel, using her best-known billing. "They said I could wait here. You must be Mr. Dale."

"Yes. Are you with the show, Mrs. Merriwether?"

"Well, not officially. I try to go to a lot of Phil's shows. I have time for it, you see, because I'm a widow." She threw in a laugh. "Footloose and fancy free, you might say. I used to go to Merv Griffin's show in Hollywood, but he always seemed to pay more attention to Dorothy Miller and those other old bags who've been there for so many years. I hope I don't sound catty."

"Not at all."

"But I figured if it was all right for those others to spend so much time traveling around with Merv Griffin and Steve Allen and whoever then I could do the same thing on Phil's show. And you know," she said, "it's really been an education. I mean all those other fellows just interview a lot of actors and singers, but Phil has the most *interesting* people. I mean he has psychiatrists and people who are experts on crime, and rape and sex and a lot of serious problems."

"I see," said Roger, pretending he didn't notice her coquettishness. He found an easy chair across from where she sat.

"It's really such a pleasure to meet you," said Mabel. "May I call you Roger?"

"Please do."

"It must be fascinating to be a detective."

"It has its moments," he said (Burglar alarms, rent-a-cops, he thought. Salesman from some company the other day wanting him to put fire extinguishers and smoke alarms in. It'd be false noses and glasses next—the kind that made you look like Bani-Sadr of Iran).

"I watch the detective shows on TV all the time," said Mabel.

"Well"—he smiled—"our business isn't really the way it usually is on TV. Not nearly as exciting."

"It isn't? How about these murders that happen every time you go on a TV show?"

"That was only once. Pure coincidence."

"I understand you're going to find this murderer. Have you got any clues yet?"

"Not really. And I haven't exactly promised to find him. That part of it's mostly Ronnie Fordyce's idea."

"Oh, him. Is he—you know—like they say?"

"I wouldn't care to guess. Not my business."

"I can see *you're* not that way," said Mabel, showing what she clearly intended as a seductive smile. "Are you married, like everybody else?"

"Not yet," said Roger.

Mabel nodded. "Men shouldn't marry too early," she said. "I know all about marriage. I could give you some marvelous tips on how to make it work when the time comes. If you'd like to have dinner tonight and talk it over, my hotel's really very nice—"

Despite his experience Roger was honestly, though slightly, shocked. "Uh—thank you, Mrs. Merriwether. But I can't, really."

"Busy, I suppose." Mabel skimmed the top off her disappointment with a long sigh.

Roger didn't answer. With a half smile and a nod, he'd put Mabel off without actually lying to her, no easy trick, and he wanted to keep his small victory pure. The lie, if he'd had to tell it, would have been relatively harmless and socially acceptable enough, but Roger had a theory about lies, including little white lies. Even telling little ones could give you a habit. Like chipping with smack. First thing you knew, it became mainstreaming.

He thought about this as Mabel continued talking. It was more diverting than whatever it was she was saying, though he took care not to let her realize this.

The door opened again, and Charley Higgins, his huge moustache bristling like the antenna of some creature finding its way in the dark, came in. To Roger's rescue.

"There you are, Mrs. Merriwether! Audience coming in now. Better grab a seat."

"It was a pleasure to meet you, Mr. Dale," Mabel said, smiling, on her way out.

Roger showed her an answering smile and a courtly half bow right out of an operetta laid in gaslight Vienna.

Jinny Cantu, directed by a pleasant and more or less faceless female secretary, entered the office of Norman Calhoun, who, as she appeared, looked up from the drawing board over which he had been hunched. Jinny, looking at him, saw a tall, lithe black man, obviously well dressed, even in his shirtsleeves, and said, in a voice with an overtone of uncertainty in it, "Mr. Calhoun?"

"That's me," said the man pleasantly.

"I'm Jinny Cantu, from the Dale Security Agency."

"Oh, yes!" Calhoun pushed two plastic triangles aside and laid down his Rapidograph pen. He stepped from the drawing board to his desk, indicated a straight-backed visitor's chair for Jinny, and took his own place in a swivel chair. "You wanted to identify some typefaces, right?"

"That's the general idea. I couldn't explain it in too much detail over the phone. Anyway, I appreciate the time you're taking."

Calhoun broadened his smile. "No problem. Any excuse to take a break."

"That's nice of you, Mr. Calhoun."

"Norm," he said. "And you're Jinny, right?"

"Right the first time."

"The first time," Calhoun said, "was on the phone. I didn't know then whether or not it would be worth remembering. Though I must say, your voice was kinda nice. Was. Is."

Jinny laughed a little. "Phone voices do fool us, don't they, sometimes? I hadn't the faintest idea what *you'd* be like."

Taking the slightest pause before he spoke, Calhoun said, "Didn't know I'd be a brother, was that it?"

"Well, now that you mention it, yes."

"In fact," said Calhoun, reaching for a pipe in a rack of several on his desk, "you probably figured I was not."

"I don't know that I figured one way or the other," said Jinny.

"You know what I mean. Here's a guy with the title of art director in a big printing house, with a straight middleclass accent, and you assume right away he's WASP, or close to it. Like you say, without even stopping to figure."

Jinny nodded. "True enough. And the point you're making, I suppose, is that we still have a long way to go."

"That's the point," said Calhoun. "Not that I beat it into the ground. But it—you know—it comes up all the time. It's what we live with."

"And never really get used to," said Jinny, her smile flickering.

"R-i-i-ight!" said Calhoun, drawing out the word with a put-on touch of jive intonation as he showed a sardonic grin. "Well, anyway, shall we get down to business?"

"Might as well," said Jinny. She reached into the envelopelike briefcase she carried, took the note with the pasteup letters from it, and slid it across the desk to Calhoun. Swiftly, she repeated the explanation she'd already made over the phone, this time fleshing it out a bit. "So I asked around," she said, "and everybody said Norman Calhoun was the man, and here I am."

Calhoun nodded and studied the note. "Didn't know my reputation was that big," he said, obviously pursuing this vector of the conversation with one part of his mind and concentrating on the cutout letters with another part. "I have to admit it feels pretty good. You know, when I was a kid—in I guess what you'd call a ghetto—my mama and all my teachers, and all the kids in the gang, even, were always telling me what a waste of time my drawing was. Though I will say this for Mama: she did the equivalent of scrubbing floors to put me through art school. God love her. It wasn't one of these la-di-da art schools—strictly commercial. That's how I got on to lettering. Loved it from the first. Well, long story short, and here I sit."

"Good story. I'd like to hear the long version sometime."

Calhoun looked up. "You must have a long story yourself. I never met a private detective before. That's what you are, isn't it?"

"Yes. We come in all shapes and sizes."

"So I see." He grinned and gave her a comedy Groucho leer.

"Why, *Mister* Calhoun," said Jinny, laughing, going along with it.

"What do you look like without those glasses?" Calhoun was studying her now instead of the pasteup note.

"I don't know. When I take 'em off and look in the mirror I can't see myself without 'em. Part of the long story."

"Got to hear it, then," said Calhoun. "Look, are you busy tonight?"

"I'm hardly busy any night. Unless I'm working overtime. Roger—that's my boss—can be a slavedriver. But he's a *nice* honky who knows his place, so maybe I shouldn't put it that way. Anyway, Calhoun—may I call you by your last name? I like it better—why don't we get back to the typefaces and save the storytelling for later? Like eating all your spinach so you can have dessert."

"R-i-i-ight!" said Calhoun. "I can hardly wait."

Phil Donahue was wandering among the predominantly female audience, microphone in hand, showing his easy half smile, picking up the questions for Roger, who sat on what amounted to a dais, feeling faintly uncomfortable in this conspicuous location, but enjoying it just the same.

The woman Phil had selected now to stand and speak her piece had long straight hair, wore granny glasses and a kind of frontier dress. A late-blooming pseudo-hippie, who lived in a house rather than a commune, Roger guessed, and dressed that way to show the world her contempt for the establishment, the system, God, herself, and various other institutions. "I would like to ask Mr. Dale," she said, "what he thinks of capital punishment."

"What was that?" Roger cocked his head forward. He'd thought she'd said capital punishment, but they hadn't been talking about that.

"She wants to know," said Phil, "what you think of capital punishment." His faint smile showed that he was used to people who came up with irrelevant axes to grind, and was passing the question along only out of common courtesy that, in itself, was a soft rebuke.

"I *don't* think about it," said Roger.

"What's that supposed to mean?" the woman said, frowning.

"What I'm interested in is identifying wrongdoers, not in the disposition of their cases."

"But everybody ought to be interested in that! It's a barbaric practice which reveals the unacknowledged cruelty of our society—the same society that forces young people to commit murder by going to war, and terrorizes innocent demonstrators for trying to express an opinion!"

"There is some of that, of course," said Phil, smoothly. "But it's really not what we're discussing here, is it?" He swung away before the young woman could continue. The mike, which he carried like a scepter, swung to a pleasant, round-faced woman with nicely coiffed blue hair and a beige suit.

"I'd like to get back to this freedom-of-information

issue," she said. "My son was picked up one time for having marijuana in the car, though it wasn't his—some friend of his had left it there. They held him down at the station house and we had an awful time finding out why. They wouldn't tell us anything. We finally had to hire a lawyer and everything and it was quite expensive."

"Was your son convicted?" asked Phil.

"No, they finally let him go. But it was just awful at first, with him in a cell and everything, and they wouldn't even tell us why. Now, I don't think the police ought to do that, do you, Mr. Dale?"

Roger frowned thoughtfully. "I don't know all the circumstances, ma'am, but there are bound to be cases where the police step on constitutional rights or even common courtesy. You have to look at it from their standpoint. They're busy, and everybody's yammering at them from all directions. What they're mainly interested in is getting their job done as quickly as possible. It just can't be done nicely all the time, with everybody's feelings unhurt."

"If that's the way you feel about it," said the woman, "why are you complaining because the FBI won't tell you anything in this murder case you're working on?"

"Good question," said Phil, smiling. There was a scattering of applause.

"I suppose," said Roger, "it's because I'm on the same team as they are, and I think there ought to be a little teamwork."

"That's really the issue, isn't it?" said Phil. "They seem to feel that they're the only players. And—I don't know—since they're professionals, perhaps they ought to be. But what bothers all of us, I think, especially in a democracy, is any one agency being permitted to cloak its operations in such secrecy. There's too much danger that they may get to control more than we want them to control. Start to affect all of our lives. The FBI, the CIA—" The microphone went to a stocky woman with iron-gray hair and what was probably a bargain-sale dress with a floral print. "Yes?"

"I would just like to say that the Bible says, 'Thou shalt not kill,' " she said.

Much applause. The Bible always got applause. Phil kept smiling and let it run out. Even he couldn't point out that the lady's remark, though well intentioned, was completely irrelevant. It made no sense to fool around with the Bible that way.

After the broadcast, Roger went with Phil to an office up the hall from the studio. The audience was still filing out. There was a retinue of assistants and coworkers on hand, people Roger had been introduced to briefly but probably wouldn't remember once he'd departed. There was coffee for all hands in the office. Phil helped Roger to a cup.

"Well, how do you think it went?" asked Roger.

"Nicely enough," said Phil. "Not a blockbuster, but I'm satisfied. Those women can be pretty sharp, can't they?"

"Yes. And I think that must be largely how you got where you are. By not underestimating them."

Phil nodded. He thumbed down the lever on the urn to pour his own coffee. "There's something I wanted to ask, but didn't have time to get in. Do you really think, Rodge, that you're going to catch this talk show killer all by yourself, as you did those others? I realize you can't know for sure, but what I mean is, are you confident about it?"

"Oddly enough, yes," said Roger. "Though not for any clear-cut, logical reasons. On the order of a hunch. Or maybe there is some logic to it that hasn't crystallized yet. As a matter of fact, maybe that's what a hunch *is*. You see, I'm building a psychological profile on this guy and I have this growing feeling of getting to know him. I'm starting to see his quirks. One of them is almost standard with a psychopathic killer. In his heart, he *wants* to get caught. The guilt bit—the subconscious craving for punishment. What's more, *he wants to get caught by me*."

"Oh? How come?"

"I think I symbolize something or other to him. When I find out what it is, I'll be even closer to him."

"If he *wants* to get caught, the case is in the bag, then. All you have to do is wait."

"It's not that simple, unfortunately," said Roger. "He's split—aren't we all?—and the other side of him is working *not* to get caught. That side of him could still win."

"Heady stuff," said Phil, smiling. "Not the usual sort of thing you hear from a cop or private eye."

"You'd be surprised," said Roger, "how sensitive or even mystical some cops are. Terman and Miles, at California, did a study of what they called 'masculine' and 'feminine' sides of personality. Engineers are masculine, for example; artists feminine—it has nothing to do with sexuality. Know where most cops scored? Way on the feminine side."

Phil laughed. "I know where talk show hosts must be. In the middle, as always."

A uniformed studio guard bustled into the room, looking worried. He was an older man with a deeply lined face—probably a retired law enforcement officer. Roger saw the collar insignia of a much larger rival agency on the man's collar and vaguely wondered if he might not be able to get the studio account for his own office sometime, maybe by low bidding, even taking a little loss for the sake of prestige. Another of those business decisions that always bored the hell out of him—

"Mr. Donahue—"

"Yes?"

"I think you better come out to the studio for a moment."

"Oh? Something the matter?"

"There's a dead woman in one of the seats," said the guard.

Phil and Roger stared at each other. Phil said, "You don't think—"

"I do," Roger said. "Come on, let's get out there."

VIII

"Charleen," said Roger into the squawk box, "please—no more calls."

"Okay, Rodge," said Charleen's kittenish voice, and in some odd way, Roger thought he could detect the immense swelling of her breasts in it. "If you say so. That goes for everybody?"

"Everybody. And his brother."

"How about clients?"

"Oh. Well, clients are different. So are potential clients. It's these media people I want out of my hair."

"How am I supposed to tell who's what when somebody calls?"

"The clients will be polite."

"Okay," said Charleen, a sigh in her voice. "I'll try."

After Roger had leaned back from the intercom, Jinny looked at him from her desk, squinting a little as though switching to a telescopic lens that would pick him up at twelve feet and when she finally got him into her field of view, she said, "Feast or famine, right?"

"What?" Roger's mind was still off on a business trip.

"A few days ago you were *wishing* some media people would call so you'd get some publicity."

Roger nodded. "That's how it goes. Hardly ever anything just right. Ever since Goldilocks and the three bears. You know, I've been thinking of bringing Meg Arlington in here to handle the media."

"Meg? She's nice."

"That's the trouble."

"Trouble?"

"Publicity people, along with agents and business managers and such, sometimes have to be just a *little* bastardly. I hate to say this, because you know how fond I am of Meg, but she might not be able to hack it. And how could I tell her that?"

"By being just a little bastardly," Jinny said. "By the way, boss, can I leave early today?"

"Sure. What's up?"

"Heavy date."

"Glad to hear it. You know, I never gave much thought to your love life, though I should have. Somebody special?"

Jinny smiled. "He might be. If things work out. Guy named Calhoun."

"Sounds like an Irishman."

"If he is," said Jinny, laughing, "he's what they call a 'black Irishman.' He's the one who gave me the dope on the pasteup letters in that note, which, come to think of it, I haven't had time to pass on to you yet. This Mabel Merriwether certainly opened up a box of bees when she got herself killed. I don't even know her, but I feel sorry for her. Or for anybody that gets murdered, I guess. Even the ones that deserve it."

"People who really deserve it rarely get it," Roger said. "Anyway, poor Mabel felt no pain, I guess. Something like a hatpin from behind, right into her medulla oblongata."

"You couldn't just say 'brain,' could you?"

"Let us be precise," said Roger, with a mock scowl. "Anyway, the M.E. had a hell of a time finding the wound. They need Jack Klugman up there. Who the hell would have a hatpin in this day and age?"

"Damned if I know. Though I suppose you could find one if you really needed it. In some studio prop room, or maybe a wardrobe room. Could it have been a shish kebab skewer? That might make our killer a gourmet of sorts."

"Crazy as it sounds," said Roger, "we'd better crank this into the P.P. Killer has access to prop rooms or is possible gourmet. Or whatever else such a weapon suggests. You know, this one's really weird when it comes to modi operandi. You nearly always get a pattern there—nothing more habit-forming than one's favorite weapon. But what does our unknown friend do? A Mickey in a vodka glass the first time, a blow-gun dart the second time, and a hatpin, or something like it, the third time. Still, this in itself tells us something about him. Him, her, whoever. He stays loose; he can extemporize. Only why, suddenly, Mabel Merriwether? Practically an innocent bystander, a studio audience regular like Dorothy Miller, or Steve Allen's Lillian Lillian. What would she have in common with Elmo Finstetter and Sonny Pearson?"

"I don't know," said Jinny. "Does that make me a lousy sounding-board?"

"Not at all. Nobody I'd rather have more. Holmes had Watson, Nero Wolfe had Archie, Damon had Runyon, and so on. Where were we?"

"Pasteup note."

"Ah, yes. And what did you learn from the estimable Calhoun, whoever he might be?"

"Calhoun," said Jinny, somewhat dreamily, "is the GLEE when it comes to typefaces."

"The what?"

"GLEE—Greatest Living Expert Ever. The latest in acronyms. You should keep up with Living English, Roger. Anyway, what Calhoun does, in that printing house, is design type they put out for printers all over. All he can talk about is roman and gothic and serifs, whatever they are, and—"

"The serif is very interesting," interrupted Roger. "It's the little stroke on roman letters. There because they were originally done in stone with a chisel. When the Goths began to invade Rome and take it over, they introduced the—"

"Another lecture?"

"Sorry," said Roger. "Continue."

"Well, the first thing Calhoun said was that all the cutout letters in the note from the killer—if it is from him—came from the same printing run—probably a single issue of a magazine. What's more, he's got a good guess as to what kind of magazine."

"Oh? What kind?"

"There's a printer and binder right here in L.A. that specializes in manufacturing west-coast specialty magazines. You know, *Dune Buggies*, *Van and Camper*, *Redwood Handicraft*, that sort of thing. It so happens that this printer ordered and got the series of typefaces Calhoun identified in the note. Something about the line being discontinued before anybody else got it. I forget the details."

"Did you go see the printer?"

"Way ahead of you. I got a list of the magazines he does. And samples."

Roger smiled. "Might have known. What we have to do now, of course, is go through all their subscription lists and see if we can match up some names with anybody connected with our victims. Dreary job, but that's how police work goes sometimes."

"I've already begun on that, too," said Jinny.

"You are a jewel," Roger said. "With a lovely type face. Neat but not Goudy."

Jinny groaned good-naturedly.

"Oh, you like jokes about printing?" Roger said, pretending not to have heard her oh-no reaction. "Did I ever tell you about an Italian called Twelve-point Bodoni? He was a bold-face type, if I ever saw one."

The squawk box came to life. "For you on line three," said Charleen's voice.

"Charleen," said Roger, "I thought I said no calls."

"This one I think you'll want, Rodge. Very insistent person. A Mr. Griswold of the FBI."

"You're right," Roger said. He punched the button for line three. "Dale here."

"This is Griswold, Mr. Dale."

"Yes. What can I do for you?"

"Can't tell you over the party line. You know, security. Can you drop around to my hotel?"

"You're in town?"

"Yes. The Wickford. What the hell room number? Let me look at this key. Yeah. Twenty-oh-four. These damn rooms are all the same. I wake up in one, some mornings, and for a few seconds I don't know what town I'm in."

"Ask the chick beside you. They always know."

"That was not only unfunny but uncalled for. Just get over here. Twenty minutes?"

"Make it an hour. L.A. traffic."

After Roger had hung up, Jinny blinked at him. "What's he want, I wonder?"

"Whatever we've got on the talk show murders, for a guess, which he ain't gonna get nohow. Two can play at this game of his."

"Be careful of Griswold, Rodge. I'd guess he bites."

"So he does. Well, hold the fort."

At the hotel, Roger announced his arrival over the house phone; Griswold said, "In the bar." When the assistant director appeared a few minutes later he had two men flanking him like bodyguards. There was a moment of déjà vu in which Roger thought he'd been brought into the presence of Mickey Samish all over again. There were mumbled introductions and Roger heard and promptly forgot the names of Griswold's cohorts, who were special agents of the L.A. office—large, athletic-looking men with a machinelike pleasantness to them.

Seated in the booth, in the bar, which was quiet and dim, the three FBI men ordered coffee. "And keep it coming," said the slightly taller one, who reminded Roger a little of Varsity. The other was a blond beast who would have been perfect on a recruiting poster for Hitler's Wehrmacht.

"I'll have MacKeckneigh's Dew of Killduggan on the rocks," said Roger. Mickey Samish couldn't be all bad—he'd given Roger a taste for the stuff.

"We haven't got that," said the waitress, a pretty girl in panty hose and a short wine-red skirt fluffed out by starched linen underneath.

"Chivas Regal?"

"That either," she said, frowning dully and suddenly looking less pretty.

"The best you have, then," said Roger.

"Yes, sir." She shifted the gum she tried not to chew in front of the customers from one side of her mouth to the other and swung away to fetch everybody's drinks.

"Sure it'll be only coffee," asked Roger, a vague ethic of his surfacing to disapprove of his drinking alone.

"We never drink on duty," said Griswold.

"Try it sometime. Might loosen you up. What's on your mind?"

"Against my better judgment, Dale," said Griswold, "I've decided to cooperate with you."

"Glad to hear it. What brought about the sudden change of heart? Wait a minute—let me guess. Somebody brought you in on the carpet and said, 'What's all this in the press about us withholding information?' "

"You just can't be nice, can you?" said Griswold. "I called you in to tell you you can have that lab report of ours you asked for. Or our printouts on some of the people connected with the talk show murders."

"What's the catch?"

"No catch." Griswold shifted heavily in the booth. "Of course, we also expect a look at any evidence you might have run into, by accident, or whatever."

"That's the catch," said Roger.

"Now who's being uncooperative?"

Roger shrugged. "I am."

"Mr. Dale," said Griswold, "let's just say what we mean here, okay?"

Miss Panty Hose came back with the Scotch and coffee. Everybody waited until it had been set on the table.

"Got any peanuts?" the blond FBI man said.

"Popcorn," she said.

He frowned his way through this major decision for a moment, then nodded and said, "That'll do."

She went off.

"End of time out," said Roger, looking at his watch.

Griswold sipped his coffee. "Damned stuff," he said. He put his cup down. "Know what the occupational diseases of bureau agents are? Stomach trouble from coffee and high blood pressure from all the assholes we have to deal with."

"I wouldn't doubt it," said Roger, looking at him levelly. "Quite a few around, I'm sure. Which kind do you mean? Mafia guys? Commies? Or maybe civil-rights attorneys who have this sentimental notion that the founding fathers were serious about the First Amendment?"

"Christ," said Griswold, "I mighta known we'd hear some of that liberal crap from you."

"Look, Griswold," said Roger, "you're not Joe McCarthy and I'm not Norman Cousins, though each of us, perhaps, leans a little in opposite directions. Let's stick to the point, whatever it is, okay?"

"The point," Griswold snapped, "is this: will you cooperate with us?"

"Who says I'm not?"

"Never mind who says it. Are ya or ain't ya? I've met guys like you before. You're not out there doing it all for good old justice and decency. You're out there to make a buck and a reputation. And if you have to undermine the image of the legitimate law enforcement establishment to do it, I don't think you'd hesitate a minute."

"I think you're getting paranoid," Roger said. "Look, it's like this. I've got my methods, and data I've collected, which you wouldn't use my way if you had it.

I'm building something, slowly, and I think maybe you'd tear it down if you tinkered with it. Once it all starts to show a little shape—if it ever does—well, then it'll be different. As soon as I've got something definite, something conclusive, it's yours. For whatever credit you can get out of it. For whatever arrests you or any other official agency care to make. It's not as though I'm trying to take the collar away from you, speaking of making a reputation."

"Then you won't cooperate."

"If that's the way you see it," said Roger.

"I once reminded you, Dale," said Griswold, "that obstructing justice is a crime. So is withholding evidence. I don't suppose we'd get you sent to jail for it— hardly anybody goes to jail for anything anymore—but we could, by God, get your license revoked. In fact, we could probably do that right now if we wanted to. A good, thorough background investigation always turns something up. Who among us has lived a clean life, one hundred percent?"

"Who, indeed? Come to think of it, making threats like this on a citizen is also a crime."

"As long as you get the message," said Griswold.

"Nice talking to you, sir," said Roger, rising. "Thanks for the Scotch. Put it on the expense account. I'll help pay for it next April, when I file."

"Be sure you do," said Griswold, glaring. "Be sure you do everything nice and clean, and by the book."

"I'd be sure of that, anyway," said Roger, disapproving of himself a little for playing the game of getting the last word in, but unable to resist.

He could feel eyes on his back as he left the bar.

IX

The *dojo* of
Kazu Hashimoto was much like a small gymnasium
except that there were tatami mats instead of polished
oaken planks on the floor.

Roger said, "*Ha!*" He brought his hands up and put
his left foot forward so that he was in the *hanmi* position.

Kazu Hashimoto, in the same position, also said
explosively, "*Ha!*"

Roger charged.

Old Kazu threw him easily.

Roger picked himself up, sighed, and tightened his
red obi. He had a long way to go before he'd be
qualified to wear a black one.

"You rusty, Roger-san," said Kazu. "No *ki* inside.
Inside, you're all fuckupu now."

"That could be it," said Roger.

Kazu was small and gnomelike. The wrinkles all
over his face were like the crazing of fine Satsuma
porcelain. "Come. We meditate," he said.

In a moment they were squatting cross-legged in
suwari, facing each other. Roger tried to clear his mind

—to change it, in effect, into a blank, virgin sheet of *getsumei* on which Kazu might deftly brushstroke some wisdom.

It wasn't easy. He should have been thinking about nothing, nothing at all, but he kept thinking about Kazu. Kazu Hashimoto, the stress in the first name on the first syllable—it irritated him to be called Ka-*zoo*, as he inevitably was here in America. The old man was one of the few living practitioners of *ninjitsu*, the ancient Japanese martial art of espionage. It had developed during the period of the warlords almost a thousand years ago, when each employed his own army and his own elite corps of special troops, the *ninja*. It included all the better-known martial arts— karate, aikido, judo—plus all the dirty tricks of spying, and a nebulous philosophy, largely borrowed from Zen, that always seemed to be floating in some kind of mist just beyond Roger's comprehension.

Kazu had been brought to the United States almost thirty years before by his daughter, who had married a G.I. stationed in Japan. He managed to get back to his homeland every two or three years for a visit, but on the whole, he loved it in America. Back in Japan he was just another *ninjitsu* expert, to be honored for it, of course, but nothing really remarkable. In America he was extraordinary and by most of his students deeply revered. Besides, he was crazy about hamburgers and tacos and the Los Angeles Rams.

"How many strokes," asked Kazu, "you need to draw picture of empty air?"

"Oh, I don't know," said Roger. "One or two?"

"God damn!" said Kazu. "That is koan. You not supposed to answer!"

"I forgot," said Roger. "Sorry."

Picture of empty air . . . sound of one hand clapping.

The koan. Roger never did really get it. But it seemed to work with Kazu, who could always throw him, so he hung on.

Kazu reached out and smacked Roger smartly atop the head with a bamboo stick.

"Thank you, *Sensei*," said Roger, as he'd been taught. *Sensei*—teacher—was a term of honor in Japan, like maestro. There was a difference in culture for you.

"That better," said Kazu. "Now you tell me. How come you so fuckupu now?"

"Well, I guess maybe it's this case I'm working on," said Roger. He told Kazu, in swift summary, about the talk show murders. "It started out, you see," said Roger, "as a more or less practical project. Something that would do me some good—get favorable publicity, attract clients. Now, suddenly, it's become emotional. I feel this killer is out there somewhere, laughing at me. And I want to get him. Out of pride. Ego. Whatever you call it. So now I'm not operating coolly and dispassionately, and this, I think, is interfering. You see what I mean?"

"If sparrow die, fertilize grass, horse eat grass, then sparrow eat horse turd, who eating who?" asked Kazu.

"I'll try not to answer this time," said Roger.

"Here one you can answer. Fox in forest. Always disappear. Cannot find—he too clever. What you do?"

"Set a trap?"

"Goddamn right," said Kazu. "You getting better. Okay, we meditate half hour more, then we go out and get pizza."

"Good a way as any to kill the afternoon," said Roger.

"What is best weapon to kill time?" asked Kazu.

Roger started to answer, then saw Kazu reaching for the bamboo stick again and desisted.

* * *

Mike Douglas, sitting at his desk, looking like a genial, middleaged Irish detective, cocked his head to one side and studied his visitor, trying to figure him out a little—searching for whatever scam might lie behind his bizarre proposal. Mike, like most talk show hosts, had one of those pleasant, almost unidentifiable faces. Just another nice guy you might run into. Leo Durocher had once said that nice guys finish last, but in the talk show industry this wasn't true. You had to be agreeable, compliant, tolerant, and if witty, never in a biting, sardonic way.

"Let me try to get this straight, Roger," said Mike to his visitor. "You want to set up a show that this nut might deliberately try to pull another killing on?"

"Exactly."

"This is crazy," said Mike.

"It must seem so. But if it works out the way I think it might, you've got the biggest show since they booked Ben Hur and Messala in the Coliseum. Your triumph will be on tape and you can promote hell out of it before it airs."

"When I say it's crazy," said Mike, frowning, "I'm thinking of the danger. And the moral aspect, too. Do we have the right to deliberately expose somebody to getting killed?"

"You have a point. I can't really answer it. Sometimes you have to take chances. And staking out a pigeon for bait is a time-honored custom. The cops who go out in drag to attract muggers, for example."

"They're cops. They're also being paid to take chances."

"What if I told you I have a volunteer?"

"Do you?"

"I think I may. Larry Lawson."

"Larry who?"

"Up-and-coming young comic. Just finished six weeks at the Mecca in Vegas."

"Oh. Sure. Lawson. Yeah—I caught his act. Not bad. I understand he's a wildie, a swinger. Might have been just another of those showbiz rumors."

"It's not a rumor. Larry would hump a snake if it would hold still. But it would have to be a female snake —he's at least that straight."

Douglas laughed.

"But you see," Roger said, "that's what makes him perfect for this thing."

"You've lost me," said Mike.

"Look at the victims in these murders. It eluded me for a while until suddenly, one morning while I was shaving, my subconscious came up with it. All amoral, so to speak. Elmo Finstetter and his three hundred sixty-five chicks a year. Sonny Pearson and his coveys of San Quentin quail. Even poor old Mabel Merriwether, who went around looking for gigolos all the time. See what we have here? The killer's quirk. Somehow, he's appointed himself the avenging angel to punish loose sexual behavior wherever he finds it."

"Do just three cases prove that theory?"

"No," said Roger, "but even far-out theories should be tested."

They both laughed. Roger continued his explanation, which, he reflected with some discomfort, had now become a sales pitch. "To fill you in on this, I've got a girl friend named Meg Arlington who dearly desires a public relations career. She, too, gets wild ideas and, alas, usually acts on them. She knew my theory about the killer's hangup and knew I wanted to set a trap. Without consulting me, she contacted Larry Lawson's agent—Danny Moss has taken him on, it seems—and said she could get Larry on the Mike Douglas show if they'd retain her for PR. Well, they went for it and she came to me. I was sore at her at first, but the more I thought about it the more I realized she'd come up with something. I tell you this just so all the axes we want to grind are right out in the open. I'm gambling that this will be more effective than trying to snow you."

"I appreciate your honesty, but—I don't know. There's still the danger."

"Which we'll minimize. First, a careful screening of whoever's there. I know how to check into backgrounds. And guards. I've got a lot of retired cops listed and on call for security jobs. I'll have some in uniform and some in plain clothes, watching. My expense. Remember, Mike, what I'm hoping is not that this killer succeeds—only that he makes a try. There's a chance he won't, of course, but I'm betting he will."

"I've got to talk to my people about this," said Mike, frowning.

"I wish you wouldn't," said Roger. "A very close adviser or two, if you must, but for God's sake, swear them to secrecy. We can't afford to have this get back to the killer, who is probably someone in the industry —though I'm not a hundred percent sure of that."

"I'll let you know," said Mike, keeping his frown.

Roger nodded. "I don't call you, you'll call me. Is that it?"

"Right," Mike Douglas said. "For now, anyway."

"Hello, all of you out there. Ronnie Fordyce here. I have it from an impeccable source that supersleuth Roger Dale is about to make another appearance, this time on Mike Douglas's talk show, which, like all such, is big on talk, not so hot on show. If there's anything blander and less stimulating than the average talk show, I don't know what it would be. The only excitement on talk shows usually comes by accident, as it did when Elmo Finstetter got done in on Toni Tennille's hour of glowing yogurt.

"The early viewing hours haven't been so dull since they took most of the violence out of them, an ingredient of drama, I remind you, that Shakespeare never hesitated to employ. Since Elmo's demise, which was welcome enough in some circles . . . both Sonny Pearson and a pathetic woman by the name of Mabel Merriwether were similarly done in, but we, the viewers, were never allowed to see it.

"There may be relief in sight, though. Roger Dale will be invited to make a progress report on his investigation of these murders for Mike Douglas. Also on the bill will be Raquel Welch, Senator Byrd and his fiddle, and an emerging and underdeveloped young comic named Larry Lawson, and don't tell me you never heard of him because neither have I.

"But now for my prediction. There will be another murder on this very talk show. At least there will be another attempt. Don't bother to tune in, hoping to see it, however. Anything the least bit interesting will probably be edited out, as usual, before the show reaches the air.

"I may die of ennui. If so, I'll try to do it right here in front of the camera where you can all see. You've been long enough, out there, without the violence you deserve, if only to spice up your dreary lives a bit.

"Once again, I can only say, Good viewing—if you can find it."

Larry Lawson sat with Danny Moss in Canter's delicatessen on Fairfax Avenue near the CBS studio.

Lawson was wolfing a thick hot pastrami sandwich; Danny was picking unenthusiastically at lox and scrambled eggs. Both had glasses of cream soda on the side.

"I keep wondering," said Larry, "if I really should go on the Douglas show, be a target like that."

Danny Moss looked at his client with forced patience. Even when he wasn't performing, Larry Lawson, with his rubbery face, looked funny. One of the minority of comedians who were funny offstage, Danny reflected, though he didn't try to be. He had this Woody Allen or Rodney Dangerfield look of being put upon. It might go over big one of these days—that was why Danny had taken him on as a client.

"When," Moss asked, "will you start listening to me? Do you realize what's fallen into your lap? You don't get booked on these big talk shows just because you want to; even I can't force it, and I carry a certain amount of clout. Do you know how many performers would turn in their mothers just to do a bit on the Douglas or Griffin or Carson show? Those few minutes can make or break your career. Why the hell do I knock myself out doing these things for my clients?"

"Yeah. But what if I get killed?"

"You won't. You'll be well protected. I've explained all that."

"Oh, sure. You won't be up there, waiting for it." Larry reached into the pocket of his boldly checked tweed jacket and took out four small bottles of various sizes.

"Medicine?" asked Danny. He always liked to know about the health of his clients, as he did their hangups and sexual preferences. Such things always had a bearing.

"Vitamins," said Larry. "Supplement to my diet."

"What diet?"

"The one I'm always on. Doc keeps telling me I gotta lose weight."

Danny nodded at the sandwich. "You're on a diet and you're eating that?"

"I thought just this once wouldn't hurt."

"I'll bet 'just this once' comes every day. Have you really lost any weight yet?"

"I will, as soon as I really get started on it."

"Yeah." Danny Moss looked at his polished nails for a moment. "I hate to tell you this, Larry, but you shouldn't lose weight."

"Why not?"

"You won't be as funny if you do."

"What do you mean, I won't be funny? It's what I say, not how I look, that's funny."

"I got news for you. It's how you look, too."

Larry frowned deeply. And expressively, the way he showed all emotion. "You don't understand. Chicks don't like fat men."

"What's that got to do with it?"

"Chicks. You're undersexed, Danny. You don't know how it is."

"I know very well how it is," said Danny. "But, as Sam Goldwyn used to say, include me out. And I'm afraid I'm going to have to give you the same advice I give to a lot of clients. The public eye will be upon you. The public is a puritan, which, H. L. Mencken once said, is a person with a lurking suspicion that someone, somewhere, may be happy. It's not as bad with a comedian as with a regular performer, but remember what happened to Fatty Arbuckle in the old silent days. It's still that way, to a degree. The least you can do is be discreet."

"What are you saying? I've got to ration my nooky or something? Like another goddamn diet?"

"Might not be a bad idea," said Danny.

"You still don't understand." Larry Lawson showed his the-world-is-out-to-defeat-me look. "When I was a kid in St. Louis I was the little fat kid everybody hated. The other guys had girls; I had goldfish. You ever try to kiss a goldfish? They suck back, but it's not the same. Anyway, I said that if I ever got somewhere and could afford it, I'd have all the nooky I wanted. Make up for lost time. Thin ones, fat ones, young ones, old ones. Even ugly ones sometimes. To me there's no such thing as an unbangable chick."

A woman went by their table. She was thirtyish, nicely dressed—probably some cub scout's mother. Larry swiveled in his chair to watch her pass.

"Take it easy," said Danny, touching his arm.

Larry looked at Danny again. "I imagine what it would be like with almost every one I see. It's always good."

"You've got to cut down," said Danny, shaking his head. "If you get to the top—and with that funny face you just might—you'll find it's precarious up there. You'll have to keep renewing your act, for example. In the old vaudeville days comics could do the same routine over and over again. Not anymore. The audience is—"

"Fuck the audience," said Larry. He took another huge bite of his sandwich, then looked up again. "Well, half of 'em, anyway."

"Will they ever listen to me?" Danny asked the air, sighing. He took a tiny sip of his cream soda. "You'd better start thinking about new material right now. In fact, I'd get something special, if I were you, just for the Douglas shot. Hire a good gagwriter. Sheldon Walters would be good. He's expensive, but worth it. I'll see if he's available if you like."

"If I like? Who likes? I'm already spending more on this Mike Douglas shot than I'm making. Minimum scale, for God's sake!"

They had to go outside, to Roger's car, in order to listen. It was one of the old wire-wheeled MG's, cherished by Roger and kept in good running order by a lady mechanic named Sophie who was a little on the hefty side and who made occasional uncaught passes at Roger. He sometimes felt faintly guilty at that, especially since she did such a great job with the car.

Jinny brought the cassette. They'd wondered how they'd be able to listen to it conveniently, and then Roger remembered the stereo in the glove compartment of the MG, installed there so it wouldn't get ripped off.

The car was parked in its slot along with those of the other tenants of the Fairview Business Park. It was a lovely day. "Shall we ride?" asked Roger.

"Might as well," said Jinny. "It's much too nice to walk."

They were soon on the boulevard, headed for the winding roads of the canyon. "Okay, let's hear it," said Roger.

"I wonder if it's what we think it is," said Jinny.

"You saw the name of the sender. X. Terminator. Not exactly a subtle pun but I guess he had to call himself something. Bothers me a little—not exactly in character. Anyway, it's got to be him."

"He," said Jinny.

"Dorothy Parker once said, 'All grammarians are homosexuals.' "

"Well, I'm not. Though maybe I ought to be. I'd be every oppressed minority there is, then."

"Play the tape," said Roger.

They listened.

"Greetings, Roger Dale," said the voice. "It's become quite a game between us, hasn't it? I'm enjoying it. I hope you are, too."

There was a pause. Roger and Jinny glanced at each other. To Roger's ear the voice sounded high-pitched and oddly sibilant. It could have been, he reflected, either a man or a woman.

"I'm sending you this," the voice continued, "to let you know there's going to be another one. And once more, right under your nose. Remember how Muhammad Ali used to call the rounds in which he'd knock out his opponents? That, in essence, is what I'm doing now. You'll try to prevent it, of course, but I don't think you'll succeed."

There was another pause. "It gives me the chills," said Jinny, blinking at the stereo head through her thick glasses.

"Shh!" said Roger. He was bent forward over the wheel, straining to listen.

"You're wondering why I'm doing it, aren't you, Roger? Well, a lot of reasons, actually. Some are quite personal, so I won't go into them now. One of the reasons, though, is that you've taken it upon yourself to be my nemesis. May I say that I consider you a worthy opponent? I would not say that about just anyone; the game lacks spice unless the opponent is as able as I am. Well, almost as able, because you're not going to win, you know."

"The hell I'm not," Roger muttered.

"You are also, from my standpoint," continued the speaker, "the perfect opponent. Detached, impersonal —indeed, abstract, and that is what symbols should be.

Man, as opposed to the lower animals, lives by symbols, does he not? You represent, you see, the forces I would destroy. Those that are tearing down the moral fabric of our civilization and leading inexorably to the disappearance of our species from this planet. I don't suppose I can prevent that, because it's inevitable, but I can make my gestures of protest, quixotic as they may be. That's all we live for, anyway, isn't it? To do what we can, even though it may be hopeless. To make our voices heard. The alternative is to sit back and do nothing. That, I maintain, is unthinkable."

"My God!" said Roger, during the next pause. "The guy's stark, raving nuts!"

"If that's really him," said Jinny.

"He," said Roger. "Or she. Shut up."

"I don't think I have to explain a great deal more," said the voice. "Considering those I have selected, you must have guessed, by now, why they deserve what's happened to them. As a matter of fact, Dale, you belong with them. You know very well why. But you will be spared—at least for the time being. The matador does not kill the bull right away; he waits for the moment of truth. Farewell for now, Roger Dale. It's been nice talking to you."

"I never heard anything like it!" said Jinny, staring.

Roger nodded absentmindedly. "He's made his first big mistake. He or she. Wish to hell English had a pronoun to cover both. That tape tells us a lot about 'The Exterminator,' and it's going to tell us more. Typical paranoia, the big cause, like harmful radio waves or fluoride in the water or something. With him, society's morality. He must know we can begin to see him from this tape. He's deliberately courting danger. He's compelled to."

"Aren't you getting pretty fancy with the psychology there?"

Roger shook his head. "Not at all. The guy is an absolute storehouse of hangups. The Albert Fish syndrome."

"Who?"

"Classic case in criminal psychology. Janitor in New York who committed a bunch of murders and had every aberration and perversion known to science. I think the point of this is that no matter how weird it is, if you can imagine it, it can happen to someone, sometime, somewhere."

"In a way," said Jinny, frowning, "he doesn't *sound* crazy."

"Also typical of paranoia," said Roger. "They can seem completely rational, and often, in their everyday life, they are. They can also be highly intelligent, which the Exterminator obviously is."

"What causes it, anyway?"

"Who knows? An episode of particular stress to set it off. That's another thing we might look for in our perpetrator as we reconstruct him. We're getting there, Jinny. We've got a long way to go yet but we're getting there." He glanced behind him, then swung the MG in a sudden U-turn.

"Where to now?"

"Back to the shop. Things to do."

"Like what?"

"There's a guy at UCLA. Sam Wechsler, a speech expert. He was a pfc in Vietnam when I was a corporal, so I outrank him. I'm going to turn him loose on this tape. Betcha he'll tell us not only what part of the country the Exterminator comes from but the precinct in which he was raised."

"I hate to spoil your fun," said Jinny, "but you're supposed to see those K mart people this afternoon about putting your shoplifting spotters in."

"To hell with them," said Roger.

"Move your butt over here and I'll kick it. That's what you told me to do, remember?"

"I can't right now," said Roger. "I'm driving."

X

Sam Wechsler was short, vigorous, and powerful. The black hair on his muscular forearms grew on a deep tan which he could renew anytime with only a few hours at the beach or under the sunlamp. His dark eyes gleamed with both his steel-trap intelligence and restless curiosity. He exuded energy, as though he were radioactive. There was none of your pale, studious Hasid in Sam. He was Saul, fiery-eyed and girded in armor, ready for battle. Anytime.

He greeted Roger at the door of his office in the Linguistic Sciences Building and said, "Come in, come in, Rodge! Terrific to see you again!"

His handshake was so firm that Roger had to relax a little to preserve his knuckles.

"So where have you been? What have you been doing? What's this about some murderer, talking on a tape? Did you have a nice drive here and are you getting much these days? Don't answer all those questions at once. I want you to stay awhile."

Roger, laughing—remembering how Sam always made him laugh—took the big leather chair he was steered to. Wechsler went to his desk and sat in one place as though under protest. While they cleared the decks of some other small talk, Roger looked around the room. The walls were nearly all books. Some of them, by Sam himself, filled half a shelf compartment. There were tape recorders and speakers on consoles against one part of the wall, and on another part charts showing cutaway drawings of the tongue, the larynx, the pharynx, and other 'ynxes Roger didn't recognize.

"We shouldn't be out of touch," said Sam. "You should come to the house sometime. Meet Leah. Only trouble is her mother who lives with us. She suffers in silence when she's sure someone's looking. You're not married yet, are you?"

"Still filing only one exemption. Grossly unfair."

"Take my advice. If you're looking for a wife, find some orphan. That way you won't get relatives with her. Now, what's up?"

Roger told the story of the talk show murders. Sam listened attentively, eyes narrowing in concentration. To him an intellectual challenge was like a physical challenge—to be met with a fast left hook before your opponent knew the game had started.

Minutes later, Sam had Roger's cassette in a slot and was running off a copy as he listened. The words came out of an overhead speaker, much clearer than they had been in the car stereo. Roger could now hear the popping of the Exterminator's *p*'s and *t*'s and even the breaths he drew between phrases.

"Interesting," said Sam.

"I figured you'd say at least that much," said Roger.

"Well, it is. My master's was in psych, you know, before I took my Ph.D. in linguistics. This guy is as nutty as a bar of marzipan."

Wechsler played the cassette again, listening even

more intently this time. "I'll tell you what we've got here," he said. "Somebody who's traveled around in his formative years so his original accent's worn down a little. Hardest kind to identify."

"Don't tell me I took this long drive for nothing."

"No, no—I've got some ideas about the speaker. I just can't pin him down as tight as I can some people, that's all."

"How do you do this pinning down, anyway?"

"I figured you'd know and start lecturing *me* on it. Anyway, you must have a rough idea. American speech, obviously, came originally from England. But from different parts of England, so there were different accents where each group settled. The people who settled here originally had an accent more like ours, today, than the so-called Queen's English or BBC accent we usually associate with England. *That* fancy-schmancy mode of speech came from Queen Victoria and all those Krauts around her. You know where the main New York City accent comes from? The 'toity-toid street' bit? From the Dutch, who originally settled Manhattan. You want a drink?"

"I'll pass."

"Then back to the exegesis, which always sounds to me like somebody who used to be a messiah. Accents run in what they call clines. Start in New England, where a *park* sounds like something wolves run in. About halfway down New Jersey they start to acknowl-edge the letter *r*. Off to one side, in Philadelphia, they say *warsh* for what you to do to your hands when they're dirty, and off to the other side, in Delaware, a *boat* sounds like what cowboys wear on their feet. In Maryland it starts to get southern, and just below Washington it does. Now, if we start to move out west—"

"Let's not," said Roger.

"Okay. You're waiting. But while I'm saying all this I'm putting it together in my head, everything I heard on the tape. I'm beginning to see this guy."

"You're sure it's a guy, by the way? I thought it could be a woman—a sort of baritone woman. Maybe like Tallulah Bankhead or Lauren Bacall. Even Lucille Ball, lately."

Sam nodded. "It *could* be. But the semantic patterns sound masculine. Muhammad Ali—the bullfight bit."

"So where's the guy from? Come on, Sam."

"Touch of the southern," said Sam, still ruminating, "touch of the northern. Nasalizes the *ow* dipththong a little. Tends to drop his terminal palatals. You can see what this indicates."

"No, I can't. That's why I came to you."

Sam thought for another moment. "Okay, Rodge, I'll take a wild shot at it. Stick a compass in the men's room of the Baltimore Hilton. Swing a hundred-mile circle. Somewhere in there."

"A lot of people could be from there," said Roger.

Sam shrugged. "It's a good place to be *from*, as the old line goes."

"Well, that hundred-mile circle's better than nothing. And I'm sure nobody else in the country could do better. You know, I don't think I ever asked—how did you get on this accent kick, anyway?"

"Wondering," said Sam, grinning, "why the goyim could never tell Jewish jokes good. I moved, undetected, among them for years and loined their lengvitch."

Roger laughed. "All right, I'll have that drink. Just one, if I may indulge in another cliché, for the road."

* * *

It was after five, but Jinny had not yet left the office by the time Roger got back to it. The door to the one rest room was open. She was at the mirror there, putting on a face, leaning close, so she could see herself. Roger, barely noticing her presence, went immediately to the easel that still held the oversize chart of the Exterminator's psychological profile, grabbing for a grease pencil to make new entries on the clear plastic overlay.

"Know what it's like?" he called to Jinny, without preface. "Those pictures you paint by filling in the numbers. Well, I've got a few more numbers. Long session with Sam Wechsler. Got more from it than just where the guy's from—which is the Philadelphia-Baltimore-Washington area, by the way. Are you listening, Jinny?"

"No," said Jinny, coming out of the rest room all neat and shining.

He looked at her, his eyebrows rising a little. "You're not?"

"I'm not listening because I'm on my way."

Roger checked his watch. "It *is* late, isn't it?" He looked at Jinny again. "Calhoun, I suppose."

"He'll be here any minute."

"Damn. I was hoping we could check out a few people. See who's from around Baltimore."

"Face it, Marse Roger," said Jinny. "By 'we' you mean 'me.' I'm the one who ends up doing the checking. Beware. We Mau Maus may have an uprising one of these days."

"Okay—sorry. It's just that I've got this thing going now—"

"Rodge—Are you sure it's not getting to be an obsession? Is something of the fantasy the murderer's created in his mind rubbing off on you?"

"When I want therapy," he said, "I'll go to a shrink."

"If you do," said Jinny, now gathering up her red morocco shoulder bag and heading for the door, "try Lionel Rand."

"Who he?"

"At first glance just another clinical psychologist, Ph.D. type, fifty bucks an hour, standard issue. But he's getting popular in the entertainment world. I think he has somebody doing publicity for him, which, of course, his colleagues consider unethical. I didn't have time to check into it further."

"Why did you check into it at all? What's this guy got to do with anything?"

"A pattern, Rodge," said Jinny, smiling just a little smugly. "We look for patterns, remember? What do the victims and possible suspects have in common?"

"Is that how you do it? Gee, it must be fascinating to be a detective!"

Unabashed, Jinny went on. "Elmo Finstetter went to Dr. Rand. Sonny Pearson went to Dr. Rand. Danny Moss, their agent, went to Dr. Rand. Several other people who work on talk shows went to him. I guess it's natural that people in any one group like that would recommend him to each other. Anyway, he, she, or it, and all the king's horses and all the king's men seem to go to Lionel Rand for their hangups, real and imagined. What do you think of that?"

Roger nodded seriously. "I'll run it down. Nice going, Jinny."

A horn sounded outside.

"Calhoun," said Jinny. "See you in the morning."

The morning.

Roger and Meg lay side by side, sweetly, as the

dawnlight rose, silent and pearly gray, outside the window of her apartment.

Meg smiled and ran her fingertips through the hair on Roger's chest. He turned his head to look at her with a floating smile.

"I must be more old-fashioned than I thought," Roger said.

"Why do you say that?"

"Because," Roger said, "I was just lying here—like a dummy—wishing that I was the first man who'd ever made love to you."

She lifted herself up, on one elbow, and looked down at him.

"Roger," she said, "that's the nicest thing anyone has said to me in a very long time. I thank you."

"Some literary wise man—it might have been Wilde —once said that in his heart every man wants to be a woman's first lover, and every woman wants to be a man's last."

"Good ol' Oscar," Meg said. "A wise man indeed. Anyway, I'm glad we waited to make love. I don't understand these guys—even the otherwise nice ones —who hit on you to go to bed with them about twenty minutes after you've met. I'm not talking about the morality of the thing. We've just made love and I feel good about that. But having sex with somebody you've just met really comes down to having sex with a stranger, and there's something about that I don't like at all."

Roger took her right hand in his and kissed it, gently, looking as if it were an object he'd never seen before.

"It's funny," he said, "life can seem very simple at moments like this. The fantasy of just preserving this moment, carrying it forward through time, is appealing.

And it isn't just the act of lovemaking—great as it was —it's the—" He fumbled for the right phrase.

"I know," she said, kissing him lightly on the lips. "I feel the same way."

"And out there," said Roger, glancing at the window, "the rat race is getting ready to start again. Wonder what would happen if some morning I said to all the other rats, 'Okay, guys—you go ahead without me.'"

"Nothing much," said Meg. "That's what success is, I imagine. How much they care whether you drop out or keep going."

Meg kissed Roger's ear lightly, her hot breath sending something like a slight electric charge through his bloodstream. "Did I tell you?" she said. "I'm going to move up in the rat race."

"Move up?"

"I've decided. No more spiels to rubbernecks on the tour bus. Public relations, full-time, from now on."

"Are you sure it's wise?"

"It's what I have to do. Have to take the plunge sometime. I've got several accounts now, you know. This dude in Santa Barbara who wants to be a movie actor and has his own funds, or at least his family's. A girl folksinger who pays me in fresh eggs and cabbage. She'd probably come up with some homegrown pot if I wanted it. And now this big one—Larry Lawson. That's the key—the big one. Yes, I think it's time. Today I look for an office to rent. Anything open at your business park?"

"I'll check," said Roger. "But I hope you're not going into it too early. Maybe you ought to have more clients first. And a better in with the media."

"I've got some media contacts. Ronnie Fordyce loves me. Very platonic, of course. I've had dinner with him, even. He told me all about himself. Said talking to me was better and cheaper than going to his psychiatrist."

"Ah. So Ronnie takes to the couch, too, does he? It figures. If I didn't have Kazu Hashimoto and all that Zen jazz I'd probably do the same. Which reminds me. Jinny dug up something interesting yesterday. Elmo Finstetter and Sonny Pearson went to the same therapist. Plus Danny Moss. And some others around the talk show scene: Shel Walters the comedy writer, I think, and Charley Higgins, who works for Phil Donahue. She got this more as gossip than a matter of record, so it may not be entirely accurate. But it does begin to smell oddly coincidental—at least worth looking into. They all either did sessions with this guy, or at least visited him for evaluation or counseling. A man in the Wilshire district named Lionel Rand."

Staring at Roger, Meg blinked twice. "Lionel Rand," she said, "is also Ronnie Fordyce's psychologist, or whatever."

"I'll be damned!" said Roger.

"So early in the morning?" She glanced at the window.

"It's not early in the morning. It's just a little later last night. All relative, you see." Roger looked at Meg fondly. Resting his head once more on her stomach, facing her, he said, "From this angle of vision your breasts dominate the world."

"The girls have been good to me," Meg said, laughing.

"When you laugh," he said, "it bounces my head around. And why do you call your breasts the girls?"

"I don't know," Meg said, in the way of shrugging.

"Well," said Roger, "whatever you call them I'm madly in love with them, separately and as a pair. I wonder why?"

"Why what?"

"Why are your breasts so beautiful, so important to me? As distinguished from your knees or elbows, I mean."

"Didn't Freud work all that out?"

"I suppose so. I would very much like to make love to you again."

"What a coincidence," she said, opening her arms.

In the anteroom to Dr. Lionel Rand's office, Roger looked at his wristwatch. It was five minutes after his appointment time. Roger was the only patient waiting. Well, not exactly patient. He'd called and made the appointment, vaguely implying that he was thinking of becoming a patient. It seemed best not to tip his hand—at least not in the beginning. If he told Rand he was an investigator the man might be on guard. Against what, precisely, Roger didn't know, but anyway, with an investigator's routine paranoia, which was to consider anybody capable of anything, this was the way he was playing it.

The visit, though preliminary, would still cost him fifty bucks, and would be difficult to explain away as a business expense come audit time. Also, at the moment, DSA, not yet incorporated, could hardly afford an extra fifty bucks.

Rand's receptionist sat at her desk, behind a little window, making a nice show of doing some book-keeping. Since the rest of the room was nicely decorated, Roger would have thought that Rand would also have gotten himself a decorative receptionist, but he had not. She was a thin, horsey woman. You'd probably be able to tell her age by lifting her upper lip and looking at her teeth.

Roger picked up a magazine from a side table. *Pacific Traveler.* All about where to go and what sights to see from San Diego to Vancouver, B.C. He was looking at pictures of the scenic route from Mount Shasta to Reno when, behind a closed door, another door opened and closed. "You can go in now, Mr. Dale," the receptionist said.

In a moment Roger was in a chair by Rand's desk, looking at the man, whose smile made him seem as detached and dispassionate as a psychologist is supposed to be. Subliminally, Roger also took in the brown venetian blinds on the windows, the English hunting-scene prints on the walls, the photo of a racehorse (his receptionist in a previous incarnation?), the beige file cabinets in the corner, the soft, leather-upholstered couch against one wall.

Dr. Rand had the dewlapped countenance of an Arkansas hound dog. He fingertipped his hands together and looked at Roger across them. "Well, Mr. Dale, what's the problem?"

"I don't know," said Roger. "That's why I'm coming to you. To find out. Whether you can do me any good."

"I see," Rand said. Though his accent was American, his intonation was formal, almost Shakespearean. "Everything depends on how open the patient himself is willing to be." He picked up the card the receptionist had sent in. "Occupation: actor. Many of my patients are. Is acting your principal occupation?"

"Well," said Roger, who had already formed his cover story in his mind, "I actually spend most of my time selling real estate. But TV work is what I'll be doing eventually, as soon as I get a decent break."

"A familiar problem," said Rand. "You needn't feel alone with it. I have some experience with the problems of the entertainment world."

"You mean you—er—take care of other actors or celebrities?"

"I have a few contacts in the profession."

Roger made himself brighten as though he were about to say gee whiz. Basking in reflected glory was a Hollywood pastime Rand would expect him, in the role he was playing, to indulge in. To be on speaking terms with the brother-in-law of the plumber who had once fixed Barbra Streisand's sink was not chopped liver. "I've heard some of the talk show people were your patients. In fact, that's why I looked you up. I have this friend, see, who's in the engineering end at one of the studios. Of course, I have only his word for it. Who are some of your patients from the talk shows?"

"I'm not at liberty to disclose that information. But I can say that I know a number of television people, from both sides of the camera."

"Gee, that's really something," said Roger. "You grew up with some of these people out here?"

"I'm from back east. I took my doctorate at the University of Maryland."

"Is that in Baltimore?"

"College Park. Actually the Washington, D.C., area. But we're getting off the track. Patients do that sometimes to keep from discussing something uncomfortable."

A buzzer sounded on his desk. He frowned at it. He said, "This must be important or Miss Lundquist wouldn't interrupt me in the middle of a session." He picked up the phone and there was a pause while Miss

Lundquist, who, Roger presumed, was the horsefaced receptionist, said something. Rand's frown deepened. He glanced at Roger. "I see," he said. "Thank you." He hung up.

Roger continued to look blank.

Rand stared at Roger evenly for a moment. "Mr. Dale," he said at last, "why the dirty pool?"

"What?" He knew as he said it that the jig was up.

"Pretending you're an actor or whatever. Miss Lundquist thought you looked familiar. She watches TV and reads gossip columns and that sort of thing. She just remembered who you are. I thought you sounded as though you were fishing a moment ago. It's obvious you're not here as a patient."

Roger sighed. "Hand in the cookie jar."

"All right. But why?"

"To find out something about Elmo Finstetter and Sonny Pearson, if I could. They were your patients, weren't they?"

"I still can't confirm that, ethically. And I don't see why you came snooping around this way, underhandedly."

"Let me plead my case," said Roger. "I didn't know you—didn't know what your reaction would be if I just asked for the information. I'm also aware that it's privileged information and that patients have to sign a release to let the medical insurance company know they've gone to a therapist. It seemed to me best to make a kind of reconnaissance first. Okay—it was sneaky. But three people have been murdered, and I'm trying to find out by whom, and why, and I think that's justification enough. I'll go further than that. Now that you know what the score is, I'll say it's your civic duty to cooperate."

"Mr. Dale," said Rand, almost pleasantly, "even if it were, I couldn't tell you anything about Finstetter or Pearson."

"It might be another of your patients I'd want to know about. These murders are—well, kinky, in a way. Psychological overtones. If, by any chance, the murderer himself is one of your patients, some insight into his psyche might steer me in the right direction. I know quite a bit about the symptoms of criminal tendencies."

"Some of my patients think they know more about it than I do. That's kind of a symptom, too. Anyway, I can't tell you a thing. Professional ethics, secrecy of the confessional, and all that. Which, after your little ploy just now, wouldn't seem all that important to you."

Roger's second sigh was even deeper. "I blew it, right?"

"Right."

"Let me ask you this," said Roger. "If you were to become aware that one of your patients was a killer—let's say he simply opened up and confessed it to you—are you saying that because of the quite understandable confidentiality of your operations there's nothing you can do about that, that you would just let the patient go on killing innocent people?"

"No, of course not. There's no simple answer to questions of this sort, of course, either for psychiatrists or Catholic priests. I suppose what most of us would do in that sort of a situation is to advise the patient to hire an attorney and go to the police with a confession. If there were mitigating circumstances—perhaps actual mental instability—we might do what we could to secure justice for both the patient and society."

"I see," Roger said. "But it could still be to your advantage to cooperate with me. How about publicity? I understand you're not averse to it. What if I made sure that anything you contributed got full attention? I even know someone who can place items like this. Very sharp PR person by the name of Meg Arlington. She'd be delighted to take you on, I'm sure."

"I have someone handling public relations," said Rand. "I have a whole complicated and rewarding business and private life I would not care for you to know about. Good day, Mr. Dale. Miss Lundquist will send your bill."

"Bill?"

"You've taken up my professional time."

Roger stared back, trying to penetrate the layer of Teflon that had come over Rand's eyes. "I seem to bother you more than I should, doctor," he said mildly. "Could it be there *is* something about this case you're holding back?"

Rand smiled. "I'm holding everything back. Will you leave now?"

Roger rose and walked out, trying to keep his head high and his shoulders square so he wouldn't look as shriveled as he felt.

XI

                               I still say it was Danny Moss's goof, but the hell of it is I can't be sure. Tuesday sometimes sounds like Thursday, especially if you visualize words in your mind. They both begin with a *T*. And Danny's diction, though adequate, is not of the clearest. He doesn't have a speech impediment, but a kind of ex-con's way of talking out of the side of his mouth, so the guard can't see. Not that he's an ex-con as far as I know; I think it's one of his ways of maintaining machismo.

Forgive me for dwelling on this, but there *was* a goof, and it may have been mine, so it bugs me. I could have sworn Danny said, "Steve, let's talk it over at my beach house in Malibu next Tuesday." He says he said Thursday. The point itself doesn't matter— just some talent I needed for a pilot I was thinking of putting together, and it seemed to me the beach house would be a fine place to relax, soak up some sun, and talk it over. On Tuesday.

When I got there, Moss wasn't around. In the house

were Sheldon Walters, the comedy writer, and a new comedian I'd heard of, vaguely, Larry Lawson.

We all made explanations as to why we were there, and Shel said, "Long as you came all this way, Steve, have something tall and cool. I am referring to a drink rather than a female person. To my regret. Or perhaps you'd like it better short and hot. Now I'm referring to a drink."

I said I'd be driving back soon so I'd have a gin and tonic without the gin, and Walters said, good, he'd put my portion into his.

We all went out to the patio.

As I gathered it, Lawson, on Danny's recommendation, had engaged Shel to supply him with special material for his appearance on Mike Douglas's show, which amounted, more or less, to the break he'd been waiting for. Danny was lending his beach house for the project.

We lowered ourselves into comfortable yellow-cushioned chairs on the redwood deck and looked out, in moderately wild surmise, at the Pacific Ocean, as Cortez once had done, according to the poem, anyway.

"Look at the seals out there," said Lawson.

"Yeah," said Walters. "Whelping in the kelp."

Lawson did not acknowledge the line, which in any event was not his kind of humor. In his swim trunks and with a huge straw hat shading his sunglassed eyes he was truly blubbery. Dolly Parton might have envied his breasts; Rabelais his swelling gut. Not a pretty sight.

Walters studied the gin and tonic in his hand as though all the mysteries of the universe might be frozen in its ice cubes. "My head works that way," he said, responding to Lawson's silence. "Hence, my penetrating observation with hyperbolic flavor couched, by happy serendipity, in internal rhyme."

I laughed. "That's better than doubletalk. And about as comprehensible."

"What the hell are you guys talkin' about?" Larry said.

"It mattereth not," Walters said. He looked a little sad and tired, I thought, as though he'd come here to sit in the sun because everybody said it would do him some good, but he didn't really believe it. "I go off like that sometimes. Psychologists call it a fugue."

"That sounds dirty," said Larry.

"Sometimes it is," said Walters.

"You're a funny guy," said Larry, frowning.

"I'm supposed to be."

"I don't mean that kind of funny."

"You mean screwed up, right?"

"I didn't say that," said Larry.

"You didn't have to." Walters sipped his drink. "You're right, of course. We're all a mass of hangups and rages. And we cope in our separate ways. Like drunks. Some get happy, some crazy. Some lash out, some retreat into catatonia. That is a psychological state, not a nation of cool black guys, as you might think, Larry. And you and I, Larry, we meet the slings and arrows by trying to be funny. It's probably aggression. Do you know what we're doing when we make people laugh? We're attacking them."

"Did we come all the way out to the beach to talk about this shit?" asked Larry.

"Forget it," Walters said, laughing—and he could look sad and sour even when he laughed. "It's my way of warming up the old mechanism. It could have been a sleek and purring thing, spewing out deathless literature, but it's only a joke machine that often goes clunkety-clunk."

"Jeez," Larry said, "are you smashed already?"

"Not after two lousy gin and tonics," said Walters. He reached into the pocket of a terrycloth robe, found cigarettes, lighted one. Blew smoke. Watched it become part of the troposphere. "Yes," he said, nodding. "You're perfect for it."

"For what?" asked Larry suspiciously.

"For hearing my anguished cries. Most people look for somebody sympathetic and understanding. That's a mistake. If they understand you, they have power over you. There are African tribesmen who conceal their real names for that very reason, did you know that? And so you, Larry—obtuse and a cut above the cretinous—will hear and never know."

"Are you zinging me?"

"Of thee I zing," said Walters. "Do you want to hear my troubles or don't you?"

"I don't want to hear your goddamn troubles," said Larry.

"Hear them anyway." Walters jiggled the ice in his glass. "You probably think I don't have any. Little do you reck. Remember the old Lou Holtz routine about the guy on the train? Sam Lapidus, Holtz's favorite character. There's a mixup about the ticket and the conductor says if Sam doesn't produce one he's going to make trouble for him. Sam then explains how his father's in a coffin in the baggage car, how his wife has just left him for somebody else, how he just lost his bankroll to card sharks on the train, and a whole list of other disasters, which he ends by looking at the conductor and saying, 'And you're gonna make trouble for *me*?' "

"So?" said Larry.

"I don't know," said Walters. "It was always funny when Lou Holtz told it."

"Is this one of the routines you're working up for me?"

"No, no. We'll get to that. Just listen awhile. I've had troubles Lapidus never dreamed of. My first novel, *The Darker Streets*. Everything I had in my young navel at the time, including the lint. Promising, said Nat Hentoff, Gilbert Highet, guys like that—another F. Scott Fitzgerald. Then a short story in *The New Yorker*, and a couple of poems in *The Nation*, which you never heard of. Out to Hollywood to work on the screenplay of *Streets*. Which never got out of the can —some internecine quarrel over distribution and contracts, or whatever. But there I was, in the poisonous miasma, breathing in the deadly fumes of mediocrity. Couldn't write serious. I could do it in Greek or German, maybe, but not in serious. Started doing gags for radio, Red Skelton, Edgar Bergen. Made the mistake of wisecracking at a party once. This old studio exec with a borscht accent was going to England. Better take me along, I said. For what? he asked. As interpreter, I said.

"Anyway, there I was, the new funny guy, and they all had to have me. TV, the insatiable monster, came along and they needed me more than ever. Are you listening?"

"No," said Larry.

"I am," I said, chuckling.

"You don't count, Steve. You're like those guys in kabuki plays who come out to move the furniture. They're all in black, therefore you can't see them."

"I like it that way," I said. "Off-camera, at any rate."

"Please don't divert me from the subject of my

troubles, in which I now wallow. Know why all my wives left me? For bigger pricks, that's why. I use this in the figurative sense, of course."

"Look at the bright side," I said. "If you didn't have all these troubles you wouldn't have anything to be funny about."

A seal barked in the distance. The waves of the Pacific gnoshed at the pebbled shore.

"Could you maybe start coming up with some ideas for the Douglas show now?" Lawson said wistfully.

"Anon, anon," said Walters, staring at the sea.

In Mike Douglas's studio, the ritual was about to begin. The guests and performers and all the behind-the-scenes workers were in the building, busy at their preparatory chores; the audience was filing in, smiling anticipation on most of the faces.

Ronnie Fordyce had a fantasy about it. He imagined two stranded extraterrestrials, who were beginning to develop their own genre of jokes, like Polish jokes or elephant jokes, coming upon this scene and promptly reporting it to their superiors back on Planet X as an exotic folk rite of the earthlings.

"But what do they *do*, once they gather, P-two-three-two?"

"Nothing. They just sit there and listen. They laugh a lot."

"Do they recite litanies? Partake of sacraments?"

"No, they just sit. Sometimes one of the acolytes holds up a sign that says Applause, and they do that."

"What god do they worship?"

"I'm not sure, Exalted Leader. They seem to speak of one. A female deity."

"Identify, please."

"The bitch goddess—Success."

Ronnie mused upon this as he walked toward one of the backstage entrances. Maybe good for a column sometime, or one of his TV shots. If the rubes out there would get something that whimsical. That was the trouble with squares; they were, like the eighty-percent peanuts in a can of mixed nuts, at least eighty-percent straight, and straights, for the most part, had no sense of whimsy.

At the backstage entrance there was a guard in what was to Ronnie an unfamiliar uniform. It was blue-black, like a regular cop uniform, but the collar insignia said DSA. Dale Security Agency, guessed Ronnie. Apparently Roger had managed to get a one-shot contract here for his rent-a-cops. Let him not complain again that all the publicity wasn't doing him any good.

The rent-a-cop was burly. Ernest Borgnine. That was how Ronnie thought of people—by star-casting them immediately.

"Good afternoon, sir. May I see your identification, please?"

"I'm Ronnie Fordyce," said Ronnie, and tried to push on.

"Identification, please." The guard barred his way.

"What the hell is this?" asked Ronnie.

"Sorry, I have my instructions, sir."

Ronnie scowled and began to pat himself down. Had he forgotten his wallet again? Freudian oversight —the damned thing always made an unsightly bulge no matter what pocket he put it in. "Oh, fuck," he said petulantly.

"I'm sorry, sir," said the hefty guard. "Without ID you can't get in. ID, and I gotta register you here." He showed a clipboard.

A little down the hall, inside, a figure loomed, and

a voice called, "It's all right, George! I know the gentleman."

"Roger, dear boy!" cried Ronnie. "*Au secours!* To the bloody goddamn rescue!"

A moment later Ronnie and Roger were drinking coffee from the pay machine in the corridor. Roger's quarters. He didn't mind carrying things in his pocket.

"All right, Roger," said Ronnie. "Why the janissary at Checkpoint Charley? What's it all about?"

"Security," said Roger. "You must know why."

"Well, I do, actually, but I still thought I'd ask. I don't want to miss a single, delicious ingredient of this fascinating caper. I almost hope there's another murder today."

"Not if I have anything to say about it."

"Spoilsport," said Ronnie. "I *love* murders, you know. Did I ever tell you? I've got every good mystery ever written—even the old Philo Vance books—and I belong to the Baker Street Irregulars. We believe Holmes lives. And Watson, and Billy, the page boy— he's *my* favorite character—and Dr. Moriarty and all the rest. We meet in New York every year for a banquet."

Roger studied Ronnie for a moment. "Maybe I ought to level with you, Ronnie. I've been doing some checking. On a lot of people. You caught the Finstetter show, didn't you? Toni remembers you dropped in earlier. And you could have been around when Sonny Pearson got it. At least you were nowhere else I can establish at that time."

"Roger!" cried Ronnie delightedly. "Dear Roger! So I'm a suspect, am I? How *marvelous!*"

"One of many," said Roger. "Some of you fits my psychological profile of the murderer, if you want to know the truth. Don't take this personally—just try to understand that this is how I have to do it. No stones unturned, and all that. Mind answering a question?"

"Anything!" Ronnie glowed.

"Where are you originally from?"

"What's that got to do with it?"

"Just wondering."

"You're not just wondering. It's a clue of some kind. Roger, you haven't been keeping me up to date. Anyway, I was born in Wilmington, Delaware, and raised there—the usual terrified childhood. Why?"

"I got a tape in the mail, Ronnie. Probably from the murderer. I had it analyzed. A speech expert says the speaker's from that general area."

"Delicious! Of course, half the people in California could be from there. They're not from California, anyway. That's the salient characteristic of our demography. Well, what do you want me to do? Make a voice print to prove it's not me?"

"I might. You and a few others."

"But tell me about this tape, Roger. Did you think you recognized my voice?"

"The speaker obviously tried to disguise his voice. Altered its pitch, I think. Could have been a man with a high voice or a woman with a low voice. It didn't sound *exactly* like you—or anyone I know, for that matter—yet it could have been you, as far-out as that seems. In this case, and with this brilliant, imaginative killer, the far-out may be the norm. There was one more thing. You won't get sore now, will you, Ronnie?"

"On a lovely day like this?"

"There was a hint of mint to the voice. That's why I still haven't ruled out the possibility of its being a woman."

"Too much!" said Ronnie, still laughing.

"I hope so," Roger said.

Once Ronnie Fordyce had gone off to take his place in a corner of the studio, from which he would catch the show, Roger found Jinny sitting on a corridor settee, much like those found in hospitals outside the operating rooms. She, too, had a clipboard and sheaves of papers. He liked her peach-colored slack suit. It was businesslike, yet feminine—even a little sexy. Calhoun, whom he'd have to meet one of these days, was a lucky man.

"Whatcha got?" asked Roger, sitting beside her.

The standard cop question. Strange cops came up at the scene of a crime, said that to the cops already there. That was how they recognized each other.

"Well," said Jinny, peering at her papers through her bulletproof lenses, "there are a few patterns. Some could be coincidence, so it's hard to tell just yet. First, certain people here today were also present at the other shows that had murders. I've made a separate list. Here."

Roger scanned the paper Jinny handed him. "Three people in the audience at the other shows. Interesting. I'll be sure the spotters keep an eye on 'em. And this audio man who was at Toni Tennille's studio. Changed jobs, did he? Let's check him out *real* good. Then, of course, backstage, there's Ronnie Fordyce and the ubiquitous Danny Moss."

"All of whom have good reason to be here."

"Which the murderer also, no doubt, has. Unless he's swung it this time so he's not here. Or unless he's not even going to try this time." Roger sighed. "Too many suspects, sprawling all over the place. And me, jumping to conclusions that aren't there. I'm getting so I hear somebody's name, I think he might be the one. Willoughby—that homicide detective. He said on the phone he might come around today. Griswold of the FBI, for that matter. He's three thousand miles away, but the way he stays uptight about sin and such all the time, well, nutty as it sounds, even that would fit this crazy-quilt pattern we've got."

"How are you doing with the regional accent thing?"

"Same loosely strewn pile of garbage. Ronnie, I've just learned, is from Wilmington, Delaware. Danny Moss from Atlantic City. The mysterious Dr. Rand —who may be the killer's therapist—went to the University of Maryland. Could *he* be our pigeon? Come to think of it, and as long as I'm reaching hard, Mike Douglas used to originate his show in Philadelphia didn't he? Christ, am I suspecting Mike now? That's absurd. But maybe somebody on his show who came here from Philly."

"I know how you feel," said Jinny, nodding. "I keep thinking the killer must be right under our noses. Somewhere within a hundred yards, laughing at us. That would fit his profile. He wouldn't be able to resist. And he must *know* it's a trap today."

Roger sighed again. "I almost admire the son of a bitch."

"I know. Ambivalent, isn't it?"

"Let's catch the show," said Roger, rising.

In the greenroom, which was done in daffodil, Larry Lawson stared shamelessly at blond, toy-faced Loni Anderson. Loni was in pleasant conversation with Senator Byrd (D., W.Va.), whose hoedown fiddle was in a case on the floor beside him. Of the three waiting guests in the room, Byrd looked least like what he was. Larry Lawson looked like a funny man, and

Loni Anderson looked like a sex goddess, though she fortunately didn't act like one, but Senator Byrd, slender, smiling, faintly beak-nosed, at that moment looked more like a hoedown fiddler and square dance caller than a U.S. senator.

"But I love country music, Senator!" Loni was saying brightly. "Especially the genuine kind you play."

"Glad you do," said Senator Byrd. "And call me Bob."

"You can call *me* Larry," said Lawson, trying to get in.

She glanced at him. "Uh—yes. Larry." She turned her attention to the senator again. "How did you ever learn to play the fiddle, anyway?"

"Where I come from you just pick it up naturally. Like feeding the chicks or calling the hogs."

Loni squealed with delight.

Larry Lawson retreated into the folds of his frown. What a thing it would be to make it with Loni Anderson herself! But it was obvious she hadn't the slightest interest in him. Well, that would change. Maybe after today it would change. If he made it on the Mike Douglas show it would be the turning point. Steve Martin had gone the talk show route; David Brenner, Rodney Dangerfield, all those others. First you had to get up there and really swing, and then all these gorgeous chicks would look at you twice. That's how the game is played, he told himself, nodding with the thought, compressing the pleats in his chin.

His fantasy faded, and realizing he couldn't possibly get to first base with Loni, Larry sat back and tried to concentrate on the material Shel Walters had given him at the beach house and later at his pad, and which he hoped by now he had memorized. It would help if Douglas gave him the right questions, the way Johnny Carson always set up David Brenner. Another stuck-up bastard, that Walters. Friendly enough, but Larry could see that he, like Danny Moss, like everyone else he dealt with, had contempt for what they imagined to be his lack of intellect. When Walters, out at the beach house, had finally gotten down to work, he'd explained things to Larry with a real patronizing air, the schmuck.

"It all springs from character," he'd said, like a fourth-grade teacher telling how to add and subtract. "If they think the character you establish is funny, then almost anything you say—and it doesn't have to be a biggie, per se—will seem funny. Zero Mostel could get a laugh just by looking at the audience and saying 'Hello.' George Burns by just looking and not saying anything. Jack Benny with a long pause. So do a Stanislavski, Larry. Inside, *think* funny. *Be* funny."

"Never mind that crap," said Larry. "How about those gems you're gonna give me?"

Frankly, he didn't understand all of them. "Trust me," Walters had said. "Do 'em right and they'll laugh."

For this he had forked over five hundred bucks?

The door opened and a small, young, ginger-haired girl with a clipboard—everybody around here had clipboards—stuck her head in and said, "You're on next, Mr. Lawson. Want to follow me?"

He followed, watching her keister go vlip, vlip, back and forth, as she walked. Not bad. He'd have to take another look at her face before he went on. She might be a possibility for after the show. Especially if he wowed them out there. She'd take another look at *him*, then.

* * *

Roger Dale paced the corridor. Somewhere beyond it, in the cavernous building, the Douglas show was in full swing; he could hear the swells of laughter and the ripples of applause as though they were the sounds of a crashing sea. He would make his way to the set and take a look presently, to see how everything was coming along. Jinny and his men were already out there, stationed strategically, watching. Right now he wanted to pace.

Something was bugging him, and he didn't know what. There was an elusive piece to the puzzle, he felt, which when finally grasped would allow all the other pieces to fall into place. He wished his big chart on the easel were here so he could contemplate it.

A woman came out of the door to the ladies' room, just down the hall; he recognized her stocky figure, remembering it from the time he'd called upon Toni Tennille just before he'd appeared on *The Tonight Show*, quixotically hoping to have some news about Elmo's assassin for Johnny Carson. The woman was one of Toni's coordinators. Now that Toni's show had gone off the air she might have gotten a job here. Debbie somebody. Weinberg? Something like that. Ah, he had it—Weintraub.

When people come out of restrooms and into corridors, reflected Roger, they always look right and left cautiously, the way animals do when emerging from a cave. A primeval trait, perhaps. This was what Debbie did as she came out. Looked up and down. Cautiously. Even, he thought, with an odd expression of guilt. Another person who'd been present when Elmo got it, he thought. But what motivation could she have? If there *was* any motivation to this whole screwy slaughter festival.

For a moment Debbie tried to pretend she didn't

see Roger, obviously hoping that this would mean, somehow, that he didn't see *her*. In the next moment it was clear that she realized it wouldn't work. There was an obligatory smile on Debbie's oval face as Roger came toward her. "Hi, there," he said. "Miss Weintraub, isn't it?"

"Yes. Nice to see you again, Mr. Dale."

"I thought you were with Toni Tennille. Are you working here now?"

"Not yet. I might be, though. I had to see somebody about a job today, so I thought I'd stick around and catch the show." She dipped her head to one side in a look of curiosity. "The word is that you expect the talk show killer to make another try today."

"Could be," said Roger noncommittally. "You haven't seen any killers around, have you?"

"I don't know," said Debbie. "What does a killer look like?"

"I wish I knew," said Roger.

"I wouldn't put it past some of the wolves that roam around these studios."

"Wolves?"

She laughed nervously to cover what was evidently a slip. "A personal thing. Sorry. Just that I was done dirt by somebody once. I'll get over it. In fact, I *am* over it."

"Didn't mean to pry," said Roger. But he couldn't help looking at her a little suspiciously.

"Well, it was nice seeing you again, Mr. Dale," said Debbie, almost awkwardly.

"Same here. Good luck on the new job if you get it."

Debbie nodded, then swung away and clicked on her low, businesslike heels down the corridor.

＊　＊　＊

Larry Lawson, having opened with a few strong jokes from his standard routine, was rattling off the bits and pieces that Sheldon Walters had given him, and trying to *think* funny, as Walters had instructed him. He had emerged from backstage, been introduced and greeted by Douglas, handed a mike, and with a swiftness that almost caught him unprepared was facing the audience on his own, while Douglas returned to his seat.

"Anybody in the audience wearing jeans today?" Lawson said. A few people put their hands up. One young woman called out, "Yeah!"

"Good," Lawson said, "but you know, there's a phrase that always sounds strange to me. It's *designer jeans*. Or *designer-label jeans*. The reason I don't understand that is that *every* pair of jeans in the world had to be designed by a professional designer."

The audience laughed, sensing what he was getting at.

"I mean, do you think the boss at Levi's says 'Hey, Gus, we're gonna make up some new jeans next week. Step out in the alley, would you, and see if any of the parking boys want to come in and design a few jeans for us'?"

A hearty laugh swept the studio.

"No, they're *all* designed by designers, which I hope doesn't come as too much of a shock to you. But come to think of it I don't see how much designing there is to do anyway with a pair of jeans. I mean, I can understand designing a *building*, designing a new *car*, designing a *rocket* to go into outer space. But what the hell is the big deal about designing a pair of *jeans*? Everybody's got nothing down there but two legs and a backside, right?"

The camera cut to a shot of Mike Douglas, chuckling in approval.

"Actually, all they do—these designers like Gloria Vanderbilt, Calvin Klein, and the rest of them—all they do is make the jeans *too tight*! They just follow the design of the body. What's so clever about that? And—even more importantly—what is the *purpose* of it? To make all the seventeen-year-old girls in the country more sexually attractive? That is really stupid. They're too sexually attractive already!"

Even the members of the orchestra were laughing now.

"I mean, there are maniacs out on the street at this very minute raping *old* women, *fat* women—It just doesn't make any sense to have everybody running around in tight pants.

"Oh, by the way," Lawson said, switching to a new subject, "did you read where the Smithsonian Institute announced that Karl Malden had donated his hat to the National Collection of Artifacts? A spokesman for the Smithsonian later revealed that Malden had originally *got* the hat from the Institute."

Lawson then did a couple of jokes about being overweight. They, too, were well received.

"My doctor told me that fish was good diet food so I went to one of your local fish restaurants last night, Mike. Some of the things there had terrible names. Last night they served me something called scrod. That's very big back east, ya know. In the east you can order *Boston* scrod. It's not a bad fish. But I think it's got a stupid *name*. Scrod. It sounds like a medical term. Sir, I hate to tell you this, but you've got the worst case of scrod I've ever seen. I mean that really is a dumb word. It sounds like the past tense of screwed. Boy, I really got scrod on that deal."

A reaction shot of Mike showed him laughing but

apparently, by his raised eyebrows, a bit uneasy about the word *screwed*.

"But I shouldn't be complaining," Lawson continued. "I mean things are really getting more difficult all the time, in all the major cities. In New York and Los Angeles, for example, it's very tough to get anybody to make housecalls anymore.

"I don't mean just doctors. I mean *anybody*. I called a plumber the other day. He said, 'I don't make housecalls.'

"I said, 'What do you mean?'

"He said, 'You bring the broken toilet into the shop and I'll fix it for you.'"

A wave of delight came over Larry Lawson as he realized that he was hot. His timing was perfect, and the wan, put-upon expression on his rubbery face seemed to be perfectly augmenting whatever he said. To his surprise, he now got a laugh by just pausing, standing there, and looking trammeled by the world. He picked up his spiel again at exactly the right moment, dissolving from the laughter into his next line. He was trusting his intuition and it was coming through.

Maybe that five hundred he'd paid Walters had been worth it, after all. If he could keep it up, he had it made. Carson, Merv, John Davidson—the other talk show hosts would hear about him and want him on *their* shows. Network execs would be looking, maybe even thinking of a comedy series starring Larry Lawson. Walters had tossed off an idea: Larry would play a character working in a model agency, surrounded by the world's loveliest chicks and getting nowhere with them for twenty-six minutes every week. Except that once he was a star he'd be getting everywhere with them in real life.

His stomach felt funny. Nauseous. This, Larry told himself, was no time for a goddamned attack of indigestion. Might have been that smoked whitefish and cheesecake he'd had in the delicatessen before coming up to the studio. Against his diet, of course, but he'd felt entitled to a little celebration, getting a shot on the Mike Douglas show and all. Tomorrow he'd get back on his diet—strictly. With success in his grasp, at last, he'd have the confidence and inner strength to stick to it.

"So there I was, alone in the room with her, and she says, 'Let's have a party.' Imagine that! Everything perfect, all systems go, and all she wants is ice cream and cake!"

The laughter was nervous and low in decibels. He hadn't put that one over quite right, somehow. It was this growing feeling of malaise in his stomach that was throwing him off. Damn! It was turning into pain now. A dull pain at first, then a sudden sharp stab—

Larry Lawson stared at the audience in blank surprise.

The audience stared back at him.

A glowing pearl-gray curtain seemed to come down over his eyes, and the room began to spin in ever-diminishing concentric spirals.

Larry Lawson turned bluish, dropped his microphone, and fell forward; first on his knees, then flat on his face.

XII

Roger, in a chair in front of Sergeant Willoughby's desk, met the sergeant's look with a blank-wall stare of his own. The sergeant's look was familiar, that certain policeman's look which says, "Well, here, to all intents and purposes, is a fine, solid citizen, but I'll bet you—I'll just bet you—he's got a corpse buried in a flowerbed somewhere."

It was a warm day. The smog outside was a blanket of vitriol laid over the city. Because of the energy crisis the air conditioning in the big room where Willoughby and a number of other detectives had their desks had been adjusted to a temperature suitable for raising orchids. The sweat on Willoughby's balding head glistened in the overhead fluorescent lights. Willoughby looked at his wristwatch. "Let's make this as fast we can, Mr. Dale," he said, with an impersonal smile. "I'm meeting my wife for dinner. Promised her. Everything falls apart if I stand her up again."

"I know how it is," said Roger, nodding. "When I was a cop I used to hate to catch a squeal just before change of shift. We'd let a lot of things go so we wouldn't have to stay over. The best times to commit a violation are just before eight, four, and twelve."

"Yeah." Willoughby was noncommittal. He did not attempt to match Roger's good-natured grin. His steady look said that Roger would get no special treatment just because he'd once been a cop, and Willoughby would, in fact, thank him to cut out the small talk and get right down to business.

Roger noted the wooden prism on the desk with Willoughby's name on it. Donald B. Willoughby. "Don," he said, first-naming it in another attempt to establish rapport, "I had to see you. Nobody else'll give me any answers."

"Who's nobody else? What answers?"

"I've called. This person and that person. I want some basics, that's all. Like what did the autopsy on Larry Lawson show? But all I get is 'you'll have to talk to so-and-so about that.' When I get so-and-so I have to tell my story all over again."

"I'll level with you, Dale," said Willoughby. "There's been a memo—well, from the top. We're not giving out any information."

"Oh? How come?"

Willoughby took off his big, black-rimmed glasses and wiped them with a soft, yellow cloth. "Who knows how come? I can make a guess, though. These cute little homicides with hundreds of goddamned witnesses on talk shows make us look bad. So until we actually have a suspect nailed down the best thing is just to keep our mouths shut. The media is upset about it, but they'd be upset anyway, so what the hell."

"I understand," said Roger. "Only I'm not the media. Take a good look at me, Don. Not a speck of dust."

"Huh?"

"From all the brushoffs I've been getting lately. Mike Douglas won't talk to me when I call. He's sore as hell because I talked him into the show. Nobody else in TV will talk to me. Or in the humdrum everyday world, to which most of my clients belong. I've had four accounts canceled so far. I am being not touched by everybody with ten-foot poles. Now even the cops won't talk to me."

"Tell me your troubles," said Willoughby wearily. "Look, Dale, what do you expect? You say you've been a cop. How did you like it when some outsider came around, meddling in your business, getting in your way? And let's really be on the level now. You're a suspect like everybody else at this point. At least you're in the don't-leave-town category. All that publicity you're getting could be the motivation, even if it did backfire on you this time."

"You're reaching."

Willoughby shrugged. "In this business you've got to reach sometimes. You grab at everything and sooner or later something fits. I've heard about those fancy theories of yours, man, but that's how it's really done. Patiently. Without personal involvement. Christ, I don't even take it home with me at night. And you want to know something else? I close a lot of cases that way."

"I don't doubt it. Just the same, what harm can it do to give me those autopsy results? I won't hand them over to the papers or the TV people, if that's what's worrying you."

Willoughby frowned at his watch again. "If I burn you off a copy will you get the hell out of here?"

"And never darken your door again. Well, not for a while, anyway."

"Okay." Willoughby rose. "The jacket's down in R and I, and they've got a Xerox. Come on. After that, stay out of my hair, will you?"

Roger refrained from asking Willoughby what hair and quietly followed him across the office to the corridor door.

Norm Calhoun, in the booth beside Jinny and across from Roger and Meg, grinned and said, "I've always wanted to try it."

"Try what?" asked Meg, who hadn't been listening.

"That kind of dancing." He angled his head toward the small dance floor in Augie Kretschmeyer's joint. The combo was playing "Body and Soul." A few couples were shuffling on the waxed floor. "Where you hold on."

"Come on," said Meg, laughing. "I'll give you a lesson."

Earlier in the evening they'd been to a disco joint where they'd enjoyed the dancing and the light show but where the music had been too loud for talk. Since the rationale of the double date had been for the four of them to get better acquainted, Roger had suggested the Jam Session. When Calhoun and Meg were out on the floor, looking good—Calhoun had a tall grace about him—Roger grinned and said to Jinny, "You've got a good one. Hang on to him."

"My main man," said Jinny dreamily. "He really is."

"You'll probably need him pretty soon as a provider," said Roger, with the sense of a sigh.

Jinny nodded and blinked behind her thick glasses. "I know. The security's not so hot in the security business, is it?"

"These are not exactly boom times," admitted Roger.

"Oh, well, I guess I can always operate out of some hole in the wall like a character by Raymond Chandler."

"Make like Sergeant Willoughby, Rodge," said Jinny. "Don't carry it with you. Tread water. Something's bound to break."

"I keep telling myself that, along with all the other homilies, but prayerwheeling it doesn't seem to work, either. And I'm bugged by the feeling that the answer's sitting around in plain sight, with what we've already got."

"Then let's go over it again—what we've already got."

"That'll be the hundred and forty-sixth time."

"Let's do it anyway."

"What we've got," said Roger, staring into his Scotch on the rocks, "is the hardest thing in the world to spot —what I call a rational nut. Somebody knocking off people he's not really connected with for reasons that aren't listed in the how-to books on crime solving. Somebody clever enough to avoid patterns and leave hardly any traces. Though I suppose the Borgia bit— three out of four were poisonings—could be called a pattern. Clever this last time. In Larry Lawson's vitamin capsules. One of the damned vitamins he took came in capsules. Willoughby's lab people checked out the stuff they found in his pockets. Except, how did the murderer know Lawson would pop one of the right pills just before he went on? Or was that pure luck? A corollary to Durocher's principle: nice guys finish last; bad guys have all the luck. According to that, I'm getting nicer all the time."

"If it's any comfort," said Jinny, "Willoughby and the FBI guys and everybody else must be going around in circles, too. But maybe we've got a few leads they haven't got. Haven't bothered to follow, anyway. Like the pasteup notes and those typefaces, which I'll always cherish 'cause they led me to Calhoun. Did you tell Willoughby about the notes, by the way?"

"Mentioned it." Roger shrugged. "He didn't seem to want it, or else it just got lost in the shuffle. It's routine, from a police viewpoint, for things like this to appear whenever a case has a lot of publicity. And we still can't be a hundred percent certain the killer really sent those notes. There are a million freakolas out there who might do something like that just for the thrill of acting like a murderer without actually being one."

"But the notes were a good lead. You got my memo, didn't you?"

"What memo?"

"On the subscription lists. You've been in and out so much I wrote you a note."

Roger frowned. "Didn't see it. I suppose that's a sign we're getting big when we start losing memos. Like IBM or the government. Anyway, what about the subscription lists?"

"Well," said Jinny, "you remember Calhoun identified the typeface as one sold to a printer that does a bunch of magazines printed in L.A. It's big stuff—in the fourteen-point class—used for titles and so on. Which the person who wrote the notes would want so he'd be able to cut them out. Since everything is photo offset these days it comes in negatives, and these are—"

"Never mind the treatise on printing."

"So the magazines using that typeface," continued Jinny, "were limited, and I went over their subscription lists. Which you told me to do, remember? *Dune Buggies, The Surfer's Journal, Pacific Traveler, Western*

Gardens—I never knew there were so many. Or so many places they get sent to. Would you believe a monastery in Thailand getting *Van and Camper*? I'm still wondering what for."

"Wait a minute. *Pacific Traveler*?"

"Yes. That's one of them."

"I saw a copy in Dr. Rand's office. He was a subscriber. I remember the label."

"That's right," said Jinny, nodding. "And not only Rand. I found the names of a lot of people somehow connected with the murders in those different lists. Ronnie Fordyce, the TV guy. Sergeant Willoughby. Danny Moss. Your friend Mickey Samish. He gets *Western Gardens*—would you believe it? Anyway, it's all in the memo."

"This is supposed to help? It doesn't narrow the field; it widens it."

"Well, don't jump on me. Checking the lists was your idea."

"Sorry. I jumped on you because I have to jump on somebody, and you're handy."

"I know," said Jinny.

Calhoun and Meg came back from the floor, glowing, grinning. "Nice place," said Calhoun, sitting. "Glad you brought us here. Why don't we do this more often?"

"We will," said Roger. "For as long as we can afford it."

Calhoun picked up the half-finished drink he'd left on the table, saw that its ice cubes had melted, shrugged, and sipped it anyway. "What's to afford? Bargain rates here, compared to some joints."

"Roger's looking for the worst," said Jinny, putting her hand on Calhoun's arm, lightly, but with a symbolic air of determination to never let him go. "The collapse of the Dale Security Agency. The disappearance of the world as we know it."

"All because you can't find out who's knocking off these talk show guests?" Calhoun's eyebrows shifted upward almost immeasurably, giving him an attentive look. Roger had already decided that one thing he liked about Calhoun was that the guy really listened. Another thing he approved of was that Calhoun was ruggedly black-man handsome and not imitation white-man handsome.

"I guess that sounds improbable," said Roger. "But that's just about it. Your reputation in this town seems to rest on what you did yesterday, not the day before, and if what you did yesterday wasn't at least sensational you get deserted in droves."

"Yeah," said Calhoun, "I know what you mean. As though everything here operates like show business. Exciting when you're up, real hard when you're down. And always the front everybody's putting up all the time. The big smile that pretends nothing bugs you."

"Sounds like you're speaking from experience," Meg said.

Calhoun's smile was slow in spreading. "I *was* thinking of what I've got to live with. And Jinny. And all our brothers and sisters. Don't mean to spoil the party."

Jinny squeezed his arm. "Calhoun gets on this kick once in a while. It'll go away in a minute."

"It doesn't have to," said Meg. "Say anything you want in this company, Calhoun."

He shrugged. "Nothing that hasn't been said before. A million times. It doesn't change the basic situation. No matter how intelligently you think about it, the old paranoia is still there. If Whitey's giving you a hard time, that figures. If he's nice to you, he's patronizing. I know that's not true every time, but I can't help thinking it. One part of me trying to enjoy and get on with it, another part, deep down, thinking. I guess that's what you call a split personality."

"I dig your split personality," said Jinny. "It makes twice as much of you."

Everyone laughed. An ice breaker. Roger nodded, wheels inside his head still turning. "We're all like that, aren't we? Split inside, I mean. Ever read a book on abnormal psychology and realize with a shock you've got everything in it? I'm thinking about our unknown killer now. The only real difference between him and us is that something in his psyche shifts— some kind of control mechanism that, for him, doesn't work the way it should—and he acts on these rages instead of keeping them down. I guess that's all pretty obvious, but what I'm getting at is that this guy—or gal—will seem to be, on the outside, as well behaved and rational as the rest of us. What he's got is like high blood pressure. No real symptoms."

"Meaning it could be anybody?" asked Calhoun.

Roger nodded. "And meaning we might just as well forget motivation, which is probably completely irrational, and try to fit in the other connections. Time, place, opportunity, capability. The hell of it is that this still doesn't narrow it down much."

Calhoun turned and beckoned to the waitress. "When in doubt, have another drink," he said. "I wonder if that combo knows 'Minnie the Moocher.' My mama used to sing it. That was *her* hangup. She thought she was Cab Calloway."

The atmosphere that prevailed in the office of the Dale Security Agency the next morning was not exactly that of a mass hangover, for neither Roger nor Jinny had drunk much, but there was a certain ennui. They'd split up at two A.M. Roger and Meg headed for her place this time, and Calhoun and Jinny to wherever they had decided upon, which wasn't Roger's business but which interested him just the same. He saw Jinny yawning at her desk, and of course that made him want to yawn too, so he did.

Outside, the morning sun shone on L.A. The smog was moderate; it didn't burn the eyes today, just made them water slightly. A glowing flood of traffic poured into the freeways. There was always lots of space in any direction—room to cuss a cat in, as a cowboy Roger knew had once said about the West in general —so you never felt confined in L.A. as you did in most major cities. Altogether, it was a good life-style. The only trouble was you needed money to enjoy it, and making money so occupied your attention that you could seldom sit back, relax, and just take it all in. So what it boiled down to was that life in L.A., like life anywhere else, amounted to a continuing attempt to have your cake and eat it, too.

Jinny worked on the monthly statements, deleting the clients who had recently dropped their accounts, scowling as their tribe increased; Roger pored over the subscribers' names she had given him and then, for a while, paced again and studied the P.P. of the unknown murderer still on its easel.

The phone rang. Jinny answered. "For you." Roger nodded, halted his pacing, and went back to his desk.

"Mr. Dale? This is Dr. Rand."

"Oh. Hello there. What can I do for you?" Hearing Rand's measured voice, Roger could visualize his oddly melancholy, hound dog look.

"It's what I think I can do for *you*, Mr. Dale." It sounded as though Rand were dragging the words out of himself, reluctantly. "I've thought this thing over and I'm still not very pleased with the way you barged in here and tried to be tricky."

"I had to," said Roger. "Apologies, if that makes it any better."

"Well, that's beside the point. What I've arrived at is a matter of conscience, I suppose. Professional ethics on one hand; moral duty on the other. I'm supposed to keep my patients' affairs confidential, and I do, but, well, maybe this is a special case."

"Sounds like you know something."

"I do. And I've decided to pass it on to you for what it's worth. The ethics are still important, but meanwhile the inescapable fact is that people are getting murdered. Putting a stop to that—if I can help do it—supersedes other considerations, I'm afraid."

"I'm listening."

"Not over the phone, Mr. Dale. Much too delicate. There'll be some discussion involved, I think. Can you come see me?"

"I can be there in less than an hour."

"No, no—not right now. I've got my schedule. You've no idea of all the things I have to do. Let's see—I'm just checking my appointment book here—can't make it at five this evening—have to rush off and speak at a banquet. Tell you what. I can stop off at the office on the way home tonight. How's eleven o'clock?"

"I'll be there." Roger frowned. "Want to give me a hint?"

"I don't think that would be proper at this point."

"But you suspect somebody, is that it? One of your patients."

"I'm not sure *suspect* is the word. Let's say there are certain indications—possibly some that only a therapist might recognize. Frankly, I still have mixed feelings about this. I've discussed it with a few people whose opinions I value—without mentioning names—and they all think I ought to go ahead. But, well, I doubt if you'd understand."

Roger cocked his head. "Let me ask you something, Dr. Rand. How come you're calling me about this instead of the police?"

"That was another difficult decision. The connection is, well, tenuous, we might say. The police might simply dismiss it. You, on the other hand, are probably willing to look into something that may seem far-out at first glance. Besides, if it turns out to be wrong, the egg will be on your face, not mine. Do you follow my reasoning?"

"I follow. Eleven o'clock tonight?"

"I'll see you then. Though I warn you, between now and then I still might change my mind."

Jinny, who had been watching Roger, blinked at him through her armorplate glasses after he had hung up. "Rand has something for you?"

"Maybe," said Roger. "Worth finding out, anyway."

"I wonder if it's a coincidence," she said.

"If what's a coincidence?"

She reached for a folded newspaper on the far corner of her desk. "Ronnie Fordyce's column this morning. Did you see it?"

"No. Got up in a hurry. Not even coffee till I got here."

"I'll read you the bit I'm thinking of." Jinny ruffled through the newspaper until she found the column. "Gumshoe Roger Dale," she read, "still frustrated by all those murders committed at talk shows under his very nose, will shortly be in consultation with the fashionable Hollywood psychologist, Dr. Lionel Rand, in his continuing attempt to track down the mysterious killer of four victims to date." She paused. "Know what he does in the column? Prints the names in upper case. Ronnie's not a name dropper—he's a name waver."

"I know, I know," said Roger. "Get on with it."

"By his unorthodox methods, Dale still hopes to identify the culprit before the police do. I previously predicted that he would, but now that the murderer has managed to claim another victim—comedian Larry Lawson—in spite of Dale's elaborate security precautions, I must confess that the odds seem to be turning the other way. Perhaps the celebrated Mr. Dale has met his match. Perhaps his reputation, all along, has rested on mere puffery. Perhaps—"

"The little bastard," said Roger.

Jinny shrugged. "So he makes his living *his* way."

Roger nodded and pressed buttons on his phone. Doo-dah-dee-dah-dum. Maybe there was a musician somewhere who knew his friends' telephone numbers by the tunes they played. This one was for Ronnie Fordyce's number.

"Hello, dear boy," said Ronnie, all salad oil. "Thought you'd phone. Now, don't start hopping on me about this morning's column. I call things the way I see them, friends and enemies alike. You know that."

"Ronnie," said Roger, "I could take the wounded pride, but the lacerations in the checkbook are a little harder to bear. Where the hell did you get that item on Rand, anyway?"

"A good reporter never reveals his sources."

"Come on, Ronnie. This could be important. Maybe the killer himself placed the item. You know—part of the campaign to give me the continuing shaft. Though how he found out Rand wants to see me, I don't know. I just learned it myself."

"You're way off base, Rodge. Which seems to be

your customary position lately. All right. For you, since you are so helpless and naive, I'll make an exception. The item came directly from Rand's flak."

"Who's he?"

"Not he. An importunate female by the name of Sappho Durkin. I think she was born Mary or Helen or something, but in this town who listens to anyone named Mary or Helen? Saff is always trying to get me to plug her clients—and why not? It's her job—and this time she succeeded because she had a worthwhile item."

"Then Rand must have told her he was thinking of calling me. I wonder if *he* knows about the item in your column."

"I daresay he does by now. Everybody who is anybody in this town reads me for breakfast. Meanwhile, Roger, what else is new? Any progress? You may not believe this, but I'd be very happy to make a meal of my own delicious words and say you're doing fine. If that's the way it really is."

"I'll let you know if anything develops."

"Do that. Nice talking to you."

Roger hung up and stared at Jinny.

"Well?" she said. "Where are we now?"

"Same place. Nowhere."

"Nice place to visit," said Jinny. "But I wouldn't want to live there."

XIII

The day dragged on like a sprayed cockroach limping across the linoleum. Jinny, ever efficient and at least outwardly unruffled, took care of the routine business: the scheduling of the rent-a-cops, the reports of debtors located and adulterers spied upon, the daily logs of the residential patrol. Roger paced and stewed and scowled and fidgeted and studied the P.P. on the easel until it began to look like alphabet soup. At noon, instead of taking lunch, he hied himself downtown to the old loft building behind the Cherry Blossom grocery in Little Tokyo, where lay the *dojo* of Kazu Hashimoto.

After changing to his white *judogi* of heavy cotton, which he kept in a locker there, and affixing to it the red obi to which he was entitled, Roger squatted cross-legged on the mats in front of the serene, wrinkled old man.

"Why does bird peck at rock?" asked Kazu. "To wear down rock or sharpen beak?"

Quite properly, Roger did not answer. Instead, he said, "Let me ask you one, *Sensei*. Why does everything I touch lately turn to manure? All I wanted to do when I started solving a few cases publicly was generate a little business. I wasn't even trying to get rich—just comfortable. How could I know this murderer, whoever he is, would make a personal feud out of it? And worse, start winning."

"Great General Hideyoshi, four hundred years ago," said Kazu, "wake up one night, know somebody else in dark room. He reach for match. Somebody put match in his hand."

"They didn't have matches then," said Roger. "And, anyway, what's that got to do with it?"

"Make you think, okay?"

"I'm tired of thinking. I want to do something. Find this bastard. Maybe kick him in the balls, the way Mickey Samish said. *Sensei*, all other considerations aside, I've got to win!"

"What prize you get if you win?"

Roger shrugged. "More business. Financial security. Might even get married. Not sure about that. Meg and I are having such fun not being married we hate to risk spoiling it."

Kazu consulted the air for a moment. "You want to be black-belt *ninja* someday. Okay. You use *ninja* technique."

"Like what?"

"*Ninjitsu* more than study of martial arts. *Ninjitsu* state of mind, way of life. How to bring out *ki* inside you. *Ki* goddamn powerful. Make everything happen your way. Great *ninja* Ohta Jiroshi, early Tokugawa period, look at teacups, make move across table."

"Psychokinesis? To be honest with you, *Sensei*, I doubt that I can influence events just by concentrating on them."

"That why you still red-belt," said Kazu.

Roger sighed. "If you're so hot in that department maybe *you* can put the squitch on this murderer for me."

"Maybe I try. Just for you. Just one time."

Roger shifted position to relieve the prickles in his legs. "Here I am, a more or less rational, modern guy, well exposed to the traditions of causality and the scientific method, believing maybe you really can. I wouldn't dare tell anybody. They'd send me to somebody like Dr. Rand. And by the way, I may be getting a break there. He's ready to talk. Possibly about the killer, who is possibly his patient. If he doesn't change his mind. It sounds a little like he's playing cute—or he's confused himself—and *might* change his mind. That's what I'd like to do—send the squitch waves, or whatever they are, toward Dr. Rand so he *doesn't* change his mind. You see? I'm ready for anything— even magic."

"When you realize *ninjitsu* not magic you closer to black-belt. Way to concentrate is *not* to concentrate. Let *ki* work on problem. You understand?"

"Well . . . sort of."

"You still got long way to go. What is taste of empty bowl of rice?"

"Bitter."

"Ha!" said Kazu. He reached for his bamboo stick and Roger braced himself for the blow.

Usually, Roger felt refreshed and vaguely inspired after he had left Kazu Hashimoto's *dojo*, but this day he was still dimly troubled. He headed his wire-wheeled MG toward the office, but on the way changed his mind, pulled into a shopping plaza, found a phone booth, and spilled some coins on to the little counter.

He called the office first.

"All routine here," said Jinny. "If any day in this place ever is. What I mean is, there hasn't been a break in the case. That's what *you* meant, isn't it?"

"Yes. I'm not coming back in. I'll check again later."

"May I ask where you're going?"

"I can't tell you because I don't know. More and more, lately, I don't know where the hell I'm going."

"You feeling all right?"

"Physically. But I think I'm having an attack of emotional indigestion. Gotta go somewhere and think."

"Okay. But don't forget your appointment with Dr. Rand tonight."

"I'll be there," said Roger. "Whatever's left of me."

The next call was to Meg's new number, which he found in one of his pockets, scribbled on the torn flap of a matchbook.

"Arlington Associates, Public Affairs," said a strident female voice.

"Stop holding your nose, Meg," said Roger.

"Oh. Rodge." Her normal voice sounded relieved. "I've been wondering when you'd call. Just a few more accounts and I'll get a real secretary with a real nasal voice. When are you coming to see the new office? It used to be an adult bookstore. They went out of business. Not enough adults, I suppose."

"I'll get there next time I screw up enough courage to drive to the valley. Look, dinner tonight, if it's okay with you, but for the moment I want be with myself."

"All right. Where will dinner be? Your den of iniquity or mine?"

"Since we're both broke and getting broker," said Roger, "let's go someplace expensive. There's a new joint near Santa Monica called Belle Epoque. French cuisine and a sommelier with a built-in sneer. Meet you there at eight?"

"That late?"

"You come earlier, they think you're a parvenu."

"Can't have that. All right. I'll see you later."

"Meg, do you know a PR person named Sappho Durkin?"

"Oh. *Her*. Or should I say her-slash-him?"

"That explains the name, which Ronnie seems to think is adopted. He doesn't care for her. I wonder why?"

"Not many people do. What's up?"

"Apparently she has Rand's account. She placed the item that I'm consulting Rand on the murders, which I'm not, exactly, but the exaggeration is ordinary PR, I suppose. Outside of that, I detect an offkey note. Why, for example, would Rand tell *her* he'd be seeing me?"

"Haven't the faintest. I take it you *are* seeing Rand, then."

"Tonight, at eleven. His office. Only time he can squeeze in. Actually, it sounds as though he had a change of heart about revealing the secrets of his inner temple, and maybe has something for me. The killer may be one of his patients, and he may know or have guessed what the he-slash-her-or-whatever is up to. Maybe. This whole thing's been a bucket of maybes, all along."

"Well, let's talk about it tonight," said Meg. "About it and us and the world. Like always."

"See you at eight. 'Bye for now."

"God bless, et cetera," said Meg, and hung up.

Ms. Sappho Durkin was in. Her secretary—a mousy young woman—showed Roger into her private office after only a five-minute wait. She was on the sixth floor of a big, gray building in the nine-thousand block of Sunset Boulevard, where other publicity and talent agents had their lairs. On the walls of Sappho's office were horsy prints. Her desk was neat to the point of being sterile.

"So you're the Roger Dale I've heard so much about," said Sappho, training a steady eye upon him. She was tall, dark-haired, slender, and dressed in a simple slack suit. Her glossy black hair was coiffed in short, no-nonsense style, and her eyes were right out of some mist-enshrouded castle in Transylvania. Altogether, restrained good taste; Roger had to give her that. "Well," she said, "what can I do for you?"

"It's about this item you placed with Ronnie Fordyce."

"What about it?"

"Well, it wasn't strictly accurate. I wouldn't call the fact that I'm seeing Rand briefly a consultation."

"That's because you're not in public relations. The art consists of selecting the most favorable words. It's not easy. That's why not everybody is in public relations, reaping fabulous rewards." Her low voice and impeccable diction heightened the sardonic effect of her statement. Her eyes remained hard on Roger.

"What really interests me," he said, "is why Rand decided to discuss the matter with you?"

"And why not?" Her knife-edged eyebrows formed a fine curve.

"But the whole thing—the fact that Rand thinks one of his patients might have something to do with the murders—would ordinarily be top secret, it seems to me. Why, suddenly, would he want to go beyond merely revealing it and make it public?"

"He didn't," said Sappho. "We had lunch. We have

a common interest; the races, you see. Lionel and I own a thoroughbred together and we often meet to talk about it. He mentioned your little problem, and I picked up on it."

"You placed it without his permission?"

Sappho shrugged. "When it comes to PR, Lionel doesn't know what's good for him. Most clients don't. He called me and complained when he saw the item, but I calmed him down. Someday, I suppose, he'll grasp the first principle, which is that the only really bad publicity is no publicity at all."

"I'm not so sure," said Roger, partly warming up to the conversation, partly still fishing. "The kind I've been getting lately seems to do more harm than good."

Sappho showed a faint smile. "Obviously, you need professional help. I'd take you on, but I'm not so sure we'd be compatible."

"I couldn't afford you," said Roger. "And what do you mean, not compatible?"

"There should be a special rapport between any client and his PR advisor. A similarity of outlook. I'm not talking about differences in sexual preferences, but perhaps in basic moral standpoints."

"Oh? Are we different that way, too?"

"I think we are. I might find it difficult to empathize with your attitude toward women."

"I thought it was the one purely normal trait I had."

"When you overdo something it's not normal anymore. As I understand it, Mr. Dale—forgive me if I'm wrong, but I get this impression rather strongly—you have a reputation as something of a womanizer."

"I haven't spent much time in a monastery, but what are you getting at?"

Sappho opened a cardboard pack of thin little cigars and lit one. Gold Dunhill cigarette lighter. "It's not so much chasing after girls, which most men do, as the state of mind. This is one of the tenets of the women's liberation movement, in which I've been somewhat active. Don't read significance in that—a lot of straights are active in it, too. Women, you see, are *people*, not animals or toys or objects to be sought purely for sexual purposes."

"I'm on your side there. So?"

"You say you are, and perhaps you even think you are. But it's my guess you're on the other side at heart. You see, this attitude is something both you and all the victims of these talk show murders seem to have in common. Seeing women as sex objects, possessions, chattels. The one woman who was murdered—Mrs. Merriwether—saw *men* that way. I wonder if the murderer is trying to tell us something?"

Cocking his head to one side, Roger said, "You seem to have more than a passing interest in these murders."

"Indeed I do. I would like to have committed them myself, except that murder's so much trouble. And tacky."

"I take it you could have. Ways-and-means-wise, I mean. You have access to shows, the studios, that sort of thing."

"As much as anyone in the business." She smiled. "Was I on hand when any of these murders occurred? Is that what you're asking? I don't know whether you amuse or infuriate me, Mr. Dale. I'll decide in a minute. As a matter of fact, I was there when Larry Lawson died. Does that make me a suspect?"

"Everybody is," said Roger, sighing. "That's the trouble. Anyway, as long as we're getting along so fabulously, Miz Durkin, I don't suppose Dr. Rand, who apparently confides in you, mentioned just who he thought might be the murderer, did he?"

"He did not. If he did, I still wouldn't say. Frankly, I'd rather see the person go free. Look at who he's done away with. Finstetter, Pearson, Lawson. Murderer? He—or she—is a public benefactor. But now the minute's up, Mr. Dale."

"It's getting stuffy in here." He rose, went to the door, then, turning, did a Peter Falk. "I almost forgot. Where are you from, Miz Durkin?"

"What's that got to do with it? I'm from Bethlehem."

"Really? Were you born in a manger?"

"Bethlehem, Pennsylvania. Heart of the Dutch country. I still miss shoofly pie. Though I'm Irish, not Pennsylvania Dutch. They named me Bridget, but I changed it. Answer my question. What's where I'm from got to do with anything?"

"Just small talk," said Roger.

"I doubt it," said Sappho.

"You're right," said Roger, closing the door.

The decor was of cut crystal and brocaded walls. The sommelier, who kept his aquiline nose at a haughty level, wore a huge key on a chain around his neck. "A St. Emilion with *lamb*, sir?" he said to Roger. He seemed shocked. "May I suggest something heartier for proper contrast? A good Burgundy perhaps."

"St. Emilion," said Roger firmly. "And be sure it's not a '78. Disastrous year in Bordeaux."

The sommelier departed, holding himself in.

Meg laughed. "Feel better now?"

"Much." Roger grinned. "Actually, a Burgundy would have been fine."

"Roger, you're too much. How can there be all that much difference?"

"But there is, and you'd detect it, too, if you'd made a study of it."

"Do you have to study everything?"

He shrugged. "We all have our compulsions. Sorry if it bothers you."

"You're edgy, Roger," she said, smiling to make her little criticism less bitter. "I take it you didn't have a very productive day. How went the visit with the estimable Sappho Durkin?"

"Not too well. Unless it's that I found out she fits in with the rest of the suspects. She's from Sam Wechsler's accent area, by the way. And she has the kind of voice that was on the tape, though I can't say I actually recognized it. I wish I could get voice prints."

"Why don't you?"

"Round up everyone and have them go through the test? What they do is have an oscilloscope measure the vibrations, and with each voice this makes a characteristic pattern."

"Nitty-gritty, please."

"Well, getting it done's all too complicated and time-consuming and would tip my hand. Finally, suppose I did identify the sender of the tape. That still doesn't nail him for the crime. He's probably been smart enough to establish an alibi for at least one or more of the murders. There are more ways to establish alibis than there are to skin a cat. Anyway, I'm beginning to think the only thing I can do is catch this guy—or gal—red-handed."

"That sounds as though it might be even more complicated."

Roger nodded. "I can't set any more traps. The talk show hosts don't want anything to do with me. But

I have the feeling the murderer isn't finished yet. I think he'll pull another one. And more after that. Until he runs out of talk shows. Then maybe he'll turn to straight interviews, panel shows, God knows what."

"Why?"

Roger frowned. "Let me see why I think why. Maybe it goes like this. The guy, in his twisted way, operates on symbols. The whole series of killings is, to him, a sort of art form. It calls for certain dramatic elements. Protagonist, antagonist, for one, and he's made me his antagonist. He may also need a climax, a moment of truth. It's got to boil down to a point where it's either him or me, with everything—perhaps even our lives—at stake."

"Sounds to me like you're overanalyzing again, if I may say so. I guess I may; I just did. Are you sure you're not projecting what would be *your* approach into this opponent of yours?"

"Could be," sighed Roger. "I'm no longer sure of anything." A waiter brought salad and ingredients for the dressing. Roger began to mix. "Heavy on the garlic?"

Meg smiled. "Only if you do."

"I'll go heavy," said Roger, "and we'll cancel each other out. That is, if we get around to our favorite pastime tonight. There's my appointment with Rand at eleven, and I'm not sure what I'll be doing after that. Possibly an all-night session at the office if things work out right."

"I'm becoming a police widow already," said Meg. "I wish I had enough business of my own to interfere with pleasure."

"Speaking of that," Roger said, "Sappho said I ought to have a PR counsel so all these things would stop backfiring on me. Would you be interested, on a kind of spec basis?"

"What do you mean by 'spec'?"

"That I can't pay you. At least not right now."

"I'll think about it."

"Somehow I have this feeling Rand isn't going to come through tonight. Can't explain it, but I get these precognitive stirrings once in a while. I've a theory about it. Your subconscious is a superb computer, which puts together all the probabilities without your realizing it and then comes up with the results, but not all the calculations that went into them. You're familiar with the Puthoff and Targ studies on that, I suppose."

"You know damn well I'm not. This is Earth calling, Roger. Come back."

"Okay, sorry. Rambling helps me think, that's all. I'm thinking that if Rand *doesn't* give me a good lead tonight I want to get on another talk show. Somehow."

"Sounds like an uphill job."

"It is. And this uphill job, I think, will go better with Jill working on it as well as Jack."

"Meaning me?"

"You Jill. Me Jack. Just like Jane and Tarzan. What I mean is, none of the talk show guys will listen to me now, as far as getting another booking is concerned. It seems to call for an intermediary. Like a marriage broker, or something. Somebody who can sing praises without seeming to be blowing his own horn."

"Your metaphors are getting mixed."

"So they are," said Roger. "But what's a meta for if you can't mix it once in a while? Will you stop distracting me? Look, you did pretty well persuading Larry Lawson to go on the Mike Douglas show."

She frowned abruptly. "I feel *awful* about that."

"Don't. Not your fault, what happened. But I'm thinking now you might use those persuasive powers of yours—you have a kind of innocent sincerity hardly anybody can resist, you know—to get me on another talk show. Your first job as my new public relations counselor."

Meg's frown was still with her. "I have the feeling I'm getting dragged into something."

"All right, there's a risk. But if I could set another trap—and it worked this time—your part in the caper wouldn't hurt your own career at all."

"Look, Rodge. Why don't you get your friend Steve Allen to intercede for you? He knows all those people. They'd listen to him, I'm sure."

Roger thought that over for a moment, then nodded. "Well, we're not exactly inseparable companions, but he might be sympathetic. Worth a try, I suppose. I'll work on it."

The sommelier returned. "The only thing we have in a St. Emilion, sir, is a '78," he said, with smug satisfaction.

"All right. Make it a Burgundy."

When the man had left, Roger said, "He wins. See how it goes? Nothing works. Must be the stars. Or sunspots. It's the kind of night I shoulda stood in bed. Which is not a bad idea, come to think of it. For both of us."

The rest of the dinner was drawn-out and delightful, as such an occasion should be, with Roger going off into a lecture only once—with his explanation of how the best Burgundy came only from the Côte de Nuits and not just any old part of the district. The wine, Meg thought, was very good, though, to her taste, no better than some good Californias she'd tasted. The one advantage to the expensive meal here, she decided, was that they didn't hurry you to get out and make room for other customers. And the waiter came only once to ask, 'ow was everysing? Everysing, it was fine, Roger assured him.

Tennish, they wandered out again into the comfortably cooled night. Their plan was that Meg would drive home, Roger would go to his appointment with Rand and return to her place later, when, as, and if; he'd call when he could to let her know how everything had worked out.

Roger knew there was something peculiar about his wire-wheeled MG the moment he glimpsed it, at the far end of the parking lot. In the next moment he saw that what was wrong with it was that it was no longer wire-wheeled. It sat there on its axles, helpless, like a wounded bird.

When he had finished staring and swearing, Meg said, "Oh, Roger! It's terrible! Why do they do things like that?"

"Some say out of economic necessity," said Roger, bitter, glowering. "God damn it all! What do I do now? Call the cops, I suppose." He looked at his watch. "And Rand's expecting me soon."

"I'll drive you to Rand's office. You can notify the police and talk to them later. You could phone Rand, I suppose, but I gather you don't want to rock that particular boat."

Roger nodded and sighed. "For a mere terrestrial of average intelligence you can be very right sometimes." He was a little sorry he'd recaptured his sense of humor. It hurt when he laughed.

The street in front of the downtown building where Rand had his office was deserted at this time of night and Meg pulled up in front of the building in her old

Chevvy, bravely saying something about at least having a parking place this time. She said she'd wait here while Roger went up, saw Rand, and found out how long he was going to be. Roger said that was a good idea, pecked her cheek, left the car, and went into the building.

Meg sat there and with nothing much else to do switched on the car radio. She pushed a few buttons, hearing songs about Jesus and cowboys until she found some middle-of-the-road FM disco she could listen to without really listening.

A man came out of the building shortly after Roger entered it. She didn't notice him, especially; someone came out, and she was dimly aware of this, but that was all. She did not look at him with enough attention to see whether he was young or old, slim or fat, or whatever. A man. Or maybe a woman in slacks. Vaguely. Nothing more. Plus an evanescent and largely ignored impression that the person paused for a moment to glance at her where she sat.

The person went down the street and disappeared. She forgot about it. The music got boring. She turned the key off and stepped out of the car to stretch her legs.

In the stillness of the night, and in the darkness of the deserted street, and from somewhere down near the corner of the office building, a shot rang out, and Meg, knowing somehow that it was directed toward her, slammed herself facedown on the sidewalk.

Roger stepped off the elevator at the eleventh floor. The lights were on in the halls, but the place was still tomblike. He looked at his watch. Eleven fourteen. Calling the cops and explaining everything about his stripped MG had taken more time than he'd anticipated and he was late. His luck was still running lousy.

He went down the corridor, footsteps echoing with a hollow sound on the recently swabbed tile that smelled of antiseptic. He turned a corner and saw Rand's office at the end of a shorter corridor. No light showed through the pebbled glass of the door, which meant either that Rand had not arrived yet or that he'd been there and gone. More likely the latter, dammit.

Roger came to the lifeless door and stared at the neatly lettered sign beside it: Lionel Rand, Ph.D. He frowned and looked at his watch again. Eleven seventeen now. Okay. Assuming Rand was late, how late would he be? A half hour at the most? Roger decided he'd wait till eleven thirty—well, make it eleven forty for good measure.

He tried the door. Locked. He'd supposed it would be. He swung away from it, stepped off twenty-three paces down the short leg of the corridor, counted them, pirouetted, and paced back again. He repeated this several times. He paused, sighed, and said, "This is for the birds." The empty hall echo-chambered his words.

He stared at the door thoughtfully for a moment. An ordinary Corbin lock—opening it would be no big problem. Just illegal, unethical, and bad manners, that was all. But Rand's files would be inside, and they might well contain information he devoutly wished to have—perhaps even the identity of the murderer who, perhaps, had given himself away during a soul-baring session with Rand.

The rationalization process began. Eighteen minutes earlier, and Roger would have had that information. Probably. So, since Rand meant him to have it, anyway, what was wrong with letting himself in, finding it, and taking it?

Roger knew very well what was wrong with it. He simply pretended he didn't and took his key case from his pocket. It contained several masters. Frankly, when he'd become a P.I. he didn't ever think he'd have to use any of them, but some romantic whim had prompted him to procure them so he could play his role to the hilt. He found the Corbin master, put it into the lock, and wiggled it delicately until the tumblers fell.

He opened the door, entered, snapped on the light in the reception room. It was the same place in which he'd waited before: same glassed-in cubicle for the receptionist, same sofa and chairs, same low table with copies of *Pacific Traveler* and other magazines upon it. He crossed to the door of Rand's private office, pushed it open, flipped on the wall switch. The overhead fluorescents blinked, then shone.

Roger halted and stared, frozen, at Rand's desk across the room. Rand was in a chair behind it. He was in a slumped position, his head thrown back, hanging. His eyes were wide open and very still. His dewlaps hung, flaccid. He wore a dinner jacket, and the white front of his lacy shirt was soaked with blood.

Rushing to Rand's side, Roger quickly felt his carotid artery for a pulse. Dead, all right. He hastily scanned the rest of the room. Nothing unusual, no furniture overturned, nothing out of place as far as he could determine. Whoever had done it had done it quickly and efficiently, probably walking right in, finding Rand in his chair, and pumping shots into him without further ado. They'd hardly be heard in the street below and certainly not anywhere else in most of the office building.

There was a sheaf of typed papers on the desk in front of Rand. Roger glanced at them and saw the title: *Aspects of Suppressed Rage.* The banquet speech he'd made that evening, probably. He looked again at the corpse.

Taking another glance around the room, Roger noticed that a drawer in one of the corner file cabinets was partly pulled out. He went to the cabinet, looked at the folders in the drawer, and saw that they were apparently case histories of patients, alphabetically arranged.

This was a break!

There were two possibilities now. The information Rand had meant to give him would be in those files, or if the murderer had taken it, the fact that it was missing would reveal the murderer's identity. Careful to touch only the edges of the tabs, so that he'd leave no fingerprints, Roger examined the typed names on the files. He was looking for those he knew had been Rand's patients—Elmo Finstetter, Sonny Pearson, Danny Moss, Ronnie Fordyce among them. Moments later, when he found none of these names—and realized that there were several empty spaces in the files —he stepped back, frowned, and tried to imagine what must have happened.

Killer hears Rand is about to pass damning evidence on to Roger. Tipped off by Ronnie's column, perhaps. Learns that meeting is in Rand's office at eleven. How? Calls office, maybe, on a ruse and somehow finds out. Figure that out later. Comes to Rand's office tonight, sees Rand arrive, perhaps early, then walks in, pulls gun, and lets Rand have it. Goes to files and— clever as he is—pulls not only his own folder but those of *all* the persons who might have had any connections with the talk shows.

That had to be it.

Roger spent another ten minutes carefully searching

the office, hoping to find *something* helpful some-where, but as he'd already surmised, there was nothing. He sighed deeply and stepped toward the phone so that he could call the police.

A voice behind him said, "Freeze."

XIV

After she had hit the concrete, skinning her elbows and the tip of her chin slightly, Meg Arlington, still numb with all the adrenaline that had suddenly surged through her, wondered if there'd be another shot and, in terror, braced herself for it. A kind of prayer darted across the edge of her mind, like a swift bird in flight. God, please, don't let this happen. Had she done the right thing, to throw herself facedown like this? Maybe she should have tried to duck behind the car. How could she know? How could anyone know? Oh, God! Really!

There was a kind of dribbling of light along the walls of the building. The sound of a car. Its growling as it passed. And then—all this sensed as much as seen—another car coming the other way, its headlights also making momentary splashes of light in the vicinity.

Suddenly all was quiet, and, somehow, quieter than it had been before. No more shots; no sound of anyone or anything stirring. Cool night breeze still on her cheek.

She dared to move her head enough to look in the direction from which the shot had come. Nothing there. Just the empty corner of the building. Beyond it, the smaller buildings along the street. Dim glow of the nearest streetlight, which wasn't nearly as near as she would have liked. And no motion anywhere. Just stark light and shadow.

With her entire body feeling detached from the rest of her, so that she seemed to be an observer, off to the side, she got up the courage to move, press herself up from the sidewalk, and stagger to her feet. Rather than rush back to her car—and she had no idea why she chose the course she did—she plunged forward and stumbled into the office building where Roger had disappeared some minutes ago.

The directory board, with its white letters stuck into the black slots. P-Q-R—let's see—Rabelaisian Publications (what could that be?), Radio Supply Company, Rand—Lionel Rand, Ph.D. Eleventh floor.

The ability to think a little seeped back into her mind. Person shot at her (why?), got scared by headlights of passing cars, changed mind and ran off. Something like that. Whatever it was, thank God for it. Maybe prayer worked, after all—if that frightened thought of hers had been a prayer.

Too terrified to wait for the elevator, she ran to the door marked Stairs, opened it, saw them going upward, and began to climb. She'd run up them as long as she could, and then crawl the rest of the way, if necessary.

In Dr. Rand's office, Roger turned, startled, scared. A uniformed man was pointing a revolver at him, and from the pale, frozen look on the other's face it was a good bet he was scared, too. The man was a security guard; Roger recognized the gaudy khaki and lavender uniform of one of his competitors, the Great Western Security Service. He was an older person with a chinless face that resembled a turtle's, and he was holding his gun in two hands, in approved police fashion.

"For God's sake, put that thing down!" said Roger.

"Just stand there, right where you are," said the guard. His voice had lost all its lubrication.

"Okay, okay," said Roger, carefully keeping himself quite still. "You were making the rounds and saw the light on. Let's take it nice and easy, now. I'm Roger Dale—Dale Security Agency. I had an appointment with Dr. Rand and found him here this way. I was just about to call the police."

"*I'll* call the police," said the guard. "You just step to one side there. Real careful."

"Whatever you say. Relax, will you?"

"Hands on your head, fella. No funny moves."

Roger stood there, feeling ridiculous, as the guard used the phone. He read the man's nameplate above his breast pocket and just below his badge. E. J. Snodgrass. "Really, Mr. Snodgrass. Really," he said, sighing.

"No moves," said Snodgrass.

Roger listened as Snodgrass got a desk sergeant or somebody and, in not too articulate a fashion, reported the situation. He hung up, his gun still pointed at Roger. "Put it down, for Christ's sake," said Roger. "Those things go off sometimes."

"You're telling me?" said Snodgrass. "On the wall, fella. Hands high, legs spread."

"I'm not armed," said Roger.

"We'll see," said Snodgrass. As he patted Roger down he said, "Don't try anything funny. I'm a retired cop. I know what I'm doing."

"Look," said Roger, "it's all a mistake."

"Where have I heard that before?" said Snodgrass.

Finding no weapon, he stepped back, directed Roger into Rand's visitor's chair, and kept his eye on him warily while he gave the body a brief and cursory examination.

"As a doornail," said Roger, watching him.

"Just shut up, huh?" said Snodgrass.

Roger shrugged. "We've got a little wait, apparently. Does it have to be antisocial?"

"Wiseguy, huh?" said Snodgrass, glaring at him.

"All right, all right," said Roger. "Golden silence, if you'd rather."

Snodgrass stood there, gun still pointed, glaring. Roger tried to meet his look with a disarming smile, which, of course, he didn't really think would disarm him.

There was suddenly the sound of a scuffling step in the open doorway behind Snodgrass, and he whirled, swinging his gun that way.

Meg—looking white and shaken, breathing hard—stood there and stared at everything. "Oh, my God!" she said.

"No moves!" said Snodgrass.

"Moves?" said Meg. "How could I, possibly?"

"Meg! Baby! What happened to you?" said Roger, staring at her.

"Everything!" said Meg. "And it still is!"

"What the hell's up with you two, anyway?" said Snodgrass.

"Let's all calm down and find out," Roger said.

In the police headquarters building, where he found himself this time, Roger supposed that Sergeant Donald B. Willoughby, of the Homicide Division, would be along sooner or later, and at last he came.

By that time Roger had talked, he swore, to every cop in Los Angeles, spending the intervals between talks in the holding tank, which smelled of antiseptic and of persons unwashed. For some reason they had said Meg could go. She said she wanted to stay. They told her to get the hell out, and she did—with a last, apologetic look at Roger.

The clock on the wall said two A.M. Roger was again in the plain interview room with its steel table and several chairs. Once in a while an outsider would slip and call it the interrogation room. Interview room, please. They were always quick to make the correction.

"Well, well," said Willoughby, blinking through his heavy hornrimmed glasses and running his hand over his head just as though he'd had hair there to smooth down. "What do you know." He'd obviously been called out of bed, but apparently had taken the time to dress himself neatly.

"Now, dammit all, Don," said Roger, "*you* must know I didn't walk in there and blast Rand."

"Maybe you didn't," said Willoughby. "But there seem to be a couple of loose ends."

"For instance?"

"Like, how you got in. The guard checked the office on a routine round at ten thirty, approx. Rand was there, but the door was locked. Rand came to the door, spoke to him, said he was expecting somebody at eleven. You say you got there after eleven and walked right in. But as the guard remembers, Rand closed the door again—so it was probably locked. And you, to get in, would have had to use one of those master keys that are in your effects in the property room. How's that for a loose end?"

"Let me give you a looser one. Why the hell should I murder Rand?"

"Maybe you can tell *me*."

"Okay, Don," said Roger. "You're just doing your job and all that. Let me try to help you out by telling you exactly what happened. Rand told me one of his patients might be connected with the talk show murders. I was meeting him there to find out who. Evidently whoever it was got there first. Meanwhile, I checked Rand's files. Several folders missing—people I happen to know were Rand's patients. The killer was smart enough not to identify himself by pulling only his own. But all we have to do now is find out what names are missing and then check 'em out till we get the right one. This is what you ought to be doing instead of giving me the polite third degree."

"I'm way ahead of you, Dale," said Willoughby. "Miss Lundquist, Rand's receptionist, is already here, answering questions. She's putting together a list of who's missing. She gave us another interesting little goody."

"Which was?"

"Strange voice called her on the phone earlier in the day. Said it was checking on *your* behalf. Wanted to know if you had an appointment with Dr. Rand and, if so, when. Said you'd forgotten, which doesn't seem likely to me, and didn't to Miss Lundquist; that's why she remembers it. She told the voice you were seeing Rand at eleven. Did you have one of your little brownies call Rand's office?"

"I did not. But there you are. That's how the killer found out when he could get to Rand. Which, apparently, he had to, because Rand was about to blow the whistle on him. It helps explain what happened to Meg, too. He must have been coming out shortly after I went in, and must have imagined Meg, in the car, saw him, and could later identify him. She said *some-*

body came out, but actually she didn't pay any attention to who it was. He'd naturally take a few moments to screw up his courage and make a decision, and then, when Meg stepped out of the car, he saw his opportunity and took a shot at her. Crazy thing to do, but when somebody's just committed one murder and is trying to get away, his mind can't be working on all cylinders."

"Maybe," said Willoughby, shrugging. "Sounds pretty good. Alibis usually do."

"God damn it, Don, use your head! Would I call Miss Lundquist if I meant to go there and do a number on Rand? And what about the person who called? The voice. Male or female?"

"Funny thing. She says it could have been either. Or like somebody trying to disguise his voice."

"Which I would have no reason to do. So there you are. You don't need me any longer."

"Oh, I wouldn't say that."

"Why in hell wouldn't you?"

"Because I never jump to conclusions, one way or the other. Yes, the killer might be who you say. The gun this time, instead of poison, bothers me, but I suppose it could have been an emergency, from his standpoint, and guns are fast and sure. On the other hand, maybe not. I've seen too many cases where the obvious answers turned out to be wrong."

"Well, what's the bottom line? How much longer do I have to stay in this joint?"

"We're allowed twenty-four hours," said Willoughby pleasantly. "Have you called your lawyer yet?"

"Didn't think I'd have to, but now I guess I will. He won't mind the late call, by the way. He'll be very interested in the possibility of suing the ass off the city of Los Angeles for false arrest."

"That's an *alte Geschichte*—an old story. I can say it in Spanish, too. A cop picks up all kinds of things from his ethnic colleagues here and there. So while you're thinking of suing, you might as well include the United States of America. The FBI's sending a couple of guys over to talk to you. We've got to hold you at least till they get here."

"The F-B-goddamn-I?" said Roger. "How do *they* get into it?"

"They were never out of it. Standing request. Let 'em know anything that happened, right away. You really must have rubbed Griswold the wrong way."

Roger nodded. "He rubs easy. I don't think he's president of *your* fan club, either."

"But with me it's not so much of a problem. I'm one of the good guys."

"I'm one of the bad?"

"I'll let you know as soon as I decide," said Willoughby.

It was mainly lack of sleep that made the next five hours go by in a thick and oily haze; Roger endured it and kept snatching at his wits to bring them back when they tried to wander. The FBI men who interviewed him turned out to be the two he'd met in the hotel bar with Griswold. He caught their names better this time. Merriam and Sheen. Sounded like a vaudeville team. Merriam, the more animated of the two, delivered the punch lines. Sheen, who still resembled Mickey Samish's pet gorilla, Varsity, was the straight man.

"Now, Mr. Dale," said Merriam, "you say you let yourself in with a master key?"

"That's what I said."

"That is not what you first told the officers when they brought you here."

"They didn't ask."

Merriam glanced at Sheen as though Roger had just made the one fatal mistake that all criminals make sooner or later. Sheen nodded knowingly and solemnly.

"You two finished now?" asked Roger.

"Let's go over all of it just one more time," said Merriam, smiling, and settling back a little more deeply in his chair.

Roger's lawyer arrived at breakfast time. He hadn't been home when Roger called—shacking up with some chick, no doubt. His recorder had given him Roger's message. His name was Kevin McTeague and the freckles on his round face were as numerous as the shamrocks in a fine patch of Irish turf. McTeague was a bachelor, and like Roger, young and hungry. That was why his fees were reasonable. That was why Roger retained him.

"Look," said McTeague, sitting on the edge of the cot in the cell, "I'll have you out of here in a couple of minutes. That's the good news. But I also took a quick look at what they've got, Rodge, and I have to say I don't like it."

"That makes two of us." Roger shrugged wryly. "But what's a little old charge of first-degree murder?"

"If it were only that, I wouldn't worry. They couldn't make it stick. But a P.C. 459 they could."

"Breaking and entering?"

"You've got it. You see, you let yourself into Rand's office. You went through his files. That, my friend, in the myopic eyes of the law, is a big fat B and E."

"They wouldn't throw that one at me, would they?"

"Depends on how they feel. I trust you haven't made any mortal enemies around here."

"I don't know," said Roger helplessly. "Only that you can do it, apparently, without even trying."

McTeague nodded. "Just like they used to tell us in law school. There ain't no justice."

Jinny studied Roger for a while before she said, "Massa, you look beat."

"I am," said Roger.

He sat at his desk. He had showered and changed his clothes, but he still looked beat. He knew his eyes were red because they felt red. By now he'd told Jinny of the previous night's events, adding how he'd beelined himself to Meg's place after being sprung from the pokey to warn her to keep her door locked and a weather eye open at all times—the killer, who'd made one attempt on her life, might make another. He'd even offered to move in with her, but she'd firmly said no to that, quipping that such an arrangement, like getting married, would spoil the delightfully sinful relationship they now enjoyed. He admired her spunkiness, but as he left, told her to be careful.

For ten minutes he had been staring silently at the P.P. on its easel. If he'd had the energy he would have paced up and down before it.

Jinny cocked her head to one side. "Might be easier just to drop the whole thing, like they want you to."

"*What?*" Roger glared at her.

"Just a suggestion," said Jinny. She pretended to get busy again with the file cards she'd been rearranging. "The least you could do is go home and get some sleep. You'll feel better."

"Yeah, and while I'm sleeping Sergeant Willoughby just might put the arm on the killer. And where were you, Roger Dale, when the arrest was made? In bed, dreaming Freudian dreams, only about the real thing instead of symbols, that's where I was."

"Still think you can beat Willoughby to it?"

"With luck, maybe. Except that I'm one of the good guys, in spite of what Willoughby thinks, and good guys rarely have good luck. Only bad guys. It's an old dramatic principle."

Jinny shrugged and continued to shuffle the file cards. As she did so, she began to sing softly to herself, moving her head up and down slightly with the disco beat. She was singing the song that had plummeted Elmo Finstetter to fame—"Eat Your Heart Out, Baby." Roger winced, as he always did when Jinny sang. Fine soul sister, she was: couldn't sing worth a damn.

Usually, he took care not to comment on her singing. This morning, in the mood he was in, he couldn't contain himself. "Jinny," he said, "your tape's offspeed."

She looked up and said, "What?"

"Offspeed. Got a wow in it. A whole bunch of wows."

She looked hurt. "You mean the way I'm singing?"

"I mean the way you're—"

He stopped short.

He stared at the air.

"Are you all right?" asked Jinny.

"That's it!" he said.

"What's what?"

He struck the desk a mighty blow with the heel of his hand. "The tape the killer sent! Where is the damned thing?"

"Right here." Jinny opened the drawer.

"I *knew* it would come in handy when I brought the stereo here. The one in the car got ripped off along with the wire wheels, by the way. Speaking of cars, will you check today to see when mine will be finished? And did you order that rental job for me?"

"It's outside," said Jinny. "Any other menial chores you want done?"

"Knock it off. The stereo. It's got all those buttons and things. As long as it's been in my apartment, I never could figure 'em all out. Does it play variable speeds?"

"Damned if I know," said Jinny. She rose and went to the machine, which had been placed on a low table against the wall. She studied it for a moment. "Here's something that looks like a speed control. Why do these things have all these gadgets? For the real stereo nuts, I suppose."

"The guy I got it from is one of those. Tex de Armond. I think it's worth more than what he owed me. Anyway, put the tape on, will you, Jinny?" He listened to his mental playback for a moment and added, "Please."

She nodded and slipped the cassette into the slot. "I think I see what you're getting at. The person who made this tape perhaps disguised his or her voice by recording it off speed, slowing or speeding up the original delivery to compensate. Is that it?"

"Smart girl," said Roger. "Maybe we ought to get a bottle of champagne ready. This may just be the first big break in the case."

Jinny ran the tape and the Exterminator's familiar voice sounded in the room.

"Greetings, Roger Dale. This is the Exterminator. It's become quite a game between us, hasn't it?"

Jinny touched the control. The voice became a little thinner, but the speed didn't change. She tried several other controls. Still no speed change.

"Sam Wechsler," said Roger, rising quickly. "He's got all sorts of equipment. He can run it fast or slow or whatever."

"You're going all the way out there? Now?"

"I'd make it to Timbuctu, if I had to. Call Sam, will you? Tell him I'm on the way."

In the outer office he rushed past Charleen without even pausing to admire her tight-fitting knit dress. Feeling a little ignored, she stared at the blur that went by, wondering what in hell the boss was up to now.

Roger never made it to the curb. The moment he burst out of the office he found himself belly to belly with J. Duffy Griswold of the FBI.

Griswold glared at him from a stolid parade rest. "I reckon I just about found you in," he said.

"Not now," said Roger. "Whatever it is, Griswold, not now."

"Now," said Griswold. "Want to take a ride?"

"Not with you. Will you get out of the way, or do I have to call a cop?"

"Always the wisecracks," said Griswold. "You wouldn't last two minutes in the bureau. Dale, I happened to get here yesterday on other matters, and I learned this morning what happened last night. In the light of that, I've got some important things to say to you, and I mean to say 'em now. I got a bureau car here that's just dandy for a confidential talk. You comin' along or do I have to formally arrest you on suspicion of something or other?"

"Barratry on the high seas, I'll bet," said Roger. "Sorry, Griswold. I've got things to do."

"Let 'em wait."

Roger stared at the FBI man evenly. "I'm tempted," he said.

"To take a swing at me? Betcha you couldn't. I almost wish you'd try."

After a pulsebeat pause Roger said, "Okay. Your car. But how about driving me somewhere? The university. It's over in—"

"Just show me the way," said Griswold. "See? I'm not as hard to get along with as you think."

They said little until Griswold's plain blue Ford sedan was on the freeway. Griswold, driving, hunched over the wheel as though he were hoarding a bone. He glanced at Roger several times, obviously trying to figure out how to begin saying whatever it was he had to say.

"I'm waiting," said Roger.

"Yeah. Well, yeah." Griswold shifted in his seat. "The first thing I want you to know is that there's nothing personal in this."

"Fine. You've established your copout. Go ahead."

Griswold's words came through a deep scowl. "If I wanted to I could really scorch your ass, you know. Have them press charges, starting with a B and E and throwing in a couple of little ones, like obstructing justice. I figured you'd frig it up royally sooner or later."

"But you haven't pressed charges. Am I supposed to lick your hand gratefully?"

"Dale," grunted the FBI man, "I don't expect you ever will take on good manners. They seem to be old-fashioned, too, these days. Let me bring you up to date. Willoughby and his men have been checking out the names snitched from those files, but they haven't got anything yet. Everybody has airtight alibis. My own guys are working on some of the leads, but their feeling is they don't go anywhere. Anyway, they've got to come up with something before Willoughby does. Doesn't look good for the bureau to get into something and have somebody else finish it."

"So it's a three-way race now, is that it?"

"Doesn't have to be," said Griswold. "Not if you drop out of it."

"If that's what you want, forget it. I've got a deeper stake in this than either you or Willoughby."

"You sure do," drawled Griswold. "You don't know how deep. Now, let me give it to you straight, Dale. I think maybe you've got a couple of leads that might be helpful to us. Willoughby said something about a crank letter, for example, which probably ain't worth a rat's ass, but still ought to be checked out, even if Willoughby doesn't think much of it. We in the bureau are thorough; that's one reason we're good. Even the civil rights assholes can't deny that. Point is, you've got this, and maybe a couple of other things, and they might, they just might, be useful to me."

"So?"

"I want you to hand over everything you've got. Everything, no matter how unimportant it seems. Back out of this whole goddamn thing and let us take it from there."

"Why should I?"

"I can think of several reasons. Like your duty as a citizen, though I don't suppose that means much to somebody like you. I guess the biggest reason is that I'll really nail you to the wall if you don't. The setup is perfect—just what I've been waiting for."

"You mean pressing those charges?"

Griswold smiled. "Better than that. Charges don't mean much these days. What with the Civil Liberties Union and people like that you can damn near rape your grandmother and get away with it. But there is, thank God, a little matter of licensing."

"Licensing what?"

"Private investigators, for one thing. You know all the clauses about moral turpitude and all that even better than I do, probably. The state commissioner isn't tied up with a lot of First Amendment horseshit the way the courts and the cops are. The slightest breath of suspicion—like maybe just the *possibility* you committed a B and E—and he can revoke your license between his orange juice and coffee any old morning. Fact is, I've already talked to him. Cooperative fella —ol' country boy. He's just waiting for me to say the word."

Roger, trying not to show the icy shock that had suddenly come over him, was silent for a long moment. Finally he said, "You'd really do that, wouldn't you, Griswold?"

"You bet your ass I would."

Roger let a deep breath in and out. "Sorry. No dice."

"Think, Dale. Think what you're doing. No license, no business. No business, no bread. None of those fancy broads you seem to like so much. What's more, your name is mud. You'll have a hell of a time finding a job washing dishes."

Roger shook his head firmly. "I started this thing; I've got to finish it."

"You'll be sorry."

"I already am. Now, if you don't mind, Griswold, drop me off at a taxi stand, okay? With company like you I'd rather be alone."

"If you change your mind," said Griswold, sighing, "I'll be at the hotel till tomorrow morning."

"I won't change," said Roger.

Griswold scowled at him. "Maybe you won't, at that. You're as stubborn as an Arkansas mule. Maybe that's your biggest problem. Okay, Dale, you asked for it.

We'll be around with a search warrant to impound your records. We got to see 'em, anyway. So you lose. That's the way it had to be, from the beginning."

"Let's wait for the ending before you say that, Griswold," said Roger.

XV

The Margulis murder came as a surprise, not only to Roger Dale but to me, as an outsider to the investigation. I knew of Roger's reaction to it because by now he wasn't calling me as much as I was calling him. The talk show murders had more than piqued my interest; they had whacked it over the head with a two-by-four.

Although in recent years I've been concentrating on shows like *Meeting of Minds*, along with the comedy specials that come up from time to time, I was what might be called one of the pioneers of the talk show, and I've always had an abiding interest in it as an institution, a semi-art form, and a good way to hustle a buck. That's how come I played a fairly large part in putting together the Big Meeting—which was largely the result of the Margulis killing.

That brings me back to the subject. Roger wasn't anywhere near when Margulis died. He was busy getting nowhere with his lead about the offspeed cassette —as you shall see presently—and the incident kind of snuck up on all of us, which was perhaps what the killer meant it to do. I think it is best reported in this excerpt from *Newsweek* magazine, reprinted here by permission of the publishers:

Real Life Violence on TV?

Up-and-coming young actor Robert Margulis, hailed for his performance as the drug addict in *Needle Gulch*, was about to be interviewed by Dick Cavett this week. He dropped dead in a corridor of a dose of poison before he ever reached the studio, and authorities are at a loss to explain how the poison might have been administered.

It was the sixth in a series of bizarre murders on talk shows that have police baffled. Four have taken place on TV stages in full view of the audience. The gunshot slaying of Dr. Lionel Rand, a Hollywood psychologist, is thought to be connected with the others—four by poison, one by a sharp instrument thrust into the brain.

"The m.o.'s lack a pattern," said Los Angeles Police Department chief of detectives Harwood Dykstra. "Even the killer's motives are obscure. Apparently, for some twisted reason, he hates TV performers."

Margulis, the latest victim, had been named lately in a number of paternity suits, and had publicly made a joke of it, saying that he was out to break Errol Flynn's record.

The other victims, to date, have been rock-star Elmo Finstetter, tennis champion Sonny Pearson, a TV talk-show fan named Mabel Merriwether, comedian Larry Lawson, and therapist Rand, who was thought to have information concerning the killer in his files.

"Some of the doctor's files seem to have been

removed," said Dykstra, "but we're still working on the Rand angle."

Another odd aspect of the case is that the FBI is also investigating. Assistant FBI director J. Duffy Griswold was present, onstage, at the Pearson murder, apparently done with a blowgun, and this has been interpreted as an assault on Griswold, giving the agency jurisdiction.

Viewers hoping to witness a homicide on a TV talk show will be disappointed. Although portions of the first murder, on the Toni Tennille show, were shown, and the second murder, on the Johnny Carson show, was broadcast by tape delay the same night, all shows are now being taped and edited.

"We worked like hell," said Rick Ludwin, NBC programming spokesman, "to cut down violence on TV, and now look. Well, at least they can't blame us for this one."

*Jeffry Flasch and Lark Meadows
in Los Angeles*

So the Margulis murder was kind of a straw that broke the cliché's back and made everybody cry "Enough already!" I'm not sure who first came up with the idea of the Big Meeting. Some of us in the talk show industry were calling and cross-calling each other to discuss the situation and the thing seemed to spring into being, full-blown.

It was a regular Appalachia of a meeting.

We rented one of these small banquet rooms at a hotel; there were canapés, Danish and coffee, and drinks for those who wanted them, but it was strictly business.

Nobody was formally appointed, but I suggested Jack Paar chair the meeting. Although Dinah Shore had gone off the air some time earlier, she was there, too. Johnny Carson was on hand, and Mike Douglas, and Phil Donahue, and Merv Griffin, Dick Cavett, David Frost, Tom Snyder, David Susskind, and, relatively new to our racket, John Davidson and Toni Tennille.

"Gentlemen," said Jack Paar—apparently forgetting Dinah and Toni—and perching with nervous energy on the edge of his chair, the way he does, "I'm glad you all agreed to come, and I certainly hope, among us, we'll be able to figure out what to do. Because the talk show business faces its greatest crisis since it started about thirty years ago."

There were nods and murmurs of agreement.

"You all know what the situation is," continued Jack, "but let me review it for you anyway. Somebody out there—or maybe somebody under our noses—is knocking off talk show guests right and left. The media are having a field day with it. But the effect—which none of us anticipated—is that this nut, whoever he is, is destroying the venerable institution of the talk show. This—well, as Fred Allen once said about radio, 'This sham, this fraud, this gold mine.'"

"There was a funny man," interrupted Johnny Carson.

"Stick to the subject, Johnny," said Tom Snyder, grinning.

"And lose his standing as a talk show host?" David Frost said.

Everybody laughed.

Jack Paar frowned. "Are we gonna perform for each other or are we gonna do what we came here to do?"

"Go on, Jack," said Mike Douglas. "We're all together in this thing."

"Okay." Jack nodded. "Now, what's happening is this. Lots of stars—the really important guests—are now afraid to appear on talk shows."

"Right," Davidson said, looking boyish and enthusiastic. "They all think they're going to get murdered."

"Exactly. You guys have been getting turndowns all over the place," said Jack.

"Of course," Merv said, patting down a wild lock in his gray hair, "they never give the real reason—it's always excuses like prior commitments or whatever—but we all know what they're thinking."

"In a way you can't blame them," said Cavett, showing his earnest frown.

"Right," said Paar. "But meanwhile, what's happening? You're all being reduced to using unknown newcomers and gong-show acts. The viewers are going in droves to the old movies. There was a while when they thought they might witness a murder on a talk show, but now most of them are wise to the taping process. And with hardly anybody watching, the talk show ratings are dropping right down into the bulb. Look at some of your commercials lately. Lots more Smokey the Bear and public service stuff about the great job the Bureau of Weights and Measures is doing. Promos for the sitcoms that'll be on later—"

"Excuse me, Jack," said Phil Donahue, "but we know all this. Only too well. Let's get down to the tough question. What are we gonna do?"

"That's why we're all here," Paar said. "To come up with ideas. You've all had some time to think about it. Well? Who's got an idea? Even a crazy one. Let's brainstorm this thing."

John Davidson, looking a little shy, stirred and said, "One of my fan clubs wants me to start coming out in a bulletproof vest."

David Frost smiled. "Like Jack said—even a crazy idea."

Davidson looked at him. "Got anything better?"

"No." Frost shook his head. "Wish I had. All I can think is that in time maybe it'll blow over."

"And by that time we could all be sunk," said Carson. "Personally, I think the talk show is a solid American institution that ought to last forever, but you know how network execs are. They're already looking for something new. And just for the sake of newness. They all dream that by accident they'll come up with a formula nobody's thought of before. Except, at heart, they're afraid to try. Sometimes I think we did better in the old days when we just acted on intuition and didn't try so hard to outsmart it all the time."

"True enough," said Donahue. "But where does that get us?"

Carson shrugged.

"Look," said Paar, "you guys are right in the thick of it, and I'm off to one side just doing occasional specials, so maybe I've got a kind of perspective. Has it occurred to anybody that the real solution to this mess is to catch the murderer?"

"Okay," said Griffin, grinning a little sarcastically, "go ahead and catch him."

"The guy may be uncatchable," I chimed in.

"Not a bad title for a crime series," mused Carson. "*The Uncatchables.*"

"What I mean is," I said, "he's a smart bastard, IQ probably way the hell up there. And contrary to popular belief, people *do* get away with murder. Hundreds, every year. One of the ways this thing could go is for the killer to break off right now and sit back, smiling, forever uncaught, like Jack the Ripper, or the skyjacker who parachuted into the woods up in the Northwest. For him, they're already writing folksongs. But even if that happens it won't do us any good immediately."

Donahue looked up. "I thought the cops were about to zero in on this guy. That's the way it sounded on the news the other night."

"Well, a little hype's been pumped into it," I said. "As far as I know, nobody's really close yet. I've been following this thing; I happen to know Roger Dale, the private detective who's working on it, and he keeps me posted. It looks like this latest clue—finding the killer among those whose names were lifted from Rand's files—didn't work out. It's my guess the killer's pulled a Neutermischel."

"A what?" asked Mike Douglas.

"The old story about the two business rivals in Europe who simultaneously decide to go to a new town—Neutermischel. They meet on the train, and one says, 'Max, where are you going?' The other says, 'Gus, I'm going to Neutermischel.' 'Aha,' says the first guy. 'You say Neutermischel so I'll think you're going somewhere else, but you really *are* going to Neutermischel—so why do you lie to me?'"

"Hey, that's not bad," said Carson, chuckling.

"I didn't tell it to get a laugh," I said, "but it's what you'd call a classic example of double-reverse English. What I'm getting at is this. Could be that the killer pulled names from the files to provide a false clue—*but left his own in!*"

"Wow!" Toni Tennille said, in that big, healthy voice of hers.

"In which case the name could be found there," Dinah said, softly.

"Maybe," I said, "but maybe not. How would you know it when you saw it? Connected with the broadcast industry, perhaps, but a lot of patients in those files are."

"Steve," said Susskind, white-haired, venerable, his voice reflecting it, "you're beginning to sound like this character Dale. What's he come up with lately?"

"Not much. He has a tape that may be from the killer—one of these taunting things—but he can't pin down the voice. And it could be just a crank job. Chances are that's all it is."

"Is he really a supersleuth," asked Tom Snyder, "or is that all just more PR?"

"I'm not sure," I said. "The guy impresses me. Quick on the uptake. And he did solve those other murders. If he has a flaw, it's his way of telling you more than you wanted to know about practically anything that comes up. On the whole, good company."

Dinah Shore stirred in the love seat where she sat. "Has it occurred to you fellas," she said, "that there's no real answer to this problem? No one brilliant thing you can do? Seems to me you've just got to plug harder getting suitable guests. A *few* of the celebrities aren't afraid to go on. You just have to keep digging to find them. Maybe even hire more talent bookers to work on it."

Merv Griffin groaned. "I knew the answer, whatever it was, would cost money."

"More than money," said Johnny Carson, looking grave. "Some hard work, too. You see, we've had it fat all these years. The talk show format was so easy it worked all by itself—we didn't have to do anything much. Kind of like American industry generally when you think about it. But the hungry fighters are coming up—like foreign industry, for example—and if we don't shape up, packagers of other kinds of shows will take it away from us."

John Davidson looked up. "All this trouble just to find out we have to work harder?"

"I'd say," murmured Susskind, "that's a pretty good thing to find out, and worth all the trouble."

"If it works," said Paar, frowning. "There's still a chance that this may mean the end of the talk show as we've always known it."

XVI

We sat in a snack bar on Hollywood Boulevard. I had a Danish in front of me and Roger Dale had a piece of banana cream pie topped with what looked like Gillette foamy shaving cream. We were both drinking our coffee, but neither of us was doing much with the pastry. We had to buy something, that's all, or the management would have glared at us for sitting there for anything over five minutes.

How we happened to meet in this place is more or less beside the point—it was a question of when each of us, going here, going there, could get someplace near the other at a time fairly convenient to both of us.

"Inspector Clouseau couldn't botch things up worse than I've been doing," said Roger. "Nothing works, dammit. People aren't in when I call, my car hasn't been the same since the wheels were ripped off, buttons break, zippers get stuck—"

"As Yeats put it," I said, "things fall apart, the center cannot hold."

"Right. Did you know that Yeats was little more than a minor playwright most of his life and wrote his greatest poems between the ages of fifty and seventy-five?"

"I didn't," I said. "Maybe I can work it into a *Meeting of Minds* show sometime. But go ahead."

"It started the day I drove all the way out to the university to get that tape played offspeed," Roger said, "only to find that Sam Wechsler was on vacation. So I started calling other people I thought might play the tape. They were all busy or out somewhere, or just not inclined to oblige. When I finally got a small recording lab lined up, Griswold's men barged in, impounded my records, and left me at the phone, where I spent another two days trying to find the licensing commissioner in the state capital and maybe talk him out of revoking my license—if that's what he's gonna do. I kept getting assistants and had to repeat the whole story to each one. They weren't listening—just waiting till I finished so they could pass me on to the next person. Anyway, Jinny managed to hide some of the stuff from Griswold's men, so they didn't get either the recording or the pasteup notes. Then Margulis got murdered, and when I tried to pick up some facts about it from the police they told me not to be so damned cheap and go out and buy a newspaper."

"What *is* your reaction to the Margulis killing?"

Roger shrugged. "More in line with the others. Maybe he's running out of original ideas. Aconite, just like the first time. In coffee. Margulis was drowning himself in coffee—apparently he'd just gone off the sauce and was using coffee to blank out the awful taste of cool, clear water. So again, the killer's someone within the industry, who would have known this, and who had entrée to the studio, practically without being noticed. The only thing different about this one is that the killer didn't notify me beforehand. What I think he's saying now is, 'Look, I can do this anytime, anyplace. And you can't stop me.'"

"Looks like he's right, there."

"Up to a point. Once I identify him I *know* I can maneuver him into a position where he'll give himself away. I know that because, subconsciously, he *wants* me to."

"I hope you're reading him correctly," I said.

"Trust me, I am," Roger said. "I may not know him outside yet, but inside I know him, maybe better than he knows himself. Him. Her. Whoever. I might know today. After I leave here I'm going to see somebody who can play the tape slow, fast, or indifferent. Funny —the guy was available to me all the time and I never thought of him till Jinny made the suggestion. Tex de Armond. The stereo nut. He's the one who gave me my unit in the first place. And that's what I came to see you about so urgently today, Steve."

"The stereo?"

"The fact that I'll probably know the killer's name. When I do I've got to draw him into another talk show—another attempt. I've got to be there. And this time, knowing who it is, I'll positively be able to lower the boom. That's where you come in."

"Into what?" I asked cautiously.

"As my middleman, to help place me on another talk show. In fact, I want to set one up specially for this purpose. Merv Griffin's show would be good. He does a lot of theme shows. You do his program a lot. You did your comedy specials from his theater. You know all these people; they'll listen to you."

"Yes, I know them, and I'm willing to help you if I can. But maybe you should get somebody like Ronnie Fordyce to intercede for you. He's got a lot of clout with anybody who makes a living on the tube.

And he's persuasive, which I guess means he can bug you till he wears you down. I think he went back for seconds when chutzpah was passed out." I cut off a corner of the Danish and idly tasted it. "Tell you what," I said. "You try Ronnie and if he agrees to ask Merv Griffin, I'll call Merv and second the proposition. I suggest this only because I think it may be the best way, with the best chance of succeeding. Okay?"

"That's fair enough, Steve," Dale said, nodding.

I looked at my watch again. "I think it's time for me to go. Wish I knew for sure . . ."

As I found out later—for this is how I found out all these things, by careful interviewing and, under that old literary license, careful reconstruction of all these episodes—Tex de Armond was delighted to see Roger.

Tex came to the door of his pad in cowboy boots and a shirt with pearl buttons and roses embroidered upon it, exactly as Roger had expected to see him. He was a large, fleshy man with streaky blond hair, and his handshake was sweaty. Roger had originally known him when they'd both been sheriff's deputies in Tucson; after each had drifted to L.A. they'd made occasional contact, hitting the singles bars together a few times, but this had dwindled off, primarily because, except for chicks and police work, they lacked common interests.

"God damn, it's good to see you again, pardner!" said Tex in a broad, range-fed drawl. Roger knew he'd been raised in Chicago and had developed a country-and-western twang, like all those city-born rock singers who deliberately sing like hicks. "Where the hell you been, anyway?"

"Same old place. Just busy. You know how it is."

"Sure," said Tex. "I reckon I do." His real name was Chester; he had given himself the name of Tex. "Come on in! Hunker down for a spell!"

Racks and amplifiers and turntables and speakers festooned the walls of Tex's pad, as did the shelves of the discs and tapes he had collected: country music that was twice as sweet to his ears when rendered with the highest possible fidelity and all the amplification his eardrums could take.

"Drink?" asked Tex.

Roger nodded, and presently Tex brought two glasses of Tennessee sour mash, along with a short lecture on its virtues as a beverage and a sovereign palliative for most ailments, from snakebite to psychological hang-ups. In the midst of this he stepped to a shelf of discs and began to select one.

"Hold it," said Roger. He held up the cassette. "This is what I want to hear." As briefly as he could, he told Tex why. "Can you do it? Vary the speed?"

"Easy as throwin' a newborn dogie," said Tex. He'd never thrown a dogie, but to do him justice, he *could* ride a horse. A willing one, anyway.

"Play it a little faster first," said Roger, when Tex had the cassette in a slot and his hand on a control that slid up and down.

"Greetings, Roger Dale. This is the Exterminator—"

Roger waved his hand and shook his head. "That's not it. Sounds like one of Mel Blanc's voices. Slower, okay?"

Tex lowered the control until the pitch deepened slightly and the words began to space themselves out more.

"I'm sending you this to let you know there's going to be another one—"

Roger stared at the amplifier as the Exterminator's

voice, coming from the woofers and tweeters and possibly some plain old speakers strategically placed here and there, filled the room. He was certain that the pitch of the voice he was hearing now was normal; he could detect a deliberate slowing of pace on the part of the speaker to compensate for the acceleration that had been planned.

"How's that?" asked Tex.

Roger nodded. "I think I know. The speaker's making an attempt to disguise even the normal voice—but by God, I think I know!"

"Well, who is it?"

"I don't want to say. Not right now."

"God damn!" said Tex, shutting off the machine. "You come all the way over here and get me all riled up, and then you ain't gonna tell who it is!"

"Top secret, Tex. Top, supercrisis, don't-even-think-about-it secret. I don't want the slightest chance of a leak, which could get to the person, who would then know what I know."

"Well, shee-yit! You're gonna let him know anyway, aren't you?"

"In time. Right now it wouldn't do any good. No proof. The killer's covered all the tracks beautifully, of course. There are time-and-place alibis that could take days or weeks to break down—if at all. There's only one way to break this one. A trap. Another trap."

"And how're you gonna do that?"

"At the moment, I don't know. Not precisely. Let's have another glass of that sour mash. It might give me ideas."

"It'll do that all right!" said Tex, heading for the bar.

"Dear boy!" said Ronnie Fordyce, rising from the canvas chair at the edge of the swimming pool as

Roger came on to the patio. He was in a fuchsia karate robe, and on the metal table beside his chair were scripts and notebooks. He wore heavy horn-rimmed glasses. Roger had never seen him in glasses before. Hardly anyone had—it was kind of a privilege. Ronnie took the glasses off. "Well! What brings you here!"

"Business," said Roger.

"Of course," said Ronnie. "Pleasure would probably be in bad taste this early in the morning. Can I get you a drink?"

"If it's soft. Orange juice or something."

Ronnie called toward the patio door through which Roger had just emerged. "Epifanio! A glass of orange juice, if you don't mind. And even if you do."

The man he'd addressed moved like a huge shadow across the inside of the door. Roger had had to look up to see his face when he'd been let in. He was fat and swarthy, and with a little more slant to his eyes might have been a Japanese sumo wrestler. Roger glanced at the disappearing shadow and said, "Quite a bodyguard you've got there."

"Epifanio's a gem," said Ronnie, shuffling another deck chair into place for Roger. "Don't know what I'd do without him. The best thing is, no distractions. He's a eunuch, you know. Shot there in Vietnam, poor lad. But in a way I envy him—at least he's rid of one major problem that bugs us all in one way or another. Sit down, Roger. I hope you've come to pay your honest debts. Like telling me first, before you tell anybody else, who the murderer is."

Roger sat. "I've come to ask a favor."

"Again? The balance of payments is becoming a bit lopsided, don't you think?"

Roger looked across the pool at the almost lifesize

mannequin pis that was dribbling water into it. "Didn't know you kept score that closely. Anyway, Ronnie, I think I know who's pulling off the talk show murders."

"How *marvelous*! Wait! Don't tell me right away! Let's draw this out and savor it!"

"I'm not going to tell you. Not this morning, anyway."

"Then why in the hell are you here?"

"Look, Ronnie, for reasons I don't want to go into right now I'm pretty sure I've got the killer identified. Maybe ninety-eight percent. Enough to act on, anyway. That's where you come in."

Epifanio lumbered in with a tray. Roger accepted his orange juice and Ronnie declined his with a grimace. Epifanio departed.

"All right, Roger. What do you need me for this time?"

"There has to be one more show," said Roger. "Merv Griffin, I guess. He's the only major one who hasn't had a murder yet."

"Does that make him a suspect?" Ronnie's antennae were quivering.

Roger laughed. "Stop fishing, Ronnie. You see, Merv won't talk to me. None of 'em'll talk to me."

"Why does there have to be one more show?"

"A trap."

"You tried that with Larry Lawson. It didn't work."

"But this time I *know* who the murderer is. I'll be watching."

"And you want me to try to persuade Merv to put you on?"

"That's it."

Ronnie leaned back and frowned. "Well, I don't know, Roger. What guarantees have I got that you really have fingered the culprit?"

"You'll just have to take my word for it. But if this thing works out you've got the scoop of all times. You're in on the ground floor. How you helped set up the trap can be part of your story. Real inside dope. Ronnie Fordyce does it again."

"But if this thing backfires, like all your other tries, then where am I?"

"Up the famous creek. But didn't you ever take a chance on something?"

"Never," said Ronnie firmly. "I don't even enter those sweepstakes things they keep sending you in the mail. The only bets I ever make are on sure things. Like divorce, for example, for practically anybody in this business who gets married. But if I knew a little more about this, and had reason to think you *have* identified the murderer—"

"No you don't, Ronnie," interrupted Roger. "No free info at this stage of the game. I haven't told anyone what I think I know. Not even Meg or Jinny."

Ronnie studied Roger for a moment. "You could give me a *hint*. Enough to let me know if you really have an idea who did it."

"All I can tell you is what I've worked out on my psychological profile. Very intelligent, but terribly twisted. Filled with moral indignation—brought to it by some kind of shock. And in show business."

"In front of or behind the cameras?"

"Let's not play twenty questions, Ronnie. Look, I'm not trying to con you or use any tricky techniques or apply any kind of pressure—or even make false promises. I'm appealing to your sense of what's decent and fair, and making what I hope is a straightforward request. I'm seeing you as a *person*, Ronnie. And at heart, I suspect, not a bad one at all. I'm gambling that beneath that gossamer exterior of yours there beats a heart of gold."

"It's Solingen steel, actually," said Ronnie. He shook his head as though to shift the weight of his frown. "Oh, very well, dammit," he said abruptly. "Under protest, mind you. If you *do* know the murderer this could be sensational."

"Get on the horn, Ronnie. To Griffin. Tell him I want to set up a special show, during which the identity of the murderer will be revealed. Put the pressure on him."

"No pressure," said Ronnie. "First, he wouldn't respond to it. Second, I don't pressure performers in spite of what you may have heard. And I'm not going to push him, myself, for that special show. Only that he set up an appointment with you and listen to your sad tale. It's up to you to sell him, after that."

"All right," said Roger. "If that's the best I can get, I'll take it."

"Epifanio!" Ronnie bellowed at the patio door. "Would you bring a phone out here, please? And for Christ's sake, don't break it!"

Las Vegas again.

That was where Merv Griffin was operating from at the moment. Appointment time, eleven A.M. sharp—at Caesars Palace. Plane arriving a little after nine, rented car at the airport—glances around to see if O. J. Simpson was running through it—quick stop at police headquarters to say hello to Stefan Radmilovich, then out to the hotel. Fifteen minutes at the slots, killing time. Net loss: twelve dollars and seventy-five cents.

Merv had a cabana. Smiling assistants ushered

Roger into it. Griffin was in green shorts, bare feet, and a blue terrycloth shirt. He had the papers and clippings Roger had expected to see scattered over a coffee table in front of him.

"Hello, Mr. Dale." His smile was cordial enough. "Have a good flight in?"

"Very nice-looking stew. Only she wouldn't make a date."

Merv grinned. "Some do, some don't. Sit down, Roger. That's what they call you? Roger? I know why you're here, more or less, so let's get right down to it. My time is limited, I'm sorry to say."

"Right." Roger took an easy chair across from the sofa. "Okay, as Fordyce told you—I was there when he called—I think I know who done it. But knowing and proving are two different things. Evidence could be developed, of course, but it has to be the kind they can prosecute on, and these days that means pretty airtight, which, in the last analysis, is probably a good thing. I'm shooting for the bullseye—a confession by the killer, in person. Which he or she—I won't say which right now—is not about to give voluntarily. So the only thing to do is catch the culprit off guard. Not privately—too much chance to think and wriggle out of it that way. On the air—in the midst of a show!"

"Are you saying what I think you're saying?" Merv absentmindedly reached into a lacquered bowl and took a foil-wrapped afterdinner mint from it. He was about to open this when he glanced at his midriff, scowled, and put it back. "I ought to watch my damned diet," he said. "You know what the thing is about diets? None of 'em work. What I mean is, who can stick to any of 'em? Now. About what you're saying. You want to go on my show, get the murderer on it, too, and *name* him, right there?"

"That's exactly it," said Roger. "What I want to do is have a certain list of guests, which I'll supply. They'll all be suspects in one degree or another, though I'll probably throw in a few red herrings, too. The psychological setup will be very important in affecting the murderer's state of mind. I won't go into details on that, except to say I've thought it all out very carefully. Still with me?"

"Hanging on," said Merv.

"The show will be a special. One of your theme shows. One factor might be tough for you, or at least so Ronnie tells me. The show will have to be live."

"Tough," said Griffin, "but not impossible."

"That's vital, so the killer will be off balance. I'm sure you know even better than I do the inner tension a live versus a taped show creates. Anyway, the killer will be invited, and won't dare refuse, because that would put the finger on him right away, and he'll naturally be hoping I've got the wrong person in mind, or perhaps that I'm bluffing. In fact, it's a good bet this person will assume that's the case."

"How can you be so sure what he'll assume?"

"Because," said Roger, "even before I knew this person's name I knew him inside fairly well. I built a thorough psychological profile. I won't go into that in detail right now, either. But it works—that's the point. It worked on the park strangler and those other cases. I realize I'm asking you to take some of this on faith, but now there's no other way."

Merv frowned. "I don't know, Roger. This is—as you imply—kinda far-out."

"So are the times we live in. The far-out's become the norm. Look at the last few years. Mass suicides in Guyana. A U.S. president conspiring in a B and E. The hostages in Iran. That someone would murder a series of guests on talk shows, and for quirky reasons, isn't as surprising as everyone seems to think."

"All right, you've got a pretty convincing sales pitch. Still, do you realize what you're asking?"

"A lot, I know," said Roger, nodding. "But we all stand to gain a lot. Steve Allen tells me the talk shows are in trouble—said you had a big meeting or something. This could help bring them out of it. And *your* show—if you agree—would certainly have a hell of a rating."

"If it works," said Merv, still frowning. He reached for one of the afterdinner mints and, without realizing it, removed the tinfoil and popped it into his mouth.

"Do it my way and it's *got* to work," said Roger. "My list of guests. And not just yourself as host—but all the other major talk show people as cohosts."

"What?" Merv's head came up.

"It's got to be made a huge, dramatic climax—stunning in its brilliance to everyone, including the murderer. The other talk show hosts will also widen the list of possible suspects. They're not immune, you know."

"One of *them* might be the murderer? Is that what you're saying?"

"I'm not saying anything definite right now. Just that this is the way it's got to be done."

"My God!" said Merv, leaning back. He gave it many moments of thought. Then, still frowning, he said, "All right, Roger. I'll tell you what I'll do. I'll talk to the others—Mike, Toni, John Davidson, everybody. I'll let you handle Carson. And then, if we decide to do it your way, I'll see if I can get all or most of my stations lined up to carry this one show live. Frankly I'm not sure they'll go for it. Or it may be impossible. But we'll see. Meanwhile, you'll just have to wait."

"I'm getting used to that," said Roger, with a deep sigh.

XVII

        To those unofficial oral historians of electronic show business, who gather in the bars and lunch counters, at poolsides, and in hot tubs here and there to sling the gossip and sing the sagas of the industry, it was known ever afterward as the week of the talk show decision. It outranked in intensity of interest those periods when program schedules are shifted about like musical chairs in the frantic effort of each network to oppose the others with shows that pull larger audiences. It was a week when old ulcers were exacerbated and new ones appeared in the linings of countless duodeni. It was every station for itself, and program managers the country over scrambled to line up local rights to this bizarre special the major talk show hosts were proposing.

The hosts themselves had not come to their decision easily. When the idea, originally proposed by Roger Dale, had been passed along by a series of telephone calls and personal contacts, they called and cross-called each other for careful discussion before arriving at any rash conclusions. Less fearful of the innovative or the experimental than those in the business end of broadcasting, the hosts decided in a comparatively short time to go along with the idea. As Johnny Carson put it, "What the hell; it's better than continuing to book nonstars every night. There haven't been this many no-shows since the night Steve Allen hosted the Emmy awards."

Somehow, at last, the decision was made. There were frowns and reservations, and there was cold sweat and trembling, but the upshot was that there would be a live, special show, carried on a syndicated basis by both independents and a number of affiliates of the three networks, and on it—Christ, let's keep our fingers crossed—the celebrated supersleuth, Roger Dale, would reveal the identity of the murderer.

But that factor would not be announced at first. The show would be trumpeted as a superspecial, hosted by Merv Griffin, with cohost appearances by most of his celebrated talk show colleagues.

There are hermits here and there who, for various philosophical or emotional reasons, have drawn deep into wild places and don't even own television sets. They were probably the only people in America who didn't know the show was scheduled.

The message came in the customary large manila envelope, addressed with printed letters cut out of magazines and pasted into place. It was sent to Roger's office this time. He stared at it for a moment before opening it and realized that he'd almost been expecting it.

Jinny was standing over his desk, looking as anxious as Roger himself. He took the paper out of the envelope and read aloud, "Dear Roger. Perhaps I should thank you. By bringing about this upcoming special talk show you are providing the perfect climax to my efforts. I will be there. There will be another victim. You'll be surprised when you learn who it is to be. You won't know until the last moment. For now, all good wishes."

"That's it?" asked Jinny, as Roger lowered the letter.

"That's it."

His eyebrows twisted themselves into what Jinny had come to know as his analytical frown. Somewhere in the depths of his mind synapses were popping off and currents were flashing back and forth. "A couple of glitches here," he said thoughtfully. "Did you catch them? First, in the tape he calls himself the Exterminator. In the pasteup notes he doesn't. No name—he just gives the message and lets it go at that."

"Meaning it's not the same person?"

"A possibility," said Roger, nodding. "The style sounds a little different, too—though that could be the difference between somebody ad-libbing and putting words down on paper."

"All right. If it's two different people, who sent which and why?"

"Two alternatives. One, both are crank notes. Two, at least one communication—either the tape or the notes—was not sent by the killer. Though it's still *possible* that he sent both."

"I hope all this logic of yours is giving you some kind of pleasurable fix," said Jinny. "It doesn't seem to be doing much else."

"You're right. For the moment it doesn't get us anywhere. Unless it means that the killer I think I recognize from his voice isn't the killer after all. In which case, where it gets us is back to square one, or maybe even minus one."

"Just what we need. For the whole thing to fall apart when we thought we had it knocked."

Roger shook his head firmly. "We're not dead in the water yet. Remember, I'm pointing out the possibilities, but not necessarily likely ones. The odds are still favorable that the killer is planning to knock off another victim and boldly call his shots. It fits what little we know of him, psychologically. He's risking his own destruction—working close to the bull—one part of him wanting to win, of course, but another, deeper part—and brilliant as he is, he doesn't realize this—wanting to be caught and punished for some kind of guilt feeling. That may sound contradictory, but it's actually common with criminals. Ask any criminal psychologist. Hell, ask any good cop."

"Maybe that's what we really need now. A good cop. No offense, Roger—I just mean a professional who has the resources of the law at his disposal. Wouldn't you be surer of everything if you just turned all the bits and pieces over to somebody like Sergeant Willoughby now?"

"Willoughby's a good cop," said Roger, "but he's already clogged up with preassumptions. One of them is that I'm a pain in his toosh—which I probably am —and anything I come up with is automatically wrong. Tell you what I will do, though. I'll bring him the note and let him fingerprint it. I was going to do that with the first one, but everything got screwed up and I never got around to it. I'll make the gesture, but I can almost guarantee you there won't be any prints. When this killer slips up—if he ever does—it won't be with something as obvious as leaving fingerprints. His style demands something more subtle."

Jinny sighed. "There are times, Roger, when I don't know whether you're very right or very wrong."

"Welcome to the club, not to coin a phrase," said Roger.

Ad from *TV Guide*:

The Whole Town's Talking!

Not just the town—the country, the world! About the big superspecial talk show coming up —live!—on an unprecedented 266 stations!

Yes, it's a dazzling show, to be hosted by MERV GRIFFIN, this time with a lineup of brilliant co-hosts. JOHNNY CARSON, JACK PAAR, MIKE DOUGLAS, DICK CAVETT, DAVID FROST, DINAH SHORE, JOHN DAVIDSON, PHIL DONAHUE, TONI TENNILLE—all on hand to make sparkling conversation as only they know how!

See and hear them all as they present a roster of fascinating guests—people who have made their marks in unusual and even unbelievable ways—in this star-studded two-hour special chock full of stunning surprises! Get ready for the most fascinating evening of "real people" entertainment you've ever known! Check your local schedules for times and channels now!

See you at the talk superspecial. Don't miss it for *anything!*

Metromedia, Inc.

Letter from Commissioner of Private Investigating Agencies, State Attorney General's Office, Sacramento, California:

TO: Mr. Roger Dale, Dale Security Agency, Fairview Business Park, Suite 6, Los Angeles, California 90027

SUBJECT: Hearing for Revocation of License

Dear Mr. Dale:

It has come to the attention of this office that on the dates indicated in the attached form you performed certain actions which indicate possible law violation in (a) withholding evidence in the investigation of a felony by duly-constituted law-enforcement agencies, (b) obstructing justice, and (c) committing unlawful entry into private premises for the purpose of theft as defined in the California Penal Code, Sections 459–467, as amended.

Prosecution for these alleged offenses is now under consideration. In the meantime, it is requested that you personally appear before this commission to show cause why your Private Investigator's license should not be suspended pending the resolution of these charges. In the event of conviction resulting from any of these charges your license may be permanently revoked under the provisions of the licensing regulations cited in the attached form 2377-A.

> Yours very truly,
> SYLVESTER BLAYLOCK
> Commissioner

"Mr. Griswold? This is Roger Dale."

"Yeah. I know. Secretary said so. You calling from California?"

"Right. Sixth time I've tried. You're a hard man to find in."

"To some people, maybe. What's on your mind?"

"I think you must already know. This revocation of my license—"

"Look, I gave you fair warning about that, Dale. You had your chance and didn't take it."

"I know. Maybe my mistake. Didn't you ever make any mistakes? We got off on the wrong foot, I'm afraid. But there's more to this than the license now. I need your cooperation, and the only way I know to get it is to call you, lay everything out on the table, and hope we can approach this thing like a couple of adults without playing upmanship games. Will you take one minute to listen, this time? Listen hard, I mean."

"Keep talking."

"I think I know who the murderer is. No evidence strong enough for charges, but I'm practically certain of his identity. You must have been in this particular boat yourself, lots of times. Never mind the details right now—I'll fill you in when the time comes. But meanwhile, to create an environment in which the killer will be off balance, and therefore more likely to make an actual admission, I've arranged for one last talk show—and for him to be there. You may have got wind of it by now. I want you to be there, too."

Pause.

"Are you crazy?"

"I may be getting there. But nothing else has worked, as you know, and this may be just about our only chance. I say 'we' because I'm asking you to be in on it. The bureau will receive all the credit it's entitled to, and I don't even mind if you imply, afterward, that the whole thing was your idea. There's something for everybody in this—even for Willoughby and the LAPD."

"Why are you so all-fired anxious to have me come to this show?"

"Your presence will provide added pressure on the

killer. Knock him even farther off base. Besides, it adds clout to the whole thing. Respectability, if you will."

"Well, I don't know, Dale. Seems to me if you've got some suspicions you better just pass 'em along and let us take it from there."

"I could do that. And I agree—maybe I ought to. But let me point out that doing this my way will bring more favorable publicity to the bureau than you could possibly buy with a whole year's budget. If old J. Edgar was so PR-conscious, why shouldn't you be? Whatever else we disagree on, Griswold, I know you have the best interests of the bureau in mind, and I'm hoping you'll see it this way. Come on, Duff, what do you say? Teamwork, for a change?"

"God damn it, Dale! You really take the rag off'n the bush!"

"If that means what I think it does, I guess I do. Deal?"

"Deal, dammit! And after I hang up I go right out and get my head examined."

"You people do that in Washington, too, huh?"

"All right, Dale. Let's have dates and times and all that."

"Has it occurred to you?" asked Jinny.

"Has what occurred to me?" Roger was pacing in the office again. It was another gloomy day there. They'd all been gloomy lately, with everything in suspension and little to do but wait and hope.

"That last note from the killer—if it *was* the killer. He said you'd be surprised at the victim this time."

"I'm sure I will be. So?"

"And what have all the victims been? Men about town, you might say. In Mabel's case, the female equivalent. Anyway, people the killer evidently considers sexually or morally irresponsible."

"Yes?"

Jinny primped her hair absentmindedly in an eternal feminine gesture. "Before you met Meg, *you* might have fit that description, Roger," she said quietly.

XVIII

Debbie Weintraub, dressed in a white skirt and a middy blouse of red and blue with anchors and stars on it, walked and walked until she came to berth number 155, almost at the end of the long pier, near the breakwater. The motor yacht *Silver Cloud* lay here, huge and gleaming white. Coming abreast of it, Debbie halted, blinked, and consulted the slip of paper in her hand to be sure she had the right place.

A tall, bearded young man in swabbies, a chambray shirt open by several buttons on the neck so that both a coral necklace and the thick hair of his chest could be seen, and with a battered white captain's hat tilted back carelessly on his head, stood by the stainless steel and mahogany gangplank in a loose, lounging way, lighting a stubby pipe, cupping his hands to shield the match flame from the harbor breeze. He looked over his hands as Debbie approached and halted; she caught a glimpse of his eyes and they struck her as oddly merry, as though the world to him was a meaningless situation comedy he could watch and be mildly entertained by without having to think too deeply about any of it. Inspecting him more closely, Debbie saw a gold ring on the lobe of one ear. He made clouds of smoke, lowered his hands, and said, "Looking for something?"

"The *Silver Cloud*. Is this it?"

"Sure is. Name on the bow there." He nodded forward.

"That's the front, isn't it?"

The piratical-looking young man grinned. "Right. But we don't dare say it that way. I'm Pete Koskiusco, the skipper."

"I'm Debbie Weintraub. I'm supposed to meet a bunch of others here."

"Yeah. The writers. Nobody else arrived yet. Are they always late like this? Are you a writer, too?"

"I'm one of Toni Tennille's production assistants. I'm supposed to be in on the conference. Not sure why—to fetch coffee, I suppose. Anyway, Toni sent me."

"Well, come on aboard and wait. Like to see the boat? You can have a drink and the fifty-cent tour."

"Too early for the drink, but I will take the tour," Debbie said.

She liked the look of Pete Koskiusco, even from the rear as he led her aboard the yacht. Debbie had always liked muscular men—she'd been almost unable to function the day Dinah had had Lou Ferrigno, the Incredible Hulk, on the show. "This is the fantail deck," he said, taking her aft to an area covered with an awning. "Fishing chairs, cocktail chairs, the whole bit. Might even be an anchor and a man-overboard buoy around here somewhere, like there's supposed to be. She's a relic of another age, when J. P. Morgan said if you had to ask about the price of a yacht you couldn't afford one. She's an exact replica, in modern materials, of a yacht Louis B. Mayer, the movie pioneer, once owned. Mr. Samish had her built that way, from the keel up."

"Very impressive ship," said Debbie. "I guess opulent is the word."

"It's the exact word. Opulent. Conspicuous consumption, à la Veblen. Gets his kicks, I guess, just knowing he owns her. Which is okay with me. Gives me a job and a place to sleep. It's a boat, by the way, not a ship. If you can put it aboard a ship, it's a boat."

Debbie laughed. "I always wanted to learn salty talk. How about 'Shiver my timbers?' "

"You say it just fine," said Pete. "Come on. I'll show you the pilot house."

As they moved along the side deck, Debbie said, "Is this how you spend all your time? Just being here on the boat?"

"Oh, I find things to do," he said. He glanced at her for a moment as though measuring her. Debbie almost dared not believe what she thought she saw in his eyes—interest in her. An Adonis like Pete, she told herself, could probably have slim and suave model types, if he wanted them. "Read," he said finally. "Contemplate the crazy scene. Write a little poetry."

"I love poetry," Debbie said.

"Yeah," said Pete. "Everybody does. They just don't buy it. Everybody thinks poetry ought to be free."

"Maybe it should," she said. "Maybe it's the one pure art form left."

He examined her thoughtfully, then nodded. "Good thought," he said. "There's more to you than meets the eye. Though what meets the eye is okay, too."

Debbie, to her chagrin, actually felt herself blush.

"Pilot house," said Pete, entering. "Wheel, engine telegraph—though there's never anybody in the engine room—radar, omega system, navigation computer. She can go anywhere. She just never does, that's all."

"Kind of a waste," Debbie muttered, then dared to add, "and I don't mean only the yacht."

"Me, too?" He smiled. "Maybe. But where else could I get to do my thing and eat regular, too?"

"Is that your thing? The poetry, I mean."

"All the way," he said. "Don't ask me why. Started in college, where I got an engineering degree. The Navy, after that. Some time in Vietnam. I was the only guy who thought the war was funny. In a dark and terrible way, funny. You probably find that hard to understand."

"No," said Debbie, "I think I know exactly what you mean. Somebody once said, on Dinah's show—I forget who it was—he said comedy is about tragedy. I'd like to hear some of your poetry."

"You would?"

"As long as it's free."

Pete laughed and took her arm to lead her out of the pilot house. "We're going to get along fine," he said. "Just fine."

The writers sat now, sprawled in various attitudes, most of them half-consciously meant to express not giving a damn, in the main salon of the motor yacht *Silver Cloud*. How Mickey Samish, who had been invited as one of the guests on the upcoming superspecial, had happened to offer it as a venue for the conference was a story not particularly worth hearing, and if any of them knew the details they had by now forgotten them. The pleasant atmosphere and the free drinks a Chinese steward in a white coat kept bringing were more to the point.

Hefty Pat McCormack, bearded Bill Larkin, and the

older, deceptively straight-faced Harry Crane were there, along with Sheldon Walters, who looked dryly sour, as usual, and there were three others for a lucky total of seven—none of them household names, but all known in the industry as top-ranking jokesmiths. Several production assistants from the various shows, men and women—Debbie among them—hung on the fringes and tried, with their own bright remarks, to keep up with the writers, or else gave up and just laughed. Reduced to the status of gofers for this one occasion, they swallowed their pride, consoled themselves with thoughts of their steady salaries, and went along with it.

Pete Barsocchini, Merv Griffin's producer, called the meeting to order.

"Okay, gang," he said, jiggling an ice-filled soft drink. "What we've got here is a real hodgepodge. It's up to us to pull it all together. They really want this thing to succeed, though I'm not sure pooling all your brilliant talents just this once is the way to do it."

"Just tell me one thing," Harry Crane said. "Why did Merv want comedy writers on a show like this? Why not the regular question-and-answer interview people?"

"Yeah," McCormack said. "What the hell's so funny about murder?"

"Nothing, of course," Pete Barsocchini said. "But this isn't an either-or situation. We do have our talent coordinators taking care of the straight stuff. But Merv isn't sure how this whole thing is going to play."

"Is it legit or isn't it?" asked Larkin, rubbing his beard.

"Beats the hell out of me," Barsocchini said. "Whether this Dale guy is really going to, you know, pull off a Sam Spade or Philo Vance and actually unmask the murderer with all the suspects in one room I'm not sure even he knows. But we've got to build on what we do know. And that is that everybody who is under suspicion in this case has agreed to appear on the show. So I guess Merv figures that even if Dale screws up, the thing will still get a hell of a rating."

"Wait a minute," Larkin said. "I must be missing something here. Are we saying that every guest on the show is a suspect?"

"Oh, no, no," Barsocchini said. "Only some of them are. But Dale is certain that the killer—whoever it is—will be in the room with us."

"You mean lurking in the woodwork someplace like the Phantom of the Opera?" asked McCormack.

"I don't think so," said Barsocchini. "More likely to be somebody in the audience, on the stage crew, the technical crew, somebody from the press, a security guard. Somebody like that. In other words somebody who has a legit reason for being there."

"Oh, that's nice," McCormack said, shifting his bulk in the chair. "That narrows it down to only about seven thousand people. Shouldn't take Dale more than a few seconds to figure it all out."

"I still don't know why it isn't happening on *our* show," McCormack said. "Wasn't Johnny willing?"

"I understand he was, but the network balked. It wasn't even definite for us—as you know—until forty-eight hours ago when we got word that all of Merv's stations had agreed to carry this one show live. In fact, I understand that about forty-two additional stations have jumped onto the bandwagon just for the free ride."

"Tell me one more thing," Crane said. "How the frig did you get all these guys to agree to do one show, and Merv's show at that? It's a hell of a deal for Merv, but it's no secret that these boys don't all play golf together, ya know? How the hell did you pull it off?"

"Well," Barsocchini said, "the original idea was Dale's, and of course Merv went along with it. But the actual work of getting all our lovable prima donnas together is something that I can take a bow for." He allowed a grin to overtake his words. "Knowing very well that he who bows too low may get his butt kicked."

"I figured that much," Crane said, "but *how* did you do it?"

"I knew it would be tough—and that the toughest one to pin down would be Johnny. He doesn't even like to do his own show that much anymore. So I tried him first—and what can I tell you?—he said okay. I guess he realized that it would be the publicity break of the decade and probably the biggest rating for a talk show since Tiny Tim got married on *The Tonight Show* back in the late sixties. Anyway, there's never been any particular ill feeling between Johnny and Merv, although there were a few sparks back when Merv was doing his show opposite Johnny's on CBS."

"And," Sheldon Walters said, "once Johnny agreed to come aboard, I guess the others just didn't want to be left out. So here we are."

"So what are we supposed to do?" Crane said, as seriously straight as Walters was sour. "Write the opening monologue for Merv?"

"Yeah, that's what we were thinking." Barsocchini nodded. "Plus any other lines you think he might drop in here and there through the show. Lines for Johnny and the rest, too. Actually it's a tough assignment for comedy writers—which is why we sent for you guys, 'cause you're the best. I mean, all of us are walking a fine line here on the question of taste. You can't just come out and do Hollywood Freeway or Taco Bell–type jokes about something this serious. And yet Merv feels if you guys do the job right there *will* be a place for some sort of humorous slant or approach to the whole experiment. I mean, we can hardly treat it like a documentary on Auschwitz."

"As I see it," Sheldon Walters said, staring humbly into his gin and tonic, a filter cigarette also in the hand that held it, "the lines won't be that big a problem once we figure out exactly where we're headed. Maybe it would help if we ran down the names of the guests for a minute here."

"One thing you'll have to do," Barsocchini said, "is write introductions a little longer than Merv usually gives the guests. He doesn't have to do twenty minutes when he's introducing Burt Reynolds or Dolly Parton, but none of these people are famous, so we're going to have to do a little more than usual just to bring them into focus for the audience."

"Okay," Bill Larkin said, "who've we got?"

"Well, first," Walters said, "there's this Japanese judo expert or whatever the hell he is. Kazu Hashimoto. Ever since Steve Allen all the talk show guys have gotten lots of mileage out of having various kinds of experts come on and do their thing, showing up the host as some kind of klutz, but I don't think Merv likes to do physical shtick, does he?"

"No," said Peter.

"That's more Johnny's line. Or how about Mike Douglas? Yeah, I like that. Make a note, will you, Debbie? Kazu tosses Mike. And by the way, he pronounces it *Kah*-zu, accent on the first syllable, not like the musical instrument."

Peter Barsocchini glanced at a list in his hand. "Next, Ronnie Fordyce, or as we call him, the bitch of the golden west. Him the people do know because he's on TV. As a matter of fact, you won't have to come up with anything much for him. The problem with Fordyce is shutting him up, not getting him started. Maybe he could even give one of his nasty reviews of the show itself, while it's actually going on."

"Cute idea," Walters said. "Now, what do we do with Mickey Samish?"

"What's the problem with him?" asked Bill Larkin.

"Well, the guy *is* a gangster," Harry Crane said. "We can't have Merv praising him. And on the other hand, we can't have him saying 'Folks, meet one of the great schmucks of all time.' "

"Why not?" asked Pat McCormack, looking like a tired bouncer.

Crane laughed his silent laugh, shaking his head.

"Why don't we give him some shtick to do," Larkin said, "like having him sit there flipping a coin all the way through the show, like George Raft?"

"Why don't you have him sit there flipping George Raft?" McCormack said.

"George Raft has already flipped," Crane said. "He took a cab."

"Oh," McCormack said. "Sorry. I forgot."

"Fellas," Peter said, "we're getting off the track."

"That's what we do for a living," Crane said. "Who's next?"

"J. Duffy Griswold," Barsocchini said, consulting the list. "Merv will naturally treat him as one of the good guys."

"Isn't he sort of a country-and-western type?" asked Walters. "Maybe Merv could talk to him about whatever the hell he did before he got with the FBI. Like maybe he played banjo to pay his way through college, or played football for Alabama or something."

"I'll check that out," Barsocchini said, "but I don't think Merv is going to want to go through the guy's whole story, and I don't think we should anyway. I think we ought to just follow the storyline of the show. It *is* pretty damn powerful. I mean, we've done a lot of theme shows with Merv, but never anything as interesting as this. So while we do want to be clever and creative, there's no sense in getting cutesy-wootsy."

"There never is," Crane said, and Barsocchini couldn't be sure he wasn't putting him on.

"I've got an idea," Walters said, grinning devilishly. "Griswold seems like a totally humorless type. But actually there is no such thing. Even Hitler used to do a little jig and clown around once in a while. Maybe Merv could say something like 'Mr. Griswold, you fellas in the FBI have to take care of so much serious business, but I'll bet that you've got a sense of humor just like the rest of us. What's your favorite joke?' Or 'Who's your favorite comedian?' You know, something like that."

"Not a bad idea," Barsocchini said. "I'll check it out with Merv. Give me a few things like that on paper and we'll see what happens."

"If Griswold doesn't know any jokes," McCormack said, "maybe we could lay a few on him. As a country boy he's certain to know Will Rogers's famous line that he never met a man he didn't like. Maybe he could use the old stock switch that he once had a girl friend with the same philosophy."

Harry Crane stood up, lighted a cigar, and began pacing on the narrow strip of carpet. "You know," he said, "I still can't believe this is really happening. Are grown men and women sitting here and putting together a show where somebody is really going to catch a killer? Is this thing *really* for real?"

"Harry," Barsocchini said, "I don't know a hell of a lot more about this than you do. All we know for sure is that half a dozen people or thereabouts have been killed, and this private eye, Dale—who has a pretty good track record, remember—has talked Merv into believing that (a) he already knows who the killer is, though he can't prove it, and (b) he thinks he might be able to prove it by bringing the guy out into the open, on the show. That's it, period, so let's get to work."

"Well," Sheldon Walters said, shaking his sad head and looking out the porthole at the sun-flecked water, "I just hope to hell there's not another murder. You know, in a way, I feel responsible for the killings in the first place."

"Why the hell do you say that?" asked Larkin.

"Because," Walters said, "I originally suggested Dale as a guest, and that's what seems to have set the killer off. I mean, maybe if it hadn't been for Dale being on TV and talking about how great he was at tracking down murderers—well, maybe the guy would just have knocked off Elmo Finstetter and let it go at that."

"Speaking of Dale," Larkin said, "what do we do with *him?*"

"Well," Walters said, "one thing we've got to work with is his special gimmick for solving crimes. But then, Johnny covered that pretty well with him on *The Tonight Show*. Question: Do we want to tip off the audience right at the top of the show that Dale has cooked this whole thing up so he can point the finger at the murderer?"

"Won't that idea have gotten around anyway?" Crane said. "I mean, obviously Metromedia's going to promote hell out of this show, and the only way they can tell people that it's more than just another of Merv's theme shows—it seems to me—is by telling people that they might actually see a murder case solved, right before their eyes. So how the hell do we play cute if that's the case?"

"I guess you're right," Walters said. "Look, Pete, have you got bios on all these people for us? Sometimes I think better just sitting staring at a piece of paper."

"Yes," said Barsocchini, reaching for a separate stack of papers. "We've got copies for all of you. Here, for example, is Roger Dale's bio. A degree in sociology, service in Vietnam as an MP, for a while in the Tucson sheriff's department, then his own detective agency. Dresses like Beau Brummell, drives an old MG, likes jazz—the forty-year-old kind. Oh, and he's supposed to be something of a wine expert."

"What's that got to do with solving murders?" asked Bill Larkin.

"Probably just something he tacked on to make himself more flashy. You know, part of the *bon vivant* image. On the other hand, we might have a possibility here. Why don't we think about this wine bit?"

"I don't know," Barsocchini said. "It's been about two years since we've done a wine-tasting bit—on Merv's show, anyway. But well, yes, maybe we *could* set up something like that."

"I read somewhere," Larkin said, "that the real sharp wine freakos can actually tell things like the year and the variety."

"I've always doubted that," McCormack said.

"Great," Crane said. "I think most people doubt it, so that sets up a challenge situation. Merv can say something like 'Mr. Dale, most people find it very hard to believe that you wine experts can really tell not only what brand you're drinking but the exact year, or part of the world, or the vineyard, or whatever. Can you really do that?' "

"Good," Walters said. "Whether he can or not, it's something that'll make the audience pay very close attention. And it's visual. Want to put that down, Debbie? Dale does wine-tasting bit."

"This damn thing isn't a show," Crane groaned. "It's a triptych by Hieronymus Bosch."

"Hieronymus who?" asked Larkin.

"Bosch," Crane said. "Used to work with a partner named Lomb. They were in the eyeglass business."

"I remember Lomb," McCormack said, "when he used to work with Abner. You remember Lomb and Abner?"

"Fellas," Barsocchini said, "the class will come to order."

Pete Koskiusco had moved quietly into the room, obviously for a glimpse of the world in which Debbie Weintraub moved, and was standing there, smiling, beside her. He whispered, "Do they go on like this all the time?"

"On," said Debbie, returning his smile. "On and on."

Iris Lundquist was cleaning out the office. Sadly, and for the last time. She was alone in the private room her boss, Dr. Lionel Rand, had occupied before his tragic demise, and with nobody around for her to resent or try to dominate, Miss Lundquist's face had become soft, sympathetic, and much less horsey than it usually was.

Death, when unexpected, brought unbelievable complications, and Iris had been working here, at the request of Rand's family, for several days to put everything in order so that the office could be properly vacated and someone else could take over Dr. Rand's practice. She reflected that if Dr. Rand, when alive, had only listened to her more attentively when it came to administrative matters—done things her way instead of letting his records fall and sprawl all over the place— there wouldn't be such a mess to clean up now.

She'd be hard put to find another job as suitable as hers had been, however. She'd almost despaired of finding *any* job the day she'd walked in to apply here several years ago. She knew why. She was not given to kidding herself and she knew why. Bosses wanted glamor girls, or something close to that, for secretaries and receptionists. And Iris Lundquist, alas, had always been far from that.

When very young she'd learned, through the unthinking cruelty of her playmates, that, facially, she bore a remarkable resemblance to a horse. That had been her nickname at one period—Horsey Lundquist —and God, how it had hurt, though she'd bravely pretended it didn't. Well, ironically, her equine appearance had procured her the best job she'd ever had, or probably ever would have. She'd bet even Dr. Rand himself had not been aware of the subconscious forces that had prompted him to hire her, in preference to several other applicants, at least two of whom could have been starlets. She looked like a horse and Dr. Rand had loved horses.

A tear formed in the corner of her eye.

She removed several boxes of carbon paper and a couple of reams of letterheads from the small steel cabinet Rand had used for his own stationery supplies, not liking to step into the outer office when he needed them. Another inefficiency of his she'd tried to forestall, though she hadn't succeeded.

And then, sandwiched in the pile of unused stationery, she saw a sheaf of several pages with typing on them. She recognized them immediately for what they were. Transcripts. The patients came in, couched themselves, and babbled away; Dr. Rand made note of what they said, then later had her type it up and put it into their case histories. He always said, smiling, he wasn't violating any confidences, because Iris Lundquist, a regular machine of a secretary, could type long passages of anything most accurately without absorbing any of the meaning of the text. That was quite true. She could type and type with her mind completely on other matters—usually show-business gossip, which she adored.

Thus, the pages she looked at now were, as far as she was concerned, pages she'd never seen before. They appeared to have been shuffled out of a complete transcript, and lacked the cover page that would have identified the patient who had once, in the usual agony, uttered these words. She had no idea why Rand had tucked them away here in the supply cabinet, but it didn't surprise her. She'd found patient-admission forms in the medicine cabinet in his private bathroom and checks he hadn't cashed in the wastebasket. Probably he'd put them here meaning to use them, then had become distracted and forgotten them.

With only mild curiosity she read some of what was on the uppermost page of the sheaf.

ANALYST: What do you mean when you say "they" killed your daughter? Just whom do you think of as "they?"
PATIENT: All of them. All of them out there.

She was so sweet, so clean, so innocent. Nobody knew I had her—I tried to keep them all from knowing, so they wouldn't contaminate her. But they got to her all right.

ANALYST: Certain persons?

PATIENT: You know there were no specific persons. What do you think I am, paranoid or something? It was the atmosphere. The permissiveness. The moral decay of our entire society.

ANALYST: And this is what makes you angry?

PATIENT: You're goddamned right. My daughter. Too young, too innocent. Make a list of all the things that can happen to young people these days. She had it all. VD. Hooked on smack. Pot. Alcohol. Pills. Mushrooms. Jail when she stole. A pimp who beat her and made her peddle her ass. Then the last abortion—the hemorrhage—the phone call I got in the middle of the night. Dead when I arrived. And then . . . and then I was *really* alone.

(Patient weeps.)

ANALYST: Go ahead. Crying helps.

PATIENT: But it doesn't help the way the other thing does.

ANALYST: What other thing?

PATIENT: Getting back at them. Ridding the world of them.

ANALYST: What do you mean by ridding the world of them?

PATIENT: Exactly what I say. And as a warning to the rest of the world. Young people aren't the only ones who see the value of activism.

ANALYST: You haven't told me what it is you do.

PATIENT: I've said too much already.

ANALYST: Well, we'll take up this fantasy of yours next time, all right?

Miss Lundquist finished reading the brief passage and nodded to herself. Pretty juicy stuff, though she had no memory at all of having typed it. That was probably because so many of the transcripts contained similar elements—so many patients were bugged by something and thinking about ways to get even. Thank heaven, she herself was adjusted. Normal. Completely calm. Not a hangup anywhere.

She took the papers she had found and dropped them into the wastebasket, where there was already a pile of other papers to be disposed of. She was going to turn away when she saw, upon the desk, the box of ordinary kitchen matches Dr. Rand had sometimes used to light his pipe.

Her eyes began to gleam.

She found a match, struck it, and dropped it into the metal wastebasket. The papers there caught fire, burned. The flames leapt and danced. She stared at them, her eyes becoming even brighter. The usual thrill surged through her, starting in her loins and creeping upward until it engulfed her entire being.

When the papers had all burned she shuddered, sighed, straightened a lock of her hair, opened the window to let out the smoke, and then continued with her task of tidying up the office.

XIX

They were lined up at the doors early in the afternoon, though the show, scheduled so that it would hit both coasts and the vast land in between at the best possible viewing time, airing live in New York at 11:30 P.M., would not begin till 8:30 P.M., its own time. As for those of the studio audience-to-be, some had picnic lunches and a few had camp chairs. A number of the tickets they clutched had been bought at outrageous prices from speculators.

The Las Vegas sun, shimmering, relentless, shone down on everything. The great neon signs stood along the boulevards of the oasis, quiescent now, like night flowers sleeping in the quiet brilliance of the day.

In the cool sanctuary of the hotel, squads of executives, specialists, and technicians were busy with their preparations for the big event. The ninety-minute show would originate from the huge auditorium the hotel maintained for conventions and indoor sports events. It was equipped with a control room and all the necessary gear for a TV broadcast, live and direct, as they kept saying, though what live and *indirect* is, I don't know.

Video and audio men checked circuits and pots and switches (pots are dials, not cooking utensils or drugs) and conversed with each other in their unique jargon, which consisted in part of initials, as jargons tend to do. Like if we wanted to go the same route, their unique jargon could become, to us, their U.J.

A small banquet chamber near the auditorium had been converted into a greenroom, this time actually done in green, including the wall-to-wall carpeting.

Sour-apple green, thought Roger Dale, perhaps because that was his mood today. Until now he had been too busy with his own preparations for the climactic event to become aware of the tension that had been building up inside him. Now, suddenly, it was there, like an invisible hand clutching at his gut and squeezing.

He sat, sipping coffee, Jinny beside him. Ronnie Fordyce, writing notes to himself on a steno pad—and wearing his TV glasses even though he was out in the real world—sat across from him. Cross-legged in a chair next to Ronnie, contemplating rather than drinking a gin-and-tonic in his hand, was Sheldon Walters, showing his usual acerb miniscowl.

"Well," said Roger, looking at Jinny, "what did we leave out? I keep having this feeling we left something out."

"I don't know," said Jinny. "I've gone over it and over it."

Roger had scribbled a checklist and now he looked at it. "Security. Extra tight. Griswold himself is handling it. More FBI agents out there than there were outside Ma Barker's house."

"Yes," said Jinny. "You can spot them a mile away. They all dress so neatly."

"You're right," Walters said, though he hadn't been addressed. "That started in the old *Untouchable* days when a lot of people dressed neatly; therefore they weren't so conspicuous. No more. It's slob time now."

"Oh, I wouldn't say that," said Ronnie mischievously. "A lot of us dress elegantly these days. Roger, here, for example—though perhaps he overdoes it a bit. Or myself, if I may say so. By the way, how do you like the new look?"

"What new look?" asked Walters, willing to play straight.

Ronnie ran his hand over his temple. "The short haircut. A la Sinatra and Tony Curtis. I said to myself, what would make one stand out from the crowd? But, of course, in good taste—"

"Haircuts, for Christ's sakes," said Walters. "Here we sit talking about everything but the business on hand."

"Undoubtedly because the business at hand is so ugly," said Ronnie. He glanced at Roger again. "Okay, let's be serious. Roger, don't explode now when I say this, but are you *sure* you want to go through with this?"

"Why shouldn't I?"

"Because it's all so shaky. So many chances it won't go the way you hope. And if it doesn't, we'll *all* have egg on our faces. You, for failing again, Metromedia, for coming up with a dud after all that ballyhoo, me, for helping to start the whole thing, and for all I know, the janitor who sweeps up all the horse manure after the show."

Sheldon Walters nodded. "I've got to agree with

what I think Ronnie senses. It's scattered—no theme, no integration. Too many off-key notes the way you've set it up, Roger. The guest list for the show. It's crazy. How can all those people possibly be suspects? What, for example, has that Nipponese guru of yours got to do with it? And then all these other people. Like me. We aren't guests, but you asked us to be here anyway. It doesn't figure. I'm just old-fashioned enough to want things to make sense and hang together. Like the plots of the old Bonzo movies."

"Stick around," said Roger, forcing a slight smile. "It'll make sense later."

"I hope so," said Walters, with a sigh. "If this were a scene by Agatha Christie, where all the suspects gather, she'd throw out half the characters you've cranked in. Can I be frank? It's crossed my mind that you're pulling off one gigantic, desperate bluff, figuring the publicity will somehow do you good even though you *don't* actually name the murderer. Come on. Why the hell did you ask me here anyway?"

"For the same reason I asked all the other writers who had anything to do with any of the murder shows. And not only the writers. Danny Moss is here. And Sappho Durkin, who was Rand's publicist. Everybody's here. Everybody I could think of."

"And one you didn't think of," said Jinny.

"Who?" He looked at her.

"Calhoun." She smiled. "We decided to do it, after the show. One of those tacky little chapels they have here."

"Hey, marvelous!" said Ronnie. "Best wishes, dear lady! I'll bring the champagne! And I'll cry! I always do at weddings."

"Thanks, Ronnie," Jinny said, "but we'd like it quiet and private. With Roger as best man. If he will."

"Delighted," said Roger, grinning. "If I'm still alive and kicking."

"Now what does *that* mean?" asked Ronnie, bringing his head up sharply. "Don't tell me you expect to be the next victim! My God, Roger—and there's nothing personal in this—that would be absolutely outstanding!"

"Don't get too excited, Ronnie," said Walters, laughing in spite of himself. "Maybe *you're* supposed to be the next victim."

"Impossible," said Ronnie. "Everybody loves me."

"Hang on to that illusion, Ronnie," said Walters.

"Oh, go fuck yourself," said Ronnie. "Excuse me, Jinny."

The show began with the usual orchestral bang, following the principle that all special shows should start with an earthquake and then work up to a climax. "From Hollywood," a voice shouted, "from New York—and tonight from Las Vegas—"

There were fanfares and stings and a series of kaleidoscopic shots, of the celebrated hosts, of the band, of the crowd, with titles superimposed as the action began. It was the talk show superspecial to end all superspecials, and the tone was one of controlled hysteria with thundering applause as the show got under way. (A thought crossed Roger's mind. What are they applauding for? Nobody's done anything yet.)

Having felt hemmed-in in the greenroom, Roger was now pacing the corridor outside of it, waiting for his call to go on. Jinny, as though ready to restrain him should he suddenly try to climb the walls, paced with him.

"It can't be that," muttered Roger. "Too obvious."

"Can't be what?"

"The wine I'm supposed to drink in the wine-tasting routine. Perfect for poison, of course. But he must know I'd check first."

"Unless he's pulling a fast one. Assuming you'll think it's so obvious you *won't* check."

"That'd be too chancy." Roger shook his head. "He's got something else in mind. And he'll want me to know what it was just before the curtain falls. It'll be one of those things where you say 'Of course! It was right there all the time—should have seen it.'"

"You're saying 'he' now. Is it a 'he?'"

"Since English, unlike old Anglo-Saxon, lacks an inclusive pronoun—they said *thon* in those days—I'm using the only one we've got."

"Ask a simple question, get a lecture on old Anglo-Saxon. But truly, Rodge, do you *really* know who it is? Could Walters have been a little bit right when he said you might be bluffing?"

"Oh, ye of little faith," said Roger.

Onstage, Merv Griffin was saying, "Ladies and gentlemen, as I suppose most of you have heard, we're doing a really unusual show tonight. I know that's something you hear three or four times a week, but in this case I'm talking about *really* unusual."

"A reeeally big shew!" called out Jack Sheldon, Griffin's trumpet-playing sidekick, from the orchestra, doing Ed Sullivan.

"That's right, Jack," Merv said. "And if you read the papers or watch the TV newscasts, of course, you have a general idea what's going on. Quite seriously, all of us talk show hosts—present and past—Johnny, Mike, Dick Cavett, Steve Allen, David Frost, all the rest—were very concerned about the fact that murders have actually occurred on some of our programs. So we all—and let me mention Dinah Shore and John Davidson and Toni Tennille—we've all agreed to appear here in Las Vegas this evening, not so much as a result of my personal invitation, and needless to say I extend it warmly—but because a private investigator named Roger Dale, who's been involved in this case from the beginning, felt it was necessary to have anyone present who had just about any sort of connection with these tragic crimes."

Some people at a table just to the left of the downstage area laughed. The laughter was followed by a shocked hushing.

"It's all right," said Merv. "I can understand why you laughed, though there's nothing funny about murder. But this whole thing does sound so—well, bizarre—that I wouldn't blame some of you if you thought it was all a put-on. But I assure you it's not. You already know about the terrible killings on our programs, and crazy as it sounds, Roger Dale feels he may be able to wrap up the case here this evening. I'm sure we would all appreciate seeing the murderer apprehended and justice done, if only to prevent any more such crimes."

A wave of applause and nodding of heads greeted this observation.

"Well," Griffin continued, "we've got a lot to cover in ninety minutes, so, uh, we'll get right to it. Ordinarily we might hold the fellow I'm about to introduce to one of those next-to-closing spots because he's not only a longtime television favorite but very popular here in Las Vegas, too. In fact, I think he may possibly spend more time working here than he does over at NBC."

As Merv continued his generous introduction of Johnny Carson I recalled that of all the talk show hosts he characteristically has been the most complimentary about guests, which—I suppose—indicates his own self-confidence. Jack Paar used to do more or less the same thing, but his introductions were sometimes so emotional and adjective-laden that they were hard to follow and, in any event, were usually applied to certain guests whereas Merv tends to compliment everyone.

"In any event," he was saying, "since our cohosts tonight are all headliners, we drew names out of a hat to decide on their—uh—running order. This guy has been host of *The Tonight Show* for the past couple of decades—on and off—and I'll resist saying mostly off —so let's welcome . . . Johnny Carson!"

Johnny entered as the band played the Paul Anka–written *Tonight Show* opening theme. He was wearing a dinner jacket, which contrasted oddly with Merv's blazer and tan slacks.

"Going someplace?" Merv said after the applause had died down. He was taking a broad and obvious look at Carson's tuxedo.

"No," Johnny chuckled, "I'm dressed like this—well, first of all because I've got class, Merv—but seriously, as you know, I'm working here in town myself and I go on after we finish this special of yours."

"Good," said Merv, grinning. "As long as you don't feel you're just slumming."

"Actually, I do," Johnny said, in traditional showbiz insult banter of the sort started by radio comedians of the 1930s.

The two genial multimillionaires went on gently topping each other for a few minutes center stage, after which they strolled to the guest-interview area, which was arranged differently for this one show.

Usually when his show originates from Las Vegas Merv doesn't do the sit-down interview bit but chats with his guests center stage in standard variety-show form. In this case, because of the great number of guests assembled for the special, something that looked like a cross between *The Tonight Show* chair-and-couch and a jury box had been arranged by the production's scenic designer.

Backstage, Meg caught Roger in the greenroom, where he had his eyes glued to the TV monitor. "There you are," she said as he rose to greet her. "I wanted to wish you good luck before everything starts. Or do show people usually say 'Break a leg' or something?"

"Interesting, that reverse curse," said Roger. "In World War Two, the O.S.S. agents, parachuting behind the lines, used to say to each other, for good luck, 'Merde,' which is the word of Cambronne, where one of Napoleon's marshals—"

"Roger!" said Meg, in a tone of warning.

"Sorry. Thanks for stopping me. Good luck's what I need. At least no really *bad* luck. Get a good seat?"

"Over to one side, but it's okay. If I don't get back out there quick I may lose it. But I had to see you. All this is so important—everything depending on it—"

"Everything," said Roger, nodding. "Even your piece of this crazy world."

"Mine?"

"If I win, I can take you on as my PR person. Now that you've lost Larry Lawson I may be that one big account you need."

Meg grinned. "Like they say, I'm available."

"I've been meaning to talk to you about that," Roger said with a playful smile.

"It's not my fault you've been working overtime," she said, meeting his gaze.

"Then we'll have to do something about that very

soon. But why," Roger said, "am I standing here like an idiot about to tell you how beautiful you are when I should be concentrating on the matter at hand?"

"You should indeed," Meg said, standing on tiptoe and giving him a schoolgirl kiss on the lips. "Just a sample," she said, smiling. "There's more where that came from."

"Glad to hear it," said Roger. "Be careful out there, okay?"

"Careful?"

"I mean keep your eyes open. The murderer took a shot at you once. When he thought maybe you'd seen and perhaps recognized him. I'm sure he realizes by now that you didn't, because he hasn't tried again—but, anyway, be careful."

"Rodge, do you really think—?"

"No, I don't. Still, be careful."

"I will," she said soberly, with a little shudder.

The sound from a TV monitor caught their attention. They glanced at it and saw that Merv Griffin was introducing Mickey Samish.

Merv knew very well he was walking a fence, introducing Mickey Samish, a well-known mobster, at least to a fairly large ingroup of cognoscenti—but ever the experienced talk show host, Merv was keeping his balance nicely.

"Although I'm sure Mr. Samish has never been on a talk show before, or a television program of any kind, Mr. Dale thought he would make an interesting guest. He's been something of a part-time fixture here on the Las Vegas scene for the past twenty years or so and has important real estate investments all over the Southwest. He's been well acquainted with many of the characters—some shady, some not—who have flocked to this burgeoning mecca since its inception. Here he is—Mickey Samish!"

Samish appeared, frowning uncomfortably in the glare of the spotlights. After a not-exactly-relevant introductory musical passage, bandleader Mort Lindsey took the music out, at which point Jack Sheldon, apparently on his own, played the clear, haunting trumpet notes of the *Godfather* theme. It broke Merv up— and the audience applauded. The best thing about it was that the audience, or most of them anyway, got the idea—and Merv hadn't said a word that could have been deemed libelous or in bad taste.

Samish, dapper and serious—looking more like a nervous talent agent than a mobster—was perhaps distracted by stage fright and missed the point, showing not the slightest negative reaction.

But as Merv began his conversation with Samish, Johnny Carson stuffed his cheeks with something— Kleenex, probably—and began doing Marlon Brando as the Godfather. The camera caught it. Merv turned and caught it. So did Samish. Surprisingly, he seemed to take it in stride. The shifting of his thin mouth might almost have been a smile. "All you guys," he said, "think that just because somebody starts out in one walk of life he's got to stick in that same rut from there on in. Well, you're wrong, at least in my case."

"What walk of life *did* you start in?" asked Griffin, with his usual quickness of mind.

"Listen," Samish said. "In my old neighborhood you either became a rabbi or you went to the chair, ya know?"

"I grew up in such a tough neighborhood," Johnny Carson said, "that there was a rabbi who went to the chair."

"Johnny Carson, you grew up in Nebraska," Merv

said, playing the good-natured straight. "You probably didn't even know what a rabbi was until you were thirty years old."

"I don't even know what a rabbi is now," Carson said.

"Tell you what," said Merv. "Sammy Davis Junior opens here next week. I'll have him explain it to you."

At this point, Samish, perhaps annoyed at having lost the attention of the audience, pulled a fifty-cent piece out of his pocket and began flipping it, George Raft style. This broke up both Carson and Griffin. Backstage—peering from a vantage point he'd found —grinning Sheldon Walters was glad the gag played well. It wasn't usual for writers to give guests bits of business, but what the hell, there had to be a first time for everything. He was glad Samish had enough of a sense of humor to go for the idea.

I was backstage, too, waiting to go on, watching a monitor in a dressing room. I had a sudden odd feeling—almost ESP—of the kind I suppose everybody gets once in a while. I looked at Samish, hamming it up there, as though wondering why he hadn't tasted the joys of performing before an audience before, and I visualized a *caporegime*—a boss of bosses—somewhere, scowling at the Mick clowning like this and asking his associates if maybe they shouldn't call Detroit or someplace and find out who was available to do a job.*

After a brief and somewhat stiff interview with J. Duffy Griswold had taken place (it turned out he

---

* Most of you must know by now how they found Mickey Samish's bullet-riddled body in that pizza joint in Phoenix. There was more to his murder than his appearance on the TV show; a fall-out over skimming was the rumor. I can't claim that I actually foresaw this—but it does leave a funny feeling.   S.A.

did play the harmonica, but refused to do it in public), Dinah Shore—having picked up John Davidson's wild suggestion at the summit meeting—appeared in a bulletproof vest to which had been sewn a number of sequins and spangles. "It's Cardin's latest, for talk show hosts," she quipped. "Or former talk show hosts," she added wistfully, her own series having gone off the air.

Merv made no cracks about that, treated her with nothing but fondness, and the audience responded and loved her, too. I was thinking that the pacing of the show was going well, even if only more or less by accident.

Phil Donahue, playing it straight, now took over with J. Duffy Griswold. By prearrangement he took his wireless mike out into the audience and relayed questions about the responsible use of television, about the talk show murders, about police powers, and where to draw the line, as Griswold, stolid and somewhat uncomfortable—but fielding the questions well enough—noticeably kept himself from glancing to the side at Mickey Samish. Ironically, it was what he frequently criticized the public for when it came to organized crime; don't look at it and it might go away.

Merv's next guest was yours truly. I was introduced with the cliché "the granddaddy of the talk shows" line, after which Griffin opened with an apology. "Steve," he said, "every other time you're on our show —or any talk show, now that I think of it—you always sing some new song you've written. But tonight, as you know, we've got so darn much to cover that if you don't mind we won't have you do a vocal, okay?"

"I won't if you won't," I said. "In this town people want their singers to be either Italians or rednecks anyway."

Merv laughed, as he always does so readily. "You know," he said, "I just remembered that explanation you gave me on my show a few months ago about the reason neither you nor I have ever had reputations as big, romantic singing stars. Do you remember what I'm talking about?"

"Yes," I said. "It's because, although you and I have been professional singers for over thirty years, have made vocal records, and sung a great deal on television, we have nevertheless rarely been *perceived* as singing stars, and the reason for this is that we don't *look* like singers."

"What do you think you look like?" Merv said, going back into the remembered routine.

"I look as if I teach history at a small midwestern college," I said. "I don't have that neurotic, greasy, romantic look that male singers are supposed to have."

"And," Merv asked, "what do I look like, if I don't look like a singer?"

"You look like you're in real estate," I said.

We traded a few more ad-lib pleasantries, briefly discussed the main purpose of the show, and then did a quick two-piano number sitting back to back on one shared bench. Merv plays much better piano than people generally recognize and both of us are constantly receiving requests to play, on television, more than we do. Consequently our four-hands-on-the-keyboard number, a purposely flashy rendition of the old standard "Tea for Two," was well received.

During the applause for the number Merv shouted, "We'll be right back," and the commercial powers took it away.

"Our next guest," said Merv, "is someone who hates TV, but maybe that's a good thing, because his perceptive and penetrating reviews keep us all on our toes. I think we can say that his prodding—as irritating as it is to some of us sometimes—has contributed to the excellence that you, the viewers, do occasionally find on TV, in spite of what Ronnie Fordyce claims to the contrary. And here he is, everybody—TV critic Ronnie Fordyce!"

Fordyce walked out, smooth, smiling, quite at ease. After a brief exchange at center stage, Merv led him to a desk resembling the one from which he usually made his broadcasts. There was a chroma-key screen behind it on which the fast-moving stills that were always part of his presentation would be flashed as he talked.

"I've had to meet some pretty fast deadlines before," said Ronnie, with his deceptively innocent boyish grin, "but this is the first time I've been asked to review a show while it was in progress. Well, what have we here in this big, overblown superspecial, this talk show to end all talk shows?"

He paused, his smile hanging, to let his question sink in.

"I can only say," bombshelled Ronnie, "that I hope it does."

Some of the audience didn't know whether to laugh or not.

"What we have here, ladies and gentlemen," continued Ronnie, "is a veritable treasure chest of bad taste even Chuck Barris couldn't achieve. Look at Miss Shore's outfit—a bulletproof vest done up in colors that don't even harmonize. Look at Mr. Samish over there, flipping his coin." (The camera looked, which meant the director was on his toes, for Ronnie was departing from his script a little.) "By romanticizing people like that we only play into their hands and give them greater power. But let's look at the opposing team, too. Mr. J. Duffy Griswold, of the FBI. Where are all those cops who are never around when you need them? Lately some of them are on talk shows, gulping in the publicity so they'll get larger appropriations with which to build their empires."

"The son of a bitch," Griswold murmured to himself. Fortunately the camera wasn't on him. It wouldn't have required a lip-reader to know what he said.

Ronnie went on, blithely. "But you do like it, don't you? You in the audience, and all of you out there, eyes glued to your sets, your brains dulled by the *real* opium of the people. So it's really your fault for responding to such tripe as this very show—or to the mindless game shows and sitcoms with their canned laughter—my God, they even point out for you what's supposed to be funny—that clog the eye of the tube like so many cataracts! Good luck to all of you, and to the TV industry as it stands today. You deserve each other. And good viewing—if you can find it."

The applause that followed was nervous, mixed with laughter and a good deal of booing.

In the control room, Peter Barsocchini, the producer, said to a Metromedia executive, "I don't know if that one went over or not. Maybe, in some perverse way, it did. Well, dammit, we always wanted to do something daring."

A quick playoff by the band covered what might have been a moment of uncomfortable silence. Ronnie took his place with the other guests and cohosts—talk about too many chiefs and not enough Indians—and Merv stepped to the runway again to bring on his next visitor.

"You know," Merv said, "it's interesting if you run down the list of talk show hosts—or hostesses—and think of what they all did *before* they headed up talk shows. Quite a few of us were singers. Besides Steve Allen and myself there's also Dinah Shore, John Davidson, Toni Tennille—Jim Nabors went the talk show route a few years ago—and with my memory I'm probably forgetting some others. But our next guest was a popular band singer with the great old Kay Kyser orchestra back around the same time, I guess, that I was working with Freddy Martin. Steve," Merv called out on a sudden thought, "you never sang with any big bands, did you?"

"The hell I didn't," I said. "I used to sing with Glenn Miller."

"You did not!" Merv said.

"I did, too," I said. "Of course I was lying in bed at home at the time and Glenn was on the radio, but I did sing with him."

"But all seriousness aside," Merv said, throwing my own stock line at me, "Mike Douglas did sing with Kay Kyser and he went on to great success in the talk show field, heading up his own popular syndicated show for the past umptey-klump years. Welcome, please, Mike Douglas!"

Mike walked on in a dapper navy blue suit and genial smile, snapping his fingers to the rhythm of his own theme song.

"Welcome, Mike," Merv said. "I thought it would be good to have you handle our next guest because you like offbeat sports. This should be right down your alley."

"Thank you, Merv. Yes, I am a big sports freak and I can't wait to talk to our next guest here. We've all heard about commandos and Green Berets and CIA agents of the zero-zero-seven type, but what most of us don't realize is that the art of dirty tricks was brought to a high level of refinement in Japan centuries ago. The warriors there developed something called *ninjitsu*, which encompasses all the familiar arts —karate, judo, kung fu—and adds a few lesser-known techniques. I'm told they found ways to make themselves invisible before your very eyes and even to walk on water! At least, that's what they say. Anyway, we're about to meet the last practitioner of *ninjitsu*, the remarkable"—he paused, knowing he'd get it wrong in spite of his rehearsal—"the remarkable Kazu Hashimoto!"

Yup. Wrong. Kazoo, he said, like the thing you play by humming into it. Well, what the hell.

Kazu Hashimoto came out, showing a slightly embarrassed grin, which revealed two gold-plated teeth. He walked forward lightly and with a springy step, like some exceptionally agile pastiche of a full-sized man. The spotlights deepened the myriad tiny wrinkles of his yellow-tanned parchment skin. He wore a white *judogi* and the black obi of his rank.

"Hi, there, Hashimoto-san," said Mike, walking up to him.

"Good evening, Mike Dougras-san," said Kazu, bowing.

Douglas assayed a purposely clumsy bow in return. It got a chuckle. "I like the bow bit," said Mike, "but in America we shake hands." He extended his.

"Unsanitary," said Kazu. "*Tak'san* germs. But I do, anyway." He stuck out his own hand.

In the next instant Mike was somersaulting in the air. It had been prearranged, and Kazu had carefully shown Mike how to fall without hurting himself. Grinning, Douglas got up, dusted off his new blue suit, acknowledged the applause, and returned to Kazu's side. "How did you do that, anyway?"

"Oh, you easy to frip, Dougras-san," said Kazu, also grinning. "Maybe not Griffin-san over there. He putting on weight."

A camera blinked its red eye on Merv, who feigned indignation and said, "Mike, you put him up to that!"

The audience was loving it.

Mike now began to question Kazu about the practice of *ninjitsu*, keeping it short and basic so it wouldn't slow the pace of the show. Presently—reading some of the questions off cue cards—he asked for a demonstration of the old man's prowess. "I make myself so you no can see me now," said Kazu. "I go back there." He pointed backstage, where, seen only by those onstage, several fringe personalities like Debbie Weintraub, Sheldon Walters, and Jinny were watching, grinning, and enjoying. "Pretty soon return."

Mike faced the audience as Kazu ducked into the wings. "Is he really going to make himself invisible?" he asked them, in his genial way. "Be a handy thing when the bill collectors come around. Or for those times when you tell a bum joke and wish you could disappear." He looked at Johnny Carson. "You know what I mean by that, don't you, Johnny?"

"Now, cut that out!" Carson said, purposely doing Jack Benny.

Mike glanced rearward. "Now, where's Hashimoto-san? Where did he get to?"

"Oh, here I am, Mr. Dougras!" cried Hashimoto, popping up from behind a large potted plant that had been placed, for the purpose, stage right near the orchestra. How he'd put himself there without being seen was a puzzle—perhaps it had been by misdirection when everyone's attention had been upon Mike and Johnny, or perhaps it had been a combination of sheer swiftness of movement and blending with the scenic background. Anyway, there he was, grinning triumphantly.

Mike turned to the audience. "How about that, folks?"

Prolonged applause.

And another commercial break.

Returning to center stage, Merv said, "As I mentioned earlier, a private investigator by the name of Roger Dale has impressed many law enforcement authorities by his ability to solve crimes without ever visiting the crime scene, or even necessarily interviewing a suspect. Many of you will recall the case of the park strangler, the missing heiress, and the heart attack murder, which Dale solved at long range. But Roger Dale happens to be more than a mere private eye. He is also acknowledged as one of the country's leading wine experts and often sits on panels to rate wines on behalf of the industry. And so we thought tonight he'd be willing to take part in a tasting demonstration. I'm sure you'll find it fascinating. And maybe we can also find out if he has any new theories about what have come to be known as the talk show murders. Now, since Steve Allen likes crime—as a spectator, I hope, and not a participant—and has written at least one book on the subject, I'm going to ask him to talk to Roger Dale. Steve?"

I came forward again, shook hands with Roger, then brought him back to where the chairs were lined up for our preliminary talk, during which the wine-tasting table would be set up, off to the right.

"Before we get to the wine tasting, Roger," I said, once we were seated and relaxed, "I wonder if you've made any progress on the talk show murders. We all know you've been working on it." I'd decided on straight questions—the subject matter hardly lent itself to comedy.

"As a matter of fact," said Roger, "I think I've identified the killer."

This had been worked out beforehand, and I said what I was supposed to say, which was "How?"

"Well, in a way he put the finger on himself. As for absolute proof—the kind that stands up in court—I don't have it. But I think once we know who it is that kind of proof can be dug up by the really professional policemen who have been working on the case."

"Now, wait a minute," I said, looking at the audience, taking them into my confidence, "are you saying you actually know who the killer is?"

"Pretty sure of it." Roger nodded. "Of course, nothing is ever a hundred percent certain, but I'm sure enough about it to stick my neck out."

"Then by all means go ahead and stick away. Right here, in front of God and everybody."

"The killer," said Roger—and I must say he delivered the line with excellent timing—"is here among us at this very moment."

XX

The audience didn't actually gasp aloud in perfect unison, as a stage direction might have said had this been a play, but there was, so help me, an approximation of that. I could feel sudden attentiveness coming into sharp focus—something you can't explain unless you've stood before an audience and gone through it. Like the arts, talk show interviewing is done as much with the gut as by set patterns of mind.

Now, the general outline of what would happen had been set and agreed upon by all hands, but the way it would go precisely could not possibly have been rigidly scripted. It was Merv's show, overall, but we cohosts had an equal responsibility to mold its form as it went along. Without thinking about the matter in so many words, I knew it was too early to name the murderer. Once that was done the show itself was either dead or could dissolve into chaos.

"Before you mention any names, Roger," I said, "we'd be interested to know how you arrived at your conclusions."

"Of course," said Roger. "And a certain amount of

explanation is very much in order, if only because there's still a chance—however small—that I'm wrong. There always is in any serious crime, even those which seem open-and-shut. That's why we have trials, which is as it should be. If I'm wrong—or even if I'm right and can't prove it legally—I could be opening myself for a libel suit."

Merv walked in again. "Yes," he said. "You, me, the TV stations, everybody. Sisters, cousins, aunts. Please keep that in mind."

"I will, Mr. Griffin," Roger said. "Explaining how I got to all this may make it more plausible and less— sue-able. I hope. Well, let's see. How shall I begin?"

"You might start by outlining your method of attacking a case," I said. "You've done it before, but there are probably millions watching who haven't heard it yet. And as far as I know, it's unique. I'm thinking of this psychological profile you put together on a suspect."

"All right. It's a complete work-up of whoever might have committed the crime—identity, of course, unknown at the start. Physical characteristics are entered if they're known—from witnesses glimpsing the killer, for example—and they alone solve some cases; but what really counts is the way the killer ticks inside. After I begin feeding every scrap of data I can find into a psychological profile, a person I would recognize when I saw him—or her—gradually begins to form."

"Him. Her," I said. "I take it you weren't sure which, at first."

"That's right. Only that the perpetrator was some kind of nut. Of course, we could say that *all* murders are the result of emotional disturbance, either chronic or temporary. Those of us who refrain from murdering —and perhaps we've all at least considered it at one time or another—are making the necessary adjustment to society that we regard as mental good health. But something clicks out of place in the mind of a murderer, and he translates his murderous fantasy into action. Am I getting too—?"

"No, fascinating," I said. "Keep going."

"Well, even quirky motives often have a rationale," said Roger. "One the murderer has built up in his own mind. The clue to this—in the case of the talk show murders—was in the character of the victims."

"You mean they had something in common?" I knew very well they did, but this is how you keep an interviewee going, the way you keep rolling a hoop with a stick.

"Yes," said Roger. "They all would be considered, by traditional standards, to be sexually immoral."

I saw a taping of the show later with the director, Dick Carson. Dick is highly competent at his craft, and a charming fellow. No doubt he's both tired of and accustomed to being introduced as Johnny Carson's brother, but I thought you'd be interested. Anyway, from seeing the tape I know that at this point Dick called for a close-up of Griswold, who was glaring intently as he listened. Good shot. Directors often act by instinct, too.

"So there was this pattern among the victims," said Roger, continuing, a camera now back on him, "and on top of that the killer sent me a communication that bolstered this impression."

"What form of communication was this?"

"I'll get to that in a minute." A real pro, like Merv or Mike or Johnny, couldn't have stretched it out any better than Roger was doing. The suspense was palpable. Except that I don't think Roger was doing it consciously; he was just saying what he had to say.

"The point here," he continued, "is that his communications carried the suggestion that the state of society today is far more—to use a common word—permissive than it was in the past, or than it has any right to be. It was an immediate clue. The killer was not too young. The current sense of moral breakup all around us stuck in his craw."

At that a wave of applause swept the audience.

"That applause is interesting," I said. "I interpret it to mean that a good many of you here today are concerned about the relative moral collapse of our society. At least I hope that's what you have in mind. I'd hate to think you were applauding the murderer for killing sinners."

Nervous laughter and a smattering of further applause.

"But I don't see how the moral-decay factor narrowed it down a great deal," I said. "A lot of us in the Grecian Formula set feel that way. And some young people, too. In fact, I'd say *most* Americans are dismayed by the amount of street crime, narcotics addiction, organized crime, violence, child abuse, pornography, family breakups and all that sort of thing that has become almost epidemic today."

"Indeed they are," said Roger. "And high time. But I would guess that you and I have a certain degree of compassion and tolerance for the frailty of human behavior that our killer does not have; and even those of us who don't certainly do not consider it justified to kill people whose conduct we disapprove of."

"You know," I said, "I have the impression that this case is actually one tiny piece of an enormous mosaic a pattern of increasing cruelty, sadism, and violence that touches every part of our society."

"I'm afraid you're right," Roger said. "You see it in

the increased numbers of assaults, rapes, the kind of vandalism or killing the newspapers call senseless, anti-Semitism, the resurgence of the Ku Klux Klan and Nazi groups. It's all part of a broad and very ugly picture."

"But," I said, "to return to the matter at hand, why do you suppose it is—if you're right—that our killer thinks the solution to sin is to kill sinners? Do you think this person is someone with a misinterpreted religious background, a sort of Victorian or Moral Majority attitude that—"

"Perhaps," said Roger. "But I don't think that's where the real explanation lies. No, I think the killer has suffered some sort of personal shock which he sees as *caused* by the sick state of our society. The people he's killed are—what shall I say?—are, to him, *carriers* of this sickness."

"All right. We follow your thinking. So what came next?"

"Well, it was impossible to build biographies of all the possible killers," said Roger, "all of whom were only loosely and vaguely suspect anyway. But at least signs of moral indignation could be looked for. The funny thing is, a surprising number of people met that criterion. Meanwhile, the murderer was covering his tracks. Skillfully. He had to be smart—even brilliant. At one point I even checked the local Mensa membership."

"That's the high-IQ society of those in the upper two percent, isn't it?" I said.

"Yes. I wanted to see if any names I'd recognize were there. Mensans like to say to each other, 'If you're so smart, why ain't you rich?' Because a lot of them are not, and there may be food for thought in that. One of the most brilliant guys I know—a minor novelist up in Washington state—is a life member and he's a churchmouse. But the question implies, among other things, that a high-powered mind by no means guarantees success, or even rational behavior. And there's a certain form of nuttiness, of which paranoia is one aspect, in which the subject seems to be quite normal at all times, *except* those moments when he gets into his particular fantasy. He can even make *that* sound reasonable and convincing, so that you don't wake up till afterward. The way the pitch of a good bunco artist or political candidate will grab you. These types are the most difficult to diagnose, and when it comes to crime, the most difficult to catch."

"Yes," I said. "You run into people like that in the context of not only politics but religion. They seem just as normal as you and me until you get on their pet subject and then suddenly you realize you're talking to a real cuckoo. Well, speaking personally, I'd love to hear you go on all night like this, but I see Merv over there making certain nervous circular movements with his forefinger, and I'm sure I speak for probably half the nation when I say we're waiting to hear who you think the murderer is."

That's what the transcript from the show says I said. Do I really shatter grammar that way when I'm ad-libbing? Maybe it would sound too stuffy if I didn't.

The camera at this point took a tight shot of the glamorous blonde, red-lipped Toni Tennille, sitting forward on the edge of her chair, her pretty brows knotted in an intense, concentrated frown. The shot widened out to reveal John Davidson, every hair in his boyish coiffure in place, patting her hand in an apparently unconscious comforting gesture. And when the camera pulled back even more there was Phil

Donahue, standing, like a football coach at a crucial moment in the game.

Were any of *them* suspects? Some viewers must have thought so. I wasn't too sure myself. Not about anybody. The way Roger was shaping it up, I could have been under suspicion.

"Among the killer's traits that emerged," said Roger, "was a high sense of drama—a fondness for twists and ironies. He at once saw me as his prime nemesis, and that's why he couldn't resist communicating with me directly. He didn't get in touch with the police or the FBI. He sent notes with pasteup letters which couldn't easily be traced, and then—with real daring—a tape in which he attempted to disguise his voice."

"Attempted?" I asked.

"The tape had what cryptographers call a double encipherment. He disguised his voice, then disguised the disguise itself by altering the tape speed. I stumbled on this and—finally—recognized the voice."

"You were quite sure? Still are?"

"Yes. But it's no crime to send a tape," said Roger. "Even one that borders on admission. I cross-checked carefully to see whether I couldn't establish the element of opportunity. Times and places that put the killer in clear contact with the victims. On some occasions he was, but on other occasions he was not, or else there was no proof that he was on hand. Never mind the details right now, but he took care to establish alibis for at least some of the murders, and that destroys the tape as even corroborative evidence."

"Do you go along with that, Mr. Griswold?" I asked, abruptly looking at the assistant FBI director. A camera focused upon him.

"Can't say without knowing what Mr. Dale has, exactly," grumbled Griswold. "If you mean do I think evidence should be court-admissible and effective in the prosecution, yes. Looking for that kind is what makes our job so tough."

I turned to Roger again. "I'm as anxious to hear who it is as anyone else. But let's be sure we cover everything, now. Do you know how the murderer obtained the poisons that were used?"

"Not in exact detail. But all were available, and could have been obtained in several ways by a resourceful person—especially one who appeared respectable and would not be suspected of criminal intent. One murder was by a hatpin or something thrust into the brain. This departure suggested that the killer was not a professional criminal, for they become creatures of habit and use the same m.o. over and over again. In the case of Dr. Rand—who was probably about to reveal the perpetrator's identity—the murderer had to act hastily and so used a gun."

"How did he know Rand was about to blow the whistle?"

"Everybody knew. It was in Ronnie Fordyce's column."

"All right, Roger," I said. There was no putting it off any longer. "Who done it?"

"The person," said Roger slowly, "who is ready to murder me, as the next victim, here and now."

"What?" I said. As an interviewer I'd occasionally been caught off base before—but never like this. Roger had said nothing about this part of it when we'd roughed out the show.

The silence was a rubber band just before it breaks. On a nearby monitor I saw that the director was calling for reaction shots of Johnny, Dinah, Merv—everybody.

By the time Roger and I were visible on the TV

screen again Roger said what I should have said some time ago, but by now had almost forgotten. "Shall we go to the wine table now?"

"Forget the wine table. Who done it?"

"I need the wine table to bring it out. You'll see."

"Well," I said, "we all thought that since David Frost is a man of the world he ought to officiate at the wine-tasting challenge, so we'll bring David out right now. Ladies and gentlemen, welcome, please, that charming English gentleman who is probably the only one present to have achieved stardom on two continents; for several years host of his own talk show and recently a producer of important specials for the networks—Mr. David Frost."

David entered, smiling as he acknowledged the applause and theme fanfare. He was wearing evening clothes, but of a more conservative cut than the Vegas nightclub tux Johnny Carson was sporting.

"Good evening, David," I said. "It's all yours."

"Thank you, Steve," he said. "Ordinarily, ladies and gentlemen, it would be my pleasure to entertain you, to interview you—perhaps to see if any of you might be candidates for one of our *Guinness Book of World Records* shows—but we have more important business to attend to at the moment, as I'm sure you'll all agree."

Three bottles had been set upon the table, along with three wineglasses, a corkscrew, a blindfold, a napkin, a bread knife, and a loaf of French bread. Writer Pat McCormack had suggested that Stan Kann come out and do a shtick with similar props in his clumsy way, but the idea had been voted down.

At the table, Roger said, "Okay, let's try it. Knowing I'd be tasting wine, what would the murderer do?"

"Poison it?" Frost said. "That obvious?"

"We can't dismiss it because it's obvious, Mr. Frost. He'd count on that. Mind you, I'm not *certain* the wine is poisoned, but it definitely has to be checked out."

"How?"

"I've got an expert waiting. I didn't mention him before—to anyone except Merv—because I didn't want to tip my hand. My assistant, Jinny Cantu, has him ready. He's Dr. Milton Klingerman, a toxicologist at USC. Can I bring him on?"

"By all means!" David said.

Steered by Jinny, backstage, Dr. Klingerman came into the lights with a businesslike step and a professional, serious expression. He was a small, fiftyish man in a conservative gray suit and a chaotically patterned tie of the sort some wives give their husbands for Christmas. To avoid slowing the pace Frost refrained from questioning him, even briefly, about his background; he rather looked the part of a toxicologist and that was enough.

"If there's poison in any of that wine," said Roger, "I'd taste it immediately if I wanted to try. The French bread's to munch on between sips—neutralizes the taste buds and lets you detect all the subtleties. What you look for is the percentage of Brix, which in most varieties shouldn't exceed twenty-five."

"We'll take your word on that," said Frost with a slight smile.

"Anyway," Roger continued, "even a little taste of poison would be dangerous, as I'm sure you understand." He was spinning the handle of a corkscrew, opening the first bottle. He glanced at its label before he handed it to Dr. Klingerman. "Good Lord, a Chateau Haut-Brion '47! The year of the century! If the guy's poisoned this one, that's a *real* crime!"

Klingerman poured a tot of wine into one of the glasses, then sniffed it. Frowning, he took a vial and eyedropper from his pocket and dropped a substance into the glass. He held it to the light and examined it closely. Then he looked at Roger and shook his head, mouthing a silent no.

"Are you sure?"

For an answer Dr. Klingerman brought the glass to his lips and tossed down some of what he had tested.

The audience gasped. One woman shouted "No!"

"I say," David Frost said, "that *is* professional confidence."

"Okay, the next one," said Roger, examining the label as he opened it. "An undated California Cabernet Sauvignon. It's a relatively inexpensive kind that's actually damned good, a fact some wine snobs might never learn. Did you know, by the way, Steve and David, that a hundred years ago when all the French vines were attacked by a vine louse, the *Phylloxera*, they sent them American grafts to save the vineyards? French wine, by ancestry, is really California wine."

"Believe it or not," I said, "I did know."

"Oh? Are you a connoisseur?"

"No, but actor Michael Caine is. In fact, he's in the wine business. We had dinner one evening and he contributed considerably to my education. Wait a minute, Roger—you've got *me* doing it now! Let's get on with this, shall we?"

Klingerman did his chemical routine again, and the Cabernet turned out to be unpoisoned. A camera took a tight close-up of the remaining bottle—a Sylvaner from the famed Haardt vineyards near Mannheim. Klingerman, after testing, drank this one, too. Half the audience expected him to fall down dead. It's what gives events like the Indy 500 such a high audience rating, I suppose.

"All right," said David. "They're clean."

"Thought they would be," Roger said. "Our murderer has something else in mind."

"Roger," said Merv, walking in again and signaling the others to join him, "I've got to be blunt, largely because we haven't much more time. This is too serious for strained tact or beating around the bush. Do you *really* know who the murderer is, or are you pulling off a colossal bluff, hoping he'll get scared and come forward?"

Roger met Griffin's firm stare. "I *do* know who sent me that tape, and who is probably the murderer—even if we can't prove it."

"Then," said Phil Donahue earnestly, "for God's sake name the man or you're going to have more people dying of heart attacks here in the studio than the murderer himself did away with."

A flurry of nervous laughter ran through the audience, and one young woman gave a half gasp, half teenage rock audience yelp, as if to express agreement with Donahue's point.

Roger Dale swung his eyes in a slow azimuth across the stage. "All right, Phil, I will," he said. "Unless"— a long pause—"unless the man who sent me the tape wants to come forward himself, right now. It is a man, by the way. We can say that much now."

Silence.

"Godamighty," Johnny Carson said. "The tension is beginning to make *me* feel guilty."

John Davidson's mouth hung open.

"I'm scared," said Toni Tennille.

Dinah Shore put an affectionate maternal arm around her shoulders.

"The man we're looking for," Roger said, "ought to realize that he'll be publicly identified sooner or later because we know so much about him now. Remember that I said I thought a personal shock had pushed him into his state of mind? I don't want to get into gossip, but this man once had a wife the public never knew about. For reasons that ought to be clear soon, the marriage didn't work out—in fact, it was entered into before the man realized that he couldn't be a conventional husband, even if he tried. My assistant, Jinny Cantu, dug up this information, which, under ordinary circumstances, we'd simply consider none of our business. As it happens, the wife in question behaved badly—had affairs on the side—and turned into a moral alley cat. Drinking, drugs, all the rest. So what I'm saying to the murderer now is that while we can't condone what he's done, we *can* understand why. And I hope he now realizes that his best chance of at least lessening his retribution is to give himself up, right now."

There was another pause in which the heartbeat of the universe itself seemed suspended, and then Ronnie Fordyce, in the end chair, next to Griswold's, rose slowly and with a grave expression on his face. His long-lashed eyes were so open and still that even the normal involuntary blinking was undetectable. His step was quite firm, lacking its usual Jack Benny swagger, as he walked to the wine table and came to a halt in front of Roger.

"I sent you those tapes, Roger," he said quietly.

Roger nodded. "Yes, Ronnie. I know you did."

"But," he said, "and I can prove this, I think—I didn't commit those murders."

"Oh?" The syllable was noncommittal, almost sarcastic.

It was accompanied by one raised eyebrow.

Ronnie sighed. "It was stupid. Worse, it was bad taste—I see that now. The hell of it is that I worship good taste above all other things. But just this once I lost my head—couldn't resist. Maybe I did sympathize with the murderer's purpose in attacking the epidemic of moral decay. Maybe I kind of identified with him. Mostly, it was an impulse."

"This is getting hard to swallow, Ronnie."

"How can I explain it? It seemed such a delicious idea to get into the game and really take part—I've always been fascinated by homicide, as you know. And I truly didn't think it would do any harm. Call it juvenile mischief. All I can say is *mea culpa*. I just hope this doesn't blow my whole career." He looked directly into the nearest camera. It wasn't conscious performing —he was utterly sincere. "Forgive me, everybody out there. Forgive the contempt I must have shown you from time to time. Somehow, pushing so hard, I lost sight of good manners, which is really what good taste is all about. In my heart, I really have the greatest respect for all of you—love all of you, as fellow human beings. And I wish—"

He seemed on the brink of tears.

"Ronnie," said Roger cautiously, "this hair shirt bit could be another ploy."

Ronnie shook his head. "It's not. As for the murders, I've got fifty-seven kinds of alibis for most of them. They'll stand up not only legally but to your satisfaction, too. Some may be embarrassing, with society looking upon certain activities by 'consenting adults' the way it still does, but fighting a murder charge would be a lot more embarrassing. We can go into all that later. The point I'm making now is that I'm not at all afraid of being accused because I know it's impossible to pin it on me. I'm not your man."

Roger said, "To tell you the truth, Ronnie, I had lingering doubts you were, even when it seemed likely. I called on you, remember, and hinted I knew who the murderer was. I thought I might detect a reaction. I remember thinking how incredibly cool you were, if you *were* the murderer. And—we might as well make it public—you were instrumental in setting up this show." He drew a deep breath. "All right, Ronnie. I think I believe you."

Mike Douglas chimed in. "But where does that leave us, Roger? It looks to me as though you still haven't identified the murderer, as you promised."

"Let me think," said Roger.

"All right, you do that," said Merv Griffin, not concealing his irritation, "and while you're thinking we can have a commercial."

As the commercial was rolled in and the cameras went off, Merv was the first to say what we were all thinking. He faced Roger squarely. "I'm sorry, Dale," he said. "You blew it. Frankly, the whole show falls flat on its face now. The best thing you can do now is fold your tent and steal away, silently or otherwise."

Sheldon Walters emerged from the wings and trotted onstage, up to the group around the table. His badgerlike countenance had its usual lugubrious look, only this time it was the way we all felt. "Merv," he said, "I was just talking to Pat and some of the others. You can still smooth this over. Go on with Roger's wine-tasting bit as though nothing has happened. The murderer might *still* make a play and reveal himself. I know that's a long chance, but it's the only one you've got."

David Frost shot quick looks at Merv and John Davidson. "Maybe Walters is right. What do you think?"

Merv frowned. "I don't know."

"I'm for it," said Davidson.

"So am I," Dinah said.

"Me, too, I guess," said Mike Douglas. "What's the producer think?"

"No time to find out now," said Merv, glancing at the clock over the control room. "Well, dammit, let's go on with it! We can't be any worse off than we already are!"

Merv returned to his on-camera smile in the nick of time as the little red light on the center camera came on. Off-camera, Walters scuttled backstage again, and the other hosts returned to their seats.

"Win a few, lose a few," said Merv, with perfect aplomb. "Roger Dale may not have come through this time as a detective, but he's still one of the country's real wine experts—and we're still going to watch him identify wines blindfolded." He made a wry expression. "I hope."

The audience laughed. Medium decibels.

"We've got some other bottles Roger hasn't seen yet," said David. He glanced at the table where a stage hand was putting a new set of bottles into place. "We've got some wine Roger hasn't seen yet, and this time he won't be shown the labels. To be safe, we'll have Dr. Klingerman check them out again before he tastes. Can we have somebody from the audience put a blindfold on Roger?"

There was the usual shuffle and switching of cameras until they found the necessary extrovert near the front row—a plain-looking young woman in bluejeans and a red silk blouse who was urged forward by her friends.

As she tied the blindfold around Roger's eyes, Frost was saying, "Tight now; really block his vision," and Klingerman was making quick tests of the three new bottles and nodding an okay for each.

"Okay, Roger," Frost said. "Three bottles, all ready. Toni Tennille, here, will pour and hand them to you. Let's see how close you can come to identifying them." And to himself Merv Griffin was saying (as he told me later): "Blow this one, you bastard, and *I'll* kill you myself."

Roger said, "Give me a hunk of that bread first, please, will you, Mr. Frost, The taste buds have to be clear."

Frost nodded at the loaf on the table and the knife beside it and said to the bluejeaned woman from the audience, "Go ahead, dear."

She hacked off a piece and brought it to Roger. He fumbled until he had it in his hand, then brought it toward his mouth.

He put it in his mouth.

I've often wondered if those moments in history that are major turning points don't pass largely unnoticed at the time. The first primitive who hacked off the end of a log and made a wheel out of it. Archimedes in his bathtub, watching the water overflow. Newton getting conked on the head with an apple. That innkeeper saying we're full up and you folks'll have to sleep in the barn.

In the next instant Roger spat the bread out of his mouth again.

He whipped the blindfold from his eyes.

He was—as I later learned—able to look offstage and into the wings. He saw Sheldon Walters there, staring at him. And he saw what he'd been looking for, though he didn't realize it until this moment. The expression in Walters's eyes. It was the look a pyromaniac gets as he watches a fire he has set. White rings around the iris—a burning gleam.

Roger looked directly into Walters's eyes, pointed, and said, "You!"

There was a visible jerk to Walters's head and stocky body as something intangible snapped out of place within him. With a kind of retching gasp he rushed forward—thoroughly mad for a moment, unable to control it—ran past David Frost, grabbed the bread knife from the table, and leapt toward Roger.

Roger Dale, seeing the blade flash, immediately parried with what I suppose was the short-long dragon hand or one of Hashimoto-san's other moves. He was slow by a fraction of a second. As he admitted later, it works better in the *dojo* than out in the real world. But while his reaction did not completely deflect the blow, it kept it off target, and the knife, instead of plunging into his chest, made a painful gash in his upper arm.

As Frost, Merv, the young woman, and I drew back, Walters, his eyes wilder than ever, immediately slashed again, while Roger was off balance. Then there was a blur of motion in Roger's direction. With so many people on stage it was difficult for anyone to see, in that first splinter of a second, what it was and where it had come from. In another blink of the eye it registered in everyone's consciousness that Kazu Hashimoto, moving like a tiny missile sent at unbelievable muzzle velocity, had sprung upon Sheldon Walters. Carson, Dinah, and the others shrank farther back, out of harm's way, as Walters somersaulted in the air and came down with a thud. The knife clattered to the floor some distance from him.

Hashimoto, grinning in what must have seemed to

anyone of Occidental culture a goofy way, bowed at
Walters and said, "*Sumi-masen!* Sorry!"

I'm still not sure where the two burly FBI agents
came from—somewhere in the front row, no doubt.
While most of the people watching still weren't entirely aware of what was going on—or couldn't believe
it if they were—the FBI men had Walters on his feet
again and in a firm grip between them. One fumbled
under his jacket for handcuffs.

The director in the control room told me later how
he all but flipped. "Camera two!" he said. "No—
camera three! Oh, crap, any goddamn camera! Just
stay on it—stay on it!"

And then—quite visibly—Walters's madness fell away
from him, like a spent wave that has just broken
thunderously on the shore. The sudden change was as
disconcerting as everything else that had been taking
place. Still held by the FBI men, he glared at Roger.
"How did you guess?"

"Not sure. It clicked into place. The subconscious,
I suppose. With your passion for the unexpected twist
it had to be something *other* than the wine. The bread
was the only other thing."

"It hurts," said Walters, quietly, pitifully. "Not making it again. That's what hurts."

"Want to tell us about it?" With a handkerchief
Roger was holding his arm where the blood was seep-
ing through the ripped sleeve. "You've got a pretty
big audience this time. Maybe some of them will
understand."

"Go ahead, Shel," said Merv Griffin quietly.

"They won't understand," said Walters, shaking his
head. "Nobody will. Because they're all drugged with
it—the whole damn country. Absolute moral disintegra-
tion. My daughter hooked on heroin, then that abor-

tion she died from. Sucked into it by filthy animals like Elmo Finstetter and Sonny Pearson and Larry Lawson and the rest. I *had* to make examples of them. While there was even a faint chance it would shock somebody into a realization of where we're headed! Just talking about it's no good—somebody had to *do* something!"

Roger nodded. "This'll be hard to understand, too, Shel—but it might do some good at that, when the whole story's told. You were very wrong; you must know that. You're sick, and I hope all this ends with treatment instead of life or the gas chamber. I really do—and I have an idea it will. But in the meantime, if it makes you feel any better, maybe, in a way, you won."

The first FBI agent looked at his companion and said, "Let's get this guy out of here."

"Right," said Griswold, joining them.

In the control room Dick Carson said, "What a finish! Hold the group shot right there."

And Merv Griffin stepped up to the camera, smiled, and said, "We'll be right back after this commercial."

Which we were. Just long enough to wish everybody good night. After all, after a climax like that, what do you do for an encore?